Connie Monk

WHEN THE BOUGH BREAKS

CANELO

First published in the United Kingdom in 2011 by Severn House
Paperbacks Ltd

This edition published in the United Kingdom in 2022 by

Canelo
Unit 9, 5th Floor
Cargo Works, 1–2 Hatfields
London, SE1 9PG
United Kingdom

Print ISBN 978 1 80436 106 1
Ebook ISBN 978 1 80436 054 5

Look for more great books at www.canelo.co

Printed and bound in Great Britain by Clays Ltd, Elcograf S.p.A.

1

1919-1933

One

Dennis Hawthorne wasn't a man to let his spirits be cast down easily, but as he closed the door of that dingy office and came into the bright sunshine his future held no ray of hope. This wasn't the dream that had kept him going through those hellish years of the war. Yet he ought to be thankful – he *was* thankful. Thousands of men who had lost their lives in the stinking trenches would jump at the offer he'd just turned down. But he couldn't, he *wouldn't*, waste the glories of the life that had been spared to him in that miserable, gloomy shed that called itself an office. *Look across the harbour to the open sea, listen to the cries of the gulls as they circled an incoming fishing boat…* Then without warning the scene before him seemed to be wiped out by the vision that haunted him and, even now, more than a year since it had happened, all too often dragged him out of sleep to find himself trembling, sweating, sometimes crying like a child. There by the harbour, the May morning was overtaken by the scene of his nightmare. He was shivering despite the palms of his hands being clammy; he felt the sweat break on his brow. He was climbing out of the trench, charging into no-man's-land, then the sound of the explosion seemed to be bursting in his head and he saw Ted Turner blown to pieces only yards from him. Ted Turner who had been his friend since they started infant school on the same day.

Now instinctively he raised his shaking hand and wiped his forehead, making a supreme effort to appear normal, standing there amongst the dock workers.

'You all right, son?' a kindly voice asked.

'Yes, I'm fine. Just so bright coming out from that dark shed.'

'Ah, give me the fresh air, no matter what the weather chucks at you. Been in there to see the old man about the job, have you?'

Dennis looked at the stranger with the kindly voice, a man more than twice his age. 'You work for him?' he asked.

'Ah, I work here on the dock, loading. I saw the notice in the paper for a bookkeeper. Did you get taken on?'

'I turned it down. I did right, I know I did. But God knows how long before I find anything. Couldn't do it though, couldn't be stuck in that dark hovel.'

'You home from the army I s'pose. A land fit for heroes, that's what you boys were promised. Tell you one thing, though, lad. Nothing in this world is ever what you dream it will be; but there's usually something good to be found if we look for it – a mate to work alongside, someone to have a joke with. You'll find the right thing, mayhap it's just around the next corner, eh?'

Dennis's bad moment had passed and with the stranger's optimistic comment echoing in his mind, he started up Quay Hill to catch the bus back to Exeter where he rented a bedsitting room. Yes, he'd done right to refuse. He was still free and like that chap had said, something good might be just around the next corner. Reality caught up with him when he joined the end of the queue waiting at the bus stop, for nearby was a man no more than his own twenty-one years, a man propped up on crutches with one empty trouser leg pinned up, and attached to a cord around his neck was a tray with boxes of matches. Dennis dug in his pocket for a penny and bought a box just as the Exeter bus drew up.

Two women laden with shopping baskets got on first, then with a smile and, 'Good luck, mate', to the match seller, he followed.

The bus was taking a long country route back to Exeter. It was only about midday and the thought of his bed-sitting room held no appeal. What was there to hurry for? When a couple of women got up to disembark in a village, he followed them, his nose immediately being assailed by the smell of fish and chips. So it was that with his lunch wrapped in a greasy newspaper package he turned from the village street in what he was to come to know as Sedgewood and started to walk down a narrow lane, which was signed: *To the Common*.

About a quarter of a mile on he came face to face with his future. No longer was it shrouded in impenetrable mist. On a garden gate was a faded sign: *COTTAGE AND ABOUT FIVE ACRES TO LET* The cottage stood empty, looking unloved and desolate with its painted name, Westways, so faded it was barely readable. But it wasn't the cottage that set his imagination racing, it was the land; five acres as sadly neglected as the building itself. It was like stumbling upon something held in a time warp. This was his future: Dennis had never felt as certain of anything. Pushing open the gate that hung on one hinge he walked up the weed-choked path and pressed his nose to the windows of the house. He battled his way through the overgrown land, imagining the hours he would spend restoring it. Hours? Weeks, months, he corrected himself. He remembered how he used to love to work with his grandfather on his vegetable plot and, casting a glance to the pale winter sky, wanted to believe that his decision was gaining approval.

There was no time to lose. He jotted down the name of the agent and caught the next bus back to Deremouth. By the end of the day his future had a shape: he would breathe new life into these five acres of south Devon countryside and make the house a home. Long ago someone else must have lived there, tilling the land, caring for the property, and that's how it would be again.

That was in May. He became the tenant on the first of June, and before that he had to attend an auction sale in Exeter and bid for the bare essentials of furniture. He took note of every penny he spent, for he had little enough to live on and he knew it would be some time before the land could bring him any income. But there were things he had to have: gardening tools (all bought second-hand) and his one extravagance, a motorized digger. But he had plenty of clearing to do before he could hope to use that.

That summer he worked outside seven days a week from first light until dusk. His scheme was to clear and plant out one patch at a time. That way by the time the winter crops came along he ought to be making some sort of a living. He found time to go to the village, to make friends with the shopkeepers and get the greengrocer's word that he would be prepared to take his crop assuming that it was of high enough quality.

During the winter evenings he distempered the inside walls. A stranger seeing it would have thought his home a barren and cheerless place, but to Dennis it was an object of pride. The rooms were small, a kitchen-cum-sitting room, a 'parlour' or dining room, then upstairs two bedrooms. Outside on the back wall of the cottage he kept a zinc bath, which he had to bring indoors and fill with water heated in buckets on the range. A few yards from the cottage was an earth closet. After his years in the trenches, to Dennis it all seemed like luxury and, in the beginning, even the solitude was balm to his spirit. Surely if anything could dispel the memories that tormented him it must be the work he did on the land.

For the first two years he worked alone; paying a helper's wage was out of the question. Bit by bit the ground was cleared, the earth turned with his motor digger and then planted. So often he sent up a silent thank you to his grandfather who had died during the war years and had left to Dennis what little money he had. Living frugally he survived, learnt to look after himself and gradually to eke out a living from his land.

–

It was in the summer of 1922 that something happened to change his future. Each day he delivered his boxes of vegetable to Jack Hopkins, the village greengrocer, in a handcart. With the delivery made he was just pushing his cart back along the track towards Westways when he saw a girl trying to put the chain back on her bicycle. Sometimes people from the village walked this way, taking the track that led to the common. But he'd never seen this girl before. She probably wasn't local, he decided, for from her attire he imagined she had been on a long cycle ride. Wearing grey flannel pleated shorts and a white short-sleeved shirt she might have been no more than a schoolgirl – or that was his impression until he came nearer. 'Do you need a hand?' he called as he approached her.

'I don't know what's the matter with it today. Three times the chain has come off. It's never done it before. I think I've got it on and half a mile along the road it's slipped again.'

'Perhaps something needs tightening. Have you a tool bag?'

'No – just two hands. And oily ones at that,' she answered cheerfully.

She had turned the bike upside down and had been crouching by its side to fix it. Now she stood up and he saw immediately that he'd been wrong in thinking her a schoolgirl. She was a young woman, and an attractive young woman too. At a quick glance he took her in from head to toe. His first thought was that her hair reminded him of autumn and conkers; to say it was brown made it sound ordinary but it wasn't really auburn. She was very slim, yet he was aware of her breasts under the thin cotton of her open neck blouse. Her long slender legs were bare and on her feet she wore a pair of strapped sandals little different from those of a child. Yet she certainly wasn't a child; if she were, her long hair would have been in a pigtail instead of being swept up and pinned to the top of her head. And her face? If he thought of the picture stars of the day who were considered beautiful, then she was no beauty for there was nothing 'rosebud' about her mouth. Her cheekbones were pronounced and her nose tip-tilted. Yet her wide dark eyes were like no eyes he had ever seen.

Aware that she'd seen how he was staring at her he felt raw and gauche. 'If you like, I'll take a look at it for you.' Once more he was in control. 'I live just along there in that cottage.' Then, unable to keep the pride out of his voice, he added, 'This field here, well, I say field but it's a market garden really, it's mine. I've just been out delivering the veg to the shop in the village.'

'You grow all that?' She spoke in awed admiration just as he'd hoped she would. 'Do you reckon you can fix it so that I can get back to Exeter? I'd be awfully grateful.'

He liked her more and more. Some girls would have looked on him with suspicion because he suggested she should go home with him. But not this one. She had bags of common sense; he knew it immediately. As she bent to up-end her bike, he picked it up and laid it on his cart.

'I've been cycling all day,' she told him as they started along the lane, speaking as if she'd known him for years. 'It was really exciting, all of it new to me. I've only been in Exeter for a fortnight and my day off last week was wet.'

'You've taken a job in Exeter? What do you do?'

'A sort of general bit of this and bit of that. When I left school I was needed at home so I've never trained for anything. All I really know is looking after a house and cooking – that sort of thing. I work for an elderly couple, brother and sister. Dear old things they are. They have a housekeeper, so you could call me a housemaid except that I do other things. Sometimes I read to the old dears. Neither of them can see well enough to read for themselves and they like to keep abreast with the daily news. I like doing that, because that way I get to read the paper too. I do the mending and the ironing, I go out shopping. Yesterday I made twelve pots of jam. Like I say, I just do whatever comes along. Not being trained for anything, really, I was lucky to get taken on.'

'I reckon they're the lucky ones having you there to look after them. So where have you been today?'

'I didn't have a map so it's hard to say. One place I went to was called Otterton St Giles – that was about the furthest I suppose. That's where I ate my sandwiches. Then to a bigger place, Deremouth, this side of the estuary. When it was time to start for home I followed a sign that said Exeter but got sidetracked at the end of the lane here when I read this was the way 'To the Common'. I shouldn't have attempted it, not with all these ruts in the track. I expect that's what got my chain off again. It was fine all the way from that Deremouth place.'

'We'll soon get it fixed. Here we are, in you go.' He held the gate open for her then followed her with the cart. 'Do you want to wait in the house while I see what I can do? My toolbox is in the shed over there.'

'I'd rather come and watch you, just in case I have trouble another time – unless your wife or your mother or someone is in there and will think it rude of me.'

'I have neither wife nor mother. I live on my own.' Then with a ring of pride, he added, 'And I work on my own too, can't afford any help yet. But it's all coming along really well. When I've done the bike I'll show you what I grow if you like.' She nodded, her wide mouth beaming with pleasure. 'I'd like that.'

It was more than an hour later that he walked with her to the end of the lane and saw her on her way. He'd wanted to ask her to come to Sedgewood again next time she had a day off and it didn't rain, but he was frightened to suggest it in case she refused. So all he said was, 'I work here on my own all the time. If you're ever this way drop in and say hello.'

'May I? I don't want to be a nuisance when you've got masses to do. Or perhaps you could give me some jobs. Remember I'm good at doing a bit of this and a bit of that.'

'Come soon, won't you.' The words were out before he could stop them.

'Just try and stop me! By the way, what's your name? I'm Kathie Barnes.'

'And I'm Dennis Hawthorne. Just Den does me.'

'Bye then, Den. If it's not chucking it down on us next week I'll ride over. But you must promise you'll tell me if you're too busy. I won't mind, honestly.'

He promised. But secretly they both knew that the days between then and her next free time were simply hours to be lived through.

Until the day he had chanced on Kathie, his own company had been all he'd wanted. His three years at Westways had calmed his shattered nerves, even dimmed some of the memories that would never be erased; solitude had become a habit and he was never lonely. Then meeting Kathie changed everything.

The following week he took her into the cottage, giving her the Grand Tour of the sparsely furnished rooms with their distempered walls. He even pointed out the zinc bath and the outside closet, not as features to be despised but as an accepted part of the ambience. And viewing it all, her eyes shone with admiration; there he was, a young, strong, good-looking man, thoroughly self-reliant.

As the weeks went by, each time she had her day off she cycled from the house near Exeter to Sedgewood. It would have taken more than rain to deter her, in fact she liked wet days when instead of working on the land they were in the cottage. She cooked their lunch – making sure she did enough that he had something he could warm up for supper or for the next day. For both of them, her visits were the highlight of their week. He knew so little about girls. Being with her made him aware of what a loner he had become. Most of his army compatriots had gone home to wives or girlfriends, but he'd had neither. If he'd had a sedentary job (like the one in that dingy shed by the harbour) he would have looked for female company in the evenings. Most nights when he went to bed he was too tired to miss the thing that was lacking in his life. Yet he was a normal, healthy young man and often enough his sleep would be disturbed by something he couldn't control. Knowing nothing of the realities of shared love making, even his fantasies lacked direction. All that changed when Kathie came into his life. He would find himself watching her as she reached to pick the first of the runner beans, aware that on these warm summer days she wore nothing under her cotton blouse and imagining how her small breasts would feel if only he could hold them in the palms of his hands. Then his hand might move down her flat stomach, force its way between her slender thighs, he would…

'What's up?' she said, turning unexpectedly from her task. Then, suddenly uncertain, 'Are you all right, Den? You look sort of funny.'

'Kathie, I was thinking.'

'Oh dear! Do you always look funny when you think?' she teased.

'Kathie, I've never felt like this before. Is this what being in love does to you?'

'In love?' It was barely a whisper.

The runner beans were forgotten as he came close to her and held her hands tightly in his. 'Can't think of anything but you. I want you as part of my life – all of my life – working together, living together. Kathie, what is it? Don't cry, Kathie.'

'Can't help it. So happy.' As the tears spilled from her brimming eyes, she forced her contorted face into a smile. 'Hold me tight, Den.'

Clinging to each other they knew complete happiness. With all the innocence of youth they saw their fixtures as cloudless; if they had each other nothing could touch them.

'You're only eighteen. Who has to give permission for you to marry?'

'My mother.' It came as a surprise to him that she had a relative as close as a mother. She never spoke of her family. 'She lives in Hampshire. My father died when I was just a kid but Mum and I were fine, he left enough money for us to live on. I don't mean we were rich, but she never had to worry and the house was our own. I was still at school when she met Cyril Harper, a photographer. She fell for him. She behaved as if she were less than half her age. Anyway, it was stupid; we were quite all right as we were. But they got married and he came to live in our house. He decided I was old enough to leave school and help at home. I was no more than a glorified maid in the house – not even a glorified one if I'm truthful. Mother got pregnant as soon as they were married and the next thing I was expected to be nursemaid too. Algy was a good little chap I suppose, but I resented always having to look after him, wash his nappies, everything. But Mother was intent on giving beastly Cyril everything he wanted. Before Algy was a year old she had her next, a girl they called Lily. That was back in January. I made up my mind I was going to get a job. Then with Lily only a few weeks old, Mother and her wretched man were pleased as punch because she recognized the signs; hardly up and about from Lily, she was pregnant again. They seem to want to breed like rabbits and they're not even young. Mother is *forty* and he's even more. It's *disgusting.*' She almost spat the word out.

Dennis looked at her tenderly, thinking not so much about her mother's second chance at happiness as about the hurt he knew Kathie felt.

'But they're happy together?'

'If being happy means that she gazes at him like some moonstruck youngster and talks a lot of drivel about getting pregnant so easily being proof that they are made for each other. It was as if she couldn't think of anything else. It was as if he'd cast a sort of spell on her. I didn't want to hear about it. They're old, for goodness sake! It's revolting. Anyway I saw this job in the newspaper and wrote about it, then the next thing I knew I had a letter saying they wanted me to work for them. They're a nice old couple – Mr and Miss Blackwell. They pay me ten shillings a week and my keep – it was going to be seven and sixpence but on my first pay day Mr Blackwell said they had had a little chat and decided to give me ten shillings.' She had talked fast, speaking her thoughts aloud. 'Heavens! Hark at me! Once I get started there's no stopping me.'

'I love you Kathie Barnes. I want to know everything – about your past, about your thoughts…'

'And my future?'

'And your future… every day of our lives, darling Kathie. And if what your mother says is true we shall have an army of children to help us on the land.'

She chuckled, nuzzling her head against his neck.

'I'll write to Mother this evening and tell her about us. I'll say we want to be married and ask for her consent. She'll give it right enough. She's so besotted with that pompous prick of a man that she's probably forgotten I exist at all.'

Dennis laughed at the sudden change in her tone.

'We'll be so happy that no one will have the power to trouble us. I ought to have proposed to you in the time honoured way, on one knee vowing my endless love—'

'And all that jazz,' she sang. Then meeting his gaze her expression suddenly changed again. Excitement gave way to an emotion that seemed to take her breath away. 'Den, hold me close.' She had never been kissed like this; her heart was pounding and following her natural impulse her lips parted and she moved her tongue on his mouth. For Dennis, too, this was a new experience. Often enough when he'd woken in the silence of the night he had imagined her as he followed where nature led. But that was as nothing compared with the reality of holding her.

'Your hand,' she whispered with her mouth touching his. And the next thing he knew she guided him to press it against her small, pert breast, her own hand covering his and moving his fingers backwards and forwards across the pinnacle of her nipple.

'No, Kathie,' he spoke more to himself than to her. 'Kathie, I want to touch you, every bit of you. Oh God, but I want you.'

She felt him pull his hand from her breast and moved her own with it, so that as he lowered his she still held it and together they raised her skirt then guided him to the wide leg of her knickers. Never before had he hated the narrow life he'd led as he hated it now. On leave in France he had been with some of his compatriots to what were thought of as 'naughty' shows, but never had he seen a naked woman and never had his hand explored as it did as Kathie stood close against him with one leg wrapped around him. As his finger probed he drew back his head and looked at Kathie; her eyes were closed, her lips parted and as she breathed she made a soft whimpering sound. She was as inexperienced and naive as he was, but she wasn't ignorant. With her eyes still closed she moved the hand that had lead him to his goal and eased it into the waist of his trousers. He gave a shuddering sigh as he felt it close around him.

'Kathie, no, Kathie, no.' Then, unable to stop himself, he continued, 'Yes, go on, harder, harder, oh God, coming... can't stop it.' With a convulsive movement he leant heavily on her as she felt the warm fluid on her hand, bringing her closer to filling the gaps in her knowledge and understanding. 'So sorry... tried not to...'

'I'm glad it happened. Den, I love you so much.' They had moved apart, her skirt fallen back into place and her hand retrieved. But the moment still held them; they weren't ready to let it go. He passed her his handkerchief to wipe her hand; they didn't look directly at each other. For both of them the last minutes had been a journey of discovery.

'How soon can we get married?' she asked. 'We don't have to save up for a silly honeymoon or anything, do we? And working in the garden here I shan't want a trousseau of posh clothes.'

'Before you go, give me your mother's name and address. I'll write to her this evening.'

'You, not me?'

'You can write as well if you want, of course you can. But I must ask her permission. *And* she'll want to know something about me.' Then with a sudden and boyish grin, he added, 'What a fine upstanding young fella I am.'

'What about your people? Not for permission, but they ought to know what sort of a girl you're tying yourself up to.'

'I've told you about Grandad dying while I was in France. He was all the family I had. I can't remember my parents; they were killed in a train crash when I was about three. They'd been on an outing with the church choir they both sang in. Grandad brought me up.'

'Oh Den, how sad for you.' But she'd make it up a hundredfold all that he'd missed.

'Now look here, this is no way to waste good daylight hours.' The last minutes were like a dream, but now reality was catching up with him. 'If you finish cutting and boxing up the calabrese, I'll get the handcart across and we'll push off down to the village. I've got carrots and spinach boxed up ready. I say, what a team, eh?'

They were restored to their usual friendly footing.

That evening they each wrote to Millicent, neither knowing exactly what the other had told her. The days went by and there was no reply. By Kathie's next day off they didn't try to hide their disappointment. Secretly Dennis had hoped that the news would have brought about a return to the earlier closeness between mother and daughter.

'Den, would we be able to afford to keep a pig when we're married? Mrs Hutchins, she's the cook where I work, she's been making brawn and I helped her. She's taught me so much; every week there's something different. I know how to make preserves, and bottle fruit and vegetables. It's going to be such fun. But about the pig, she said that when she was a girl her people always reared one for the table. You don't have to kill it yourself, you send it to be done and it comes back in joints, chops, and all sorts of things. We could barter in the village – a whole ham would be worth, oh I don't know, perhaps curtains for the sitting room or something. It's just that I don't know if we could afford to buy a piglet.'

'It's all extra work, Kathie.'

'I'd look after it. And think of all the edible bits you put on the compost heap every day when you prepare the vegetables to take to the shop. Once I'm here all the time I could cook it all up and make it appetizing for the lucky chap.'

'You're a glutton for work, young Kathie.'

Her chuckle was a sign of the contentment she felt. 'Work is something you get paid to do for someone else. What we do here isn't like work; the more we do, the more established Westways becomes. And Westways will be *us*. Listen, Den, there's a motor coming down the lane. If they're trying to go to the common they'll have to reverse all the way back.'

'It's stopping, whoever it is must be going to turn by our double gate.'

But they were both wrong. A minute later they heard the click of the garden gate leading to the front door of the cottage.

'I'd better go and see,' Den said, wiping his hands on his overalls.

Humming to herself, Kathie continued trimming the main crop carrots, letting her mind leap forward to when she would be turning the vegetable trimmings into pigswill.

'Kathie!' At the sound she stood bolt upright.

'Mother!' Her pretty mother! But she had never looked like this when she'd been expecting Algy or Lily. 'Mother, how did you know I'd be here? Have you been to see the Blackwells?'

'I wanted to see for myself what sort of a man it is you want to marry.'

Kathie's eyes filled with hot tears. Her mother still cared! Throwing down her knife, then laying the carrot on the pile, she hurried to hurl herself at Millicent.

'Careful Kathie, don't knock me off my feet.'

'You look as though it would take a mighty great push to do that,' Kathie laughed. 'How long have you got to wait?'

'If I got pregnant when I think I did, I'm due in six weeks.'

'You look like the cat who stole the cream.' Kathie found her old irritation surfacing.

'That's how I feel. I know I'm huge, but there's good reason. This time the doctor tells me he believes it's twins.'

'Four children! Are you alright? You're not young.' She didn't mean it as unkindly as it sounded.

'I wish I were. I wish I were twenty instead of forty. But years have nothing to do with anything. I feel young – and a thousand times happier and more loved than I did at twenty. Kathie, I wish you were living near us. Soon you'll be a wife and there's so much we could share. But just one thing: when your young man wrote he said you both want the wedding very soon, as soon as possible. Was he trying to tell me that you'd been doing things you shouldn't?'

'Things we shouldn't?'

'Shouldn't before you're married, I mean. You know I've said before that when two people are *right* together there is nothing easier or more natural than to make a baby. And in my opinion it's a gift from God whether it's before you're married or after. So you can tell me, Kathie, you mustn't be frightened.'

'No, you're wrong – about us I mean.' Then, laughing and encompassing the five-acre field with a grand sweep of her arm, she explained, 'With all this to look after we have too much to do on my day off to spend time "doing what we shouldn't".'

'Oh dear, don't be like your father. He was never interested in that sort of thing; sometimes I wonder how I conceived you at all. When he did rise to the occasion it was such a passionless performance. The only passion he knew was for the bones and treasures to be dug up of people who'd been dead for hundreds of years; the nights I've cried myself to sleep! Then after he died, I had to wait all those achingly lonely years. No wonder I fell in love with Cyril. The first time we talked I just knew that with him – well, I seemed to read his thoughts just as he read mine. I do wish you'd liked him better; you were always so scratchy to him.' Then, changing the subject, her voice alive with excitement, she continued, 'Did you hear us arrive? We drove. We've had such an exciting summer since Cyril has bought a motor cycle and sidecar.' Like a child she giggled. 'Not much space in a sidecar. If I get much bigger he'll have to get me in and out with a shoehorn. Let's go and find the men. I left him to have a talk with your young man. Then there's something else we want to tell you. Oh Kathie, who would have thought that life could be so... so thrilling?'

'And you'll write a letter giving me your consent to marry?'

'Oh but I've done that already. We brought it with us. Cyril has it in his pocket. If you think he's right for you then I'm sure he must be. You're a sensible girl – too sensible I sometimes think, too much of your father in you – but I'm sure you wouldn't lose your heart to someone who was no good. Wait until we are all together, then Cyril has some news for you.'

Kathie and Cyril greeted each other with cool courtesy, but on that occasion Millicent was too eager for his announcement to notice.

'We wish you both well for your future together. And I must say—' Cyril addressed his words to Dennis '—Millicent will have no worries leaving Kathie with you, certain that she will be in good hands. When do you hope to be married?'

'We haven't even talked about dates yet,' Kathie answered him. 'I don't see there's any reason to wait, do you, Den?'

'Today would suit me fine,' Dennis laughed, 'but I imagine your mother would prefer we wait until after the birth.'

'I hardly look like mother of the bride.' Millicent cradled her enormous hump in both hands, smiling at Cyril as if to acknowledge the part he'd played. 'But you can have a wedding without me being there. I've written my consent; Cyril will leave it with you. As soon as I'm about again after shedding my load – well you tell them Cyril darling.'

He came to her and put his arm around her and just like a teenager in the throes of first love she gazed at him in open adoration.

'We are leaving the country,' he announced. 'As soon as Millicent is ready for the journey we are moving out to California. I have a friend with a most successful photographic studio, he is renowned for his portraits – well-known people in the world of moving pictures sit for him.

He knows my work well and he has written suggesting that I take over the Californian studio as he means to open in New York. High society will flock to him; he is able to flatter even the plainest. Indeed my own work is very similar to his, but my clientele very different. I shall never reach the top of my profession where I am now. We have a buyer for the house so by the time the legal work is all completed the timing should be right. So we are off, we two, the new nursemaid is coming with us and by then the four children to keep her busy. Any more family we have will be born American. Isn't that so, my precious?'

Millicent nodded, moving his arm down and pressing his hand to the hump she carried with such pride.

Dennis said all the right things, congratulating Cyril, wishing them every happiness in their venture. But Kathie said nothing. Just for those first moments with her mother their old closeness seemed to be unchanged, but it had been an illusion. Already she was forgotten.

'Can you stay and eat with us?' Dennis invited. 'We always have something around teatime so that Kathie can cycle back to Exeter before it's dark.'

'No, we'll get on our way. I have the letter here that Millie has written. She did it before we left home so that she could see you had it safely. And now my darling we'll say our farewells. We have a long drive ahead of us. We'll find somewhere for a meal when we get most of the journey behind us.'

Five minutes later, making a great thing of what a tight squeeze it was to fit her bulk into the sidecar, Millicent blew a final kiss as Cyril started the motor. Then without a backward glance they were off.

'America's such a long way. Don't expect she'll ever come back.' Kathie heard her voice break as she blinked back the tears.

'No. It'll be a different world for them. And so will ours be different for us.'

Kathie nodded, forcing a smile. 'You get the cart and I'll finish the carrots or we shan't get them delivered in time for us to have tea before I have to start back. Now we've got the letters Den what is there for us to wait for?'

'Good girl.' He didn't enlarge on exactly why she was a good girl. 'Hey, Kathie, I reckon we ought to add something to our vows: that as we get older we won't let ourselves get… get… well, soppy, lovey-dovey.'

Kathie started to laugh. 'I'll finish the carrots.' Five minutes later they were pushing the loaded cart along the lane towards the village street. The brief and unsettling interlude with their visitors had left no scars.

It wasn't until they sat down to the bacon and egg tea Kathie cooked for them that she opened the bulky envelope her mother had left. Even then it wasn't the letter that gave her such a look of blank amazement.

'What's up, Kathie? Hasn't she made it clear?'

'The consent's fine. She's written something else. Here, you read it.'

Kathie watched as Dennis took out the contents she had crammed back into the envelope, his expression one of incredulity.

'Fifty pounds! Did she tell you what was in the envelope?'

'Not a word.' This time she couldn't blink back the tears that welled in her eyes. 'It had always been my home. That's what she says. Even with Cyril there, she didn't forget it was my home. I feel so mean – about them both.

She's so besotted with him that if he'd told her he wanted her to keep all the money for themselves – and setting up fresh in America, I'm sure they can do with it – she would have done what he said. So he must have agreed to what she was doing. Fifty pounds! Can't believe it.'

That same night, sitting up in bed she wrote to her mother, saying things she could never have been comfortable saying to her face and, above all, begging her not to let them become forced apart by the miles.

That was in September.

–

Kathie and Dennis were married in the village church on the first Saturday in November. The only people present were the Blackwell siblings, who had insisted they wanted to be there and had promised to sign the register as witnesses. So instead of making the journey on her bicycle, Kathie arrived at the church in style in the Blackwells' car with her bike and two suitcases roped to the luggage grid on the back. Only after the ceremony was the rope untied and her worldly possessions stacked against the wall of the churchyard. Then the car moved off, leaving the bridal couple at the church gate.

'I must have a guardian angel, Den. When I looked for a job it guided me to them. I shall really miss them.' She'd known the Blackwells for hardly more than seven months but their simple kindness would stay with her. Waving until the car rounded the bend at the end of the village street, she and Dennis set out for home, he carrying a suitcase in each hand while she pushed the bicycle.

'I should have insisted we at least had a weekend away. Kathie, you deserve something better than this. You ought to be wearing white and carrying flowers, not pushing your bike back home. You deserve a honeymoon in a first-class hotel.'

'Don't be daft,' came her spontaneous answer, 'that would just be a waste of time. We'd be itching to get home and start a proper life. Don't you think that most couples grasp at the chance of a honeymoon just to get away by themselves; but we never have family listening and watching what we do and say. Now, Den, we shall have all day, every day.'

'Every day and every night.'

They turned from the road into their lane that led to the common. Silently Dennis imagined the hours ahead of them, silently he begged that he would manage to do it right, right for both of them. Tonight he mustn't rush at her and bungle the whole thing. She was as much a novice as he. She wouldn't be shy, of that he was certain, but she wouldn't be any more knowledgeable than he was. Together they'd find the way.

'Let's do that, shall we?' He'd been so lost in his own thoughts he'd not listened to what she'd been saying.

'Sorry, Kathie. I wasn't listening, I was thinking about the sort of honeymoon I would like to have given you. Let's do what?'

'This evening, when we've finished outside, let's get the bath in front of the fire. Not big enough for both of us at the same time unless we stand up. Can't you just imagine, you and me standing in the water, lovely and warm, the curtains closed. Now what could a honeymoon give better than that? Mr and Mrs Hawthorne taking their first dip.'

Suddenly all his fears melted.

'Come on—' she tugged his arm in a most unbridelike fashion— 'race you home.' And she was off, pushing her bike – not cheating and riding it – and reaching her goal just ahead of him, propping the bicycle against the fence and leaning, breathless, on the gate.

'I love you Kathie Hawthorne.' At the sound of those softly spoken words her mood changed. With her lips parted she raised her mouth to his as he dumped the cases on the ground.

–

She had never lived without a bathroom and the novelty of the bathing ritual excited her. He filled two buckets with water and put them on the range, then an hour or so later he carried the bath in while she rolled away the rug in case it got splashed. She soon learnt that a four-foot zinc bath was hardly the setting for the eroticism she had half imagined – for more than half imagining was beyond her. With the buckets emptied into the bath, they undressed each other, the sight of her almost Dennis's undoing. The moment was a big step for her too, for the sight of him was evidence of what she had only half understood despite their brief encounter with desire on the afternoon he had asked her to marry him. When she had encircled his warm flesh and been secretly thrilled that she had the power to make him lose control, she hadn't imagined what she held to be as large and erect as what she now saw as he moved towards her.

This was a mistake, she thought. He wants us to make love, to do it, now. That's what I want too… but not down here on a stone floor. The water looked temptingly steamy so she put one foot in, testing the temperature.

'Lovely. Come on, Den, hop in.' She scooped up the tablet of soap which, having no dish, was getting soft in the water. 'I'll do you first.'

They were on unknown territory, more exciting than anything they had dreamed. They rubbed the tablet of soap in their hands, and then lathered each other, not once but over and over until their hands slid over the surface of their skin. Even though they were still standing, the burning coals in the range kept them warm.

Reaching to where Kathie had put towels on the table, Den wrapped one loosely around her as without a word he stepped out of the bath and pulled the kitchen chair close. Then sitting on it he held out his arms.

'Face me,' he whispered, drawing her down to him. Following instinct, she sat astride him. She left dizzy with emotion, there was nothing but *this*, her damp body pressed close to his. Secretly they had both been frightened of failure, but now she knew exactly what she had to do as she guided him then lowered herself so that he penetrated deep into her. She had wondered and imagined, she had explored with a slender finger, expecting that when the moment came that would be what she would feel. But she hadn't been prepared for *this*.

'You're deep inside me. It's as if you fill me. Deeper, Den, harder.' As she whispered, so she moved on him, lifting his hand so that his fingers caressed her telltale raised nipple. She had never known a feeling like this: joy beyond anything she had dreamed and yet she yearned for an elusive something that stayed just out of reach as with a stifled cry his climax came. In her innocence she didn't know how near she had come to grasping that elusive something, but she felt weak and shaken with love.

'Kathie,' he gasped when at last his convulsive movements were stilled, 'wonderful... God... never knew... could be so wonderful.' He shivered, suddenly realizing that they were still wet and soapy.

Nuzzling against him she started to laugh. 'What a pickle we're in. We have to bale out the tub too. Oh Den, no one could have a better honeymoon than this.'

'No one,' he agreed.

'You're shivering. Best you hop back in that water and rinse the soap off. I ought to, too. If we stay soapy we shall get itchy.'

'Love you, Kathie Hawthorne, my practical wife.'

Five minutes later, rinsed and rubbed vigorously with their towels, there was no choice but to be practical. Each with a saucepan they gradually baled out most of the water until holding one end each they were able to carry the bath outside and drain the last of it onto the patch of grass. With bare feet and their towels wrapped around them, it was a good thing they had no neighbours.

She fetched his pyjamas and her nightdress and dressing gown.

'I couldn't find your dressing gown,' she said as she put the things on the kitchen table.

'Now what would I want with a thing like that? I always go straight to bed once I've cleared away the bath.'

'We'll do that too in a minute, but first what do you want to drink, tea or cocoa?'

'Cocoa, please. I say, don't we sound *married*! Cocoa at bedtime.'

While she made the drinks he raked the fire in the range and banked it up for the night. Had she been as apprehensive as he had about how they'd manage the first time? Yet it had been so easy, so right – so wonderful.

28

What a moment for that haunting vision to come back to him: no man's land, shrieks and cries of the wounded, then the moment when he had seen Ted blown to bits. Poor bugger, no wife for him, no life, no kids to look forward to. And here am I with Kathie, with everything, our future ahead of us… I thank God from the bottom of my heart.

–

The clean sheets were cold (and unironed too, but at least he had washed them ready to bring his bride to), but it would have taken far more than a cold bed to mar their first night together. Sex had never played a paramount part in Dennis's life; he had usually been too physically weary to give it much thought unless it woke him in the middle of the night. But, relieved at the success of their first encounter, he was as ready as any bridegroom and this time with better control.

'I didn't know it could be like that,' Kathie spoke in an awed whisper when he moved off her. 'Like climbing to the peak of a high mountain, stars shining and twinkling around you.'

She was utterly sure that they were right for each other. So if what her mother had said was true, perhaps already they had made the beginning of a baby.

'Den,' she whispered, 'are you awake?'

'Um…' More truthfully he was half awake.

'When two people are right for each other the easiest thing in the world is to conceive; that's what my mother said. That's why she keeps having babies. Do you suppose it'll be like that for us?'

'Hope so,' he mumbled, consciousness fast slipping beyond recall. 'Need all the help we can get – an army of

29

sons to dig and...' Dennis slept but she was wide awake, eager for the future. With all the confidence of youth she saw it as cloudless; tragedies were things that happened to other people.

Two

They were both young and their busy lives were full of challenge so, at least in the beginning, it was possible to hold on to the expectation that the family they took for granted would be part of their future.

On a bright morning the following May a letter arrived from America with the news that Millicent, twice Kathie's age and with their latest additions to the family only five months old, was expecting her fifth child setting the seal on the family's commitment to their new country. If her belief about conception echoed in Kathie's memory, she refused to listen. Of course she and Den were right for each other. Yet already that regular monthly disappointment was beginning to cast a shadow. Each time they made love she silently begged, 'Let it happen this time. If it does, will I know? Will it be different for me?' If only she knew a woman well enough to talk to, a woman with children. If only she could ask the things she didn't understand. Occasionally as his passion mounted towards a climax something wonderful happened to her too but lately, even if she reached what she strived for, when it happened all she could think was, 'This time! It's *got* to be this time.'

She and Den worked together as partners whether it was outside on the land, or indoors where they hung wallpaper, or he built a cupboard for their clothes while she stitched curtains. Yet as the days of each month passed she came to dread the time her period was due. In the watches of the night she even imagined there must be something wrong with her that she couldn't conceive.

They had been married nearly a year and a half when, for the first time, she dared to let herself hope. She was four days late, something that had never before happened. And with each passing hour hope took a firmer hold. She hurried through the essential work in the house and went out to help Dennis where she spent the rest of the morning planting out the cabbages they had brought on in the greenhouse he had built the previous summer.

'When I've finished these, how about if I plant out another row of lettuce? Just feel the sun, Den. I bet there's no one luckier than us.'

He looked at her affectionately. How pretty she looked kneeling there with the tawny lights in her recently bobbed chestnut hair shining in the sunshine. He supposed four days wasn't very long, but there was something about her, a sort of inner glow. Never a demonstrative man, before he could stop himself he stooped down and kissed her forehead, a forehead that even so early in the season had lost its winter paleness.

'Nor yet half as lucky. Kathie, don't let yourself get tired. I mean… if… well, you know – if this really is the beginning, you mustn't risk upsetting things.'

'Silly,' she laughed, grabbing his hand and rubbing it against her cheek, 'I'm tough as old boots. If we've got the start of a baby, then I don't have to worry. Having a baby won't be a problem, as long as you've done your bit and given me one to work on.'

For a second he frowned. Was she inferring that their regular disappointment might be *his* fault? Of course it wasn't anything to do with him. Sometimes he knew he came so quickly she hadn't even got started; other times he managed to hang on until he could feel her rising excitement at what he was doing to her. Either way, when his moment came he filled her with what must be the makings of dozens of babies. If she couldn't do her part, that was hardly his fault. Den felt his manhood had been challenged.

'I hope you're right. But it's taken us all this time to get even a glimmer of hope, so don't run any risks.'

She felt cherished.

They worked until about one o'clock then went indoors to eat bread, cheese and chutney, washed down with tea. In less than half an hour they were outside again. This was their regular routine; a plot of five acres with only two people to work it didn't allow time to relax. Each of them gardened independently and yet with the comfortable knowledge that everything they did was a shared step towards their goal. As daylight started to fade he saw her put her tools in the shed then go in to start getting their meal.

'I'll knock off pretty soon,' he called. 'And Kathie, don't you carry the coal. Leave me to fill the bucket.' Bringing in enough coal for the evening and to bank the range to keep the fire in overnight was usually her job; they both understood the hidden message in his words.

That evening there was a feeling akin to celebration about their frugal meal of home-made rissoles and the jacket potatoes she had put in the oven of the range during the afternoon. Later, while he was raking the fire and banking it up for the night he hardly noticed that she disappeared upstairs.

'What are you doing?' he called after a few minutes. 'The kettle's ready for the cocoa.'

'Coming.' Yet, even from that one word he knew something was wrong.

'You all right, love?' he asked as she came back into the room (a room that, because the range never went out, had been given the name 'the warm room'). A silly question, for he could see from her face she was anything but all right.

'I thought this time would be different,' she said, not able to keep her voice steady.

'You mean…?'

She nodded. 'It's not fair,' she croaked, giving up the battle for control, 'other people have babies easy as anything, even people who don't want them. I've always been well. I'm normal and healthy. So why don't I get pregnant? What's the matter with us? Are we doing something wrong, Den?'

'I guess we just have to wait. Don't cry, Kathie. One of these days it'll happen to you – then I bet you'll be like your mother. I reckon he only has to hang his trousers over the bed rail for her to get like it. Come on, cheer up love, some people wait for years not months. Like you say, you've never had any trouble – with all that sort of thing – so you'll manage it one of these days. Come on, let's have our cocoa and get to bed. Tomorrow we'll set up the poles for the runners, shall we?'

She nodded; she even tried to smile. But his words echoed: 'so you'll manage it one of these days.' It was *her* fault. Hadn't he as good as said so?

Lying in bed, staring out at the starless night and listening to his deep, even breathing, her mind leapt back to their wedding day and the sombre voice of the vicar declaring that 'marriage was ordained for the procreation of children, to be brought up in fear and nurture of the Lord...' Was this their punishment for not going to church on Sundays? No, she wasn't going to believe it could be that. But how could anything be wrong with *her*? She was always so well, so full of energy. And yet when they made love Den always seemed to achieve the great heights of ecstasy that she never could reach; so the fault must be with her.

–

From the start Dennis had agreed that they should rear a pig, but before they built the sty they'd decided to erect a chicken run with nest boxes. Once chickens started laying they would never be short of eggs, an essential staple in the diet of those without much money; whilst a pig would certainly eat vegetation that had always gone straight to the compost, but it would be a long time before their table saw any reward for the work and expense.

Looking after the chickens was Kathie's department, so when they bought their first young pig, which they'd christened Rufus, she automatically became responsible for him, making a daily mash from the vegetable cuttings and mucking out the pigsty – her least favourite job. One thing surprised her, and that was the animal's intelligence. Had she been brought up in the country she might have been more prepared. Before Rufus had been with them for more than a week he would raise his head and listen at the sound of her step and when she unbolted the gate of his sty he would amble to meet her and she could swear that in his face she could detect a look of pleasure.

'Morning, Rufus,' she greeted him as, grunting, he ambled towards her. 'Oh look at the mess you've left me. Call yourself a friend! You're a horror, yes you are.' But despite the unsavoury offerings he had left on the ground, she talked to him with affection and he seemed to understand. She wondered sometimes if perhaps he considered the messes he daily left for her to shovel up were his contribution to their friendship.

He grew fat just as they had planned when they'd agreed to keep a pig, but somehow she conveniently forgot (or pushed to the back of her mind) what lay ahead for him. Perhaps it had been a mistake to give him a name, but when she went into his sty and called, 'Food time, Rufus', he never failed to answer with a grunt she could swear held appreciation.

Then came an evening when Den told her Rufus was being collected the next day and taken to the slaughter-house.

'I looked in at the butchers on the way back from delivering the veg this afternoon and I've arranged that when the carcass is ready Bill Chapman will joint it up for us. Incredible, you know Kathie, there'll be pretty well nothing on it that can't be used. With the sty empty at the weekend we ought to give it a good spring-clean so we can get a replacement.'

She nodded, not answering.

'Is something up, Kathie? You haven't got much to say.'

'Sorry. I expect I'm tired.'

It wasn't like Kathie to admit to being tired but, come to think of it, it hadn't been like her to look peaky either. Or had it? When did he really *look* at her? She never gave herself a chance to relax; that was her trouble.

'Tell you what, love – you go on up and get yourself an early night. I'll wash these dishes.'

She made an effort to pull her mind away from the pigsty where Rufus would have no idea he was spending his last night 'Better still, we'll do the dishes together and both have an early night.' And the sudden smile she gave him made him think that perhaps she wasn't as tired as all that and an early night might be just what they needed.

Next morning the lorry came. Rufus sensed something was afoot and decided he wasn't going to walk up the loading plank; but he lost his battle and at last he was aboard. Kathie watched from the 'warm room' window. When Den looked in to say Rufus had gone he found Kathie in floods of tears. 'Hey, Kathie love, don't cry like that.'

She hadn't heard him coming.

'He's such a nice pig,' she'd sobbed, 'knew me, always came to meet me. I should have stopped him going. I came out to say please don't send him – but I couldn't. He had to go. That's why we had him. We're country people.' Her last words were almost swallowed in her sobs.

'Hey, hey, love, this is the way we live. He won't know anything about it. Blow your nose and dry your eyes.'

She looked at him with eyes full of misery as she rubbed the palms of her work-hardened hands over her face.

'If it's going to upset you like this we'd better not have another. You've got the tough part coming when I collect the meat from Bill Chapman.'

She'd nodded, holding her chin a little higher.

'What sort of a wimp do you take me for? I've been making notes on all I have to do. It's all part of the job. 'Course I can do it.'

He probably surprised them both by giving her a sudden hug. 'Good girl. And do we replace Rufus?'

She nodded. 'Of course we do. I won't be so silly next time.'

And silently he vowed that next time he would send her on an errand to Deremouth or even Exeter to be sure that she would know nothing about it until the animal had been taken to the slaughterhouse.

–

As time went on there was no sign of the family they wanted, not even a few days of hope. Disappointment gave way to a dull sort of acceptance, something that seemed to hang between them like a shadow. It had never been in Kathie's nature to give way to depression; if things went wrong instead of crying about it she would decide on a plan to overcome the problem. But now she was faced with something outside her control. And did she imagine it or, as the early years went by, had something quenched the spontaneous passion in their relationship? In truth it probably had, but the reason was most likely to be simply that they had more work than time, sending them to bed aching in every joint and longing for the oblivion of sleep.

But it's *shared* work, she told herself, work that means the world to both of us. Westways is our life. They were neither of them ambitious for material things and even if they weren't prospering they had no real financial worries. It was early in 1928 that Dennis bought a van. No longer did he have to push his cart to the village greengrocer and, even more important, having transport meant he could take some of his more exotic produce as far afield as Deremouth. In August of that same year he engaged two fifteen-year-old boys, Bert Delbridge and Stanley Stone, both of them straight from school and good workers.

Until then, attention to the cottage had had to be pushed into second place in their workload as they had both been needed on the land but the two lads were keen and Kathie was able to turn the place into a real home. It might lack riches, but never welcome or comfort.

The money Millicent had given Kathie had been put into a Post Office Savings Account to which, little by little, they had managed to add. They had permission from the landlord to extend the cottage, so they put the work into the hands of the local builder and decorator. Whenever possible Dennis acted as his labourer, doing anything he could to keep the cost down. The 'warm room' lost the sink and became a dining room, albeit with a kitchen range, and beyond it Bob Geary built a small extension comprising a new kitchen and above it a bathroom. The small parlour had a 'face lift' with new wallpaper and, bought at an auction sale, two easy chairs, a sofa and a small table. All the interior work they did themselves. In area the cottage wasn't very much bigger, but the difference it made to their living was enormous.

With the two boys helping Dennis, Kathie had more time for cooking too. She borrowed *Mrs Beeton's Book of Household Management* from the one-evening-a-week lending library in a room behind the village hall; it became her bible. Into a thick exercise book she copied recipes and hints enough to make her a domestic treasure. Her shelves became packed with preserves, chutney, jams, mincemeat, pickled eggs and bottled fruit, peas and beans.

'You're like a squirrel collecting nuts to hoard for the winter,' Dennis teased her when he came into the kitchen to find her standing on a chair lining up her pots of blackberry and apple jelly on the high shelf. But there was pride in his voice, whether entirely for her or partly in the knowledge that through the winter months they would still be eating food they had produced themselves – or, in the case of the blackberries, picked from the brambles in the lane. 'They're collecting poor old Chummy tomorrow morning.' He went on as she climbed down from the chair, her latest array of jars lined up and neatly labelled: Green tomato chutney, 1929. The latest pig was Chummy, but as Dennis said it his mind went back to when Rufus, their first, had gone to the slaughterhouse. He could remember the scene so well. It was a long time since they had consciously looked at each other as they did now. He held her shoulders then gently drew her close. Minutes later she was ashamed at how easily she had been able to forget poor Chummy. As she raised her face to Dennis's, her lips parted and his mouth covered hers, not in the brief habitual kiss, but in a caress that told her nothing had changed between them. Only when he spoke did his words surprise her.

'There never was much of you, but Kathie you've got really skinny You work too hard.'

'Silly! I'm peasant type; I'm not the sort to sit around. You should know that.'

'Peasant type suits me fine. You deserve better than I give you though.'

'Den, darling Den,' she said with a laugh that proved another change brought by the years: he had just told her tonight's supper would be Chummy's last and she had learnt to accept that this was how they lived. Had some of her spirit been crushed? When she answered he knew that her mind hadn't gone further than what he'd been saying. 'What could be better that what we have here? I wouldn't change a thing.'

But even as she said it she knew it wasn't strictly true. After over six years of marriage they must surely accept they would never have children. Suppose the fault was with *him*. Suppose he couldn't make a woman pregnant. There were some men who couldn't; she had read an article about it on the medical page of a magazine she'd found on a side table in the library. Yet each month she believed she saw accusation in the way he looked at her. There's nothing wrong with me, again and again she told herself. What was it she had read in the article about a low sperm count? She almost wished she hadn't looked at the magazine. Now that she knew the trouble could be with the man as easily as with the woman it seemed to change how she felt when they made love. It still sometimes gave the same physical pleasure, but something really fundamental was lost. The change in her feelings was subtle; sometimes she was able to believe she imagined it.

–

She soon absorbed all she learned from Mrs Beeton. These days there was no need for her to get out her notebook and follow instructions on what to do with jointed Chummy. She could have written her own cookery book; she knew just how to cure hams and bacon, how to make good dishes from offal and how to make brawn. The only thing she rejected was the chitterlings – but Stanley Stone happily took them home, added to the chops she shared with both lads. She had learnt a good deal about the outside work, but her natural flair was in turning a house into a home, whether it was with the food she cooked, the way she arranged the greenery from the hedgerows, or the wild flowers when the season was right, or her knack of bringing a room to life with colourful cushion covers and draught excluders she made from scraps of remnants she bought for next to nothing.

Time is said to be the greatest healer and when her monthly disappointment arrived always on time it lost some of its power.

–

Then in the spring of 1933 the miracle happened. After nearly ten years of marriage she was pregnant. Her own fear that she was barren disappeared, as did her suspicion that Dennis was less of a man than he believed himself to be.

Her natural good health was given a boost by her feeling of inner joy. So through the early months of pregnancy Kathie thrived. The changes in her body were a source of excitement and pride, pride tinged with joy and thankfulness when she saw the way Dennis looked at her. Perhaps she would give him that army of sons after all. In those months often she thought of her mother with a new understanding.

With five months still to wait the second bedroom was ready for the new arrival and for Kathie it was the most natural thing in the world to spend any spare hours working out of doors. She wasn't as nimble as she had been in previous years, but any discomfort she felt (even to herself she refused to call it pain) she accepted as part of her new and exciting experience.

The latest pig, Bertram, was growing well. Pig and chickens continued to be her responsibility. As the crops flourished so she blossomed, feeling herself to be one with nature. Outside, it was a case of all four of them – Dennis, the two lads and Kathie too – working long hours right through the autumn. The baby wasn't due until towards the end of January, so she threw herself wholeheartedly into the work. As the season for each vegetable peaked she not only worked outside but indoors too as she put up her preserves for the winter.

It was in December, a grey still afternoon when the clouds hung low, when she took her shovel and outsize bucket and set to work clearing the pigsty. Although it was a job she disliked, normally she got through it with cheerful determination. But on that day every movement was an effort; over the last few hours she was sure something was different. For weeks she had silently accepted backache as a natural part of her condition, but on that day it seemed to push everything else from her mind. There was nothing, *nothing* but pain.

'Oh Bertram, I know it's not your fault, but this is a filthy smelly mess.' With a mighty effort she emptied her shovel into the bucket, then just for a moment stood straight with her hand on the small of her aching back. It had been getting worse as the months had gone on, but it was something she had accepted as normal. When Dennis said, 'Are you sure you want to help outside, you feel OK?' she always replied with the same reassuring smile and, 'Fit as a flea', or 'Just you try and stop me!' But on that afternoon in Bertram's sty she could have cried with the pain that was like nothing she'd known. It must be just the way the baby is lying, she told herself. It's never been like this. I must pull myself together; I bet some women are much worse. Oh, but I feel so awful. Pull yourself together... one more shovelful and the bucket will be full. That'll be all for this afternoon. Then I'll go indoors. Mustn't worry Den. If I lie down for a bit perhaps it'll be... 'Ouch!' she cried out aloud before she could stop

43

herself. With no one to see her she dropped her shovel then bending as near to double as her girth would allow, pressed her hands against the top of the fence of what she referred to as Bertram's garden (his or any pig's in residence at the time). She had never known such searing pain. It had woken her in the night and still been with her when she got up, but not like this. She ought to call Den and ask him to get one of the lads to carry the bucket. But Den would worry. Just because she had been so energetic all through these months that was no reason to suppose she wouldn't get pain at some stage. It must happen to all women. If other people could put up with it and not make a fuss, then so could she. Using all her willpower she stood straight, then stooped first to pick up the shovel then the heavy bucket. Bertram watched her dolefully, then as if to tell her that this was *his* space and he'd do what he liked, looking her straight in the eye he gave a satisfied grunt as he left a steaming deposit then turned his back on her and ambled indoors to lie on his clean straw. She put her spade over the wall, and then with her spare hand let herself out, closing the gate securely. Now to carry the load to the far end of their five-acre plot.

The rough grass track at the edge of the field had never felt like this before, so uneven that she wasn't sure where her feet were going to touch ground. She'd have to stop for a moment. No, she'd get beyond the last row of sprouts before she let herself rest. Why didn't the plants stay still? Why did they sway like that? Nearly at the last row of them, then I'll... but she knew no more.

-

Perhaps she only lay on the ground for a minute or two, or even only seconds, she was aware of nothing until she felt herself being lifted and heard Dennis say, 'Now we've got her up, I can manage her. Take the pail, Stan, and empty it in the ditch right at the end. I'll carry Kathie to the house.'

'Are you sure? She must have got pretty heavy.'

'She's coming round. We'll manage.'

Kathie was making a huge effort to gather her wits. Why was she being carried?

'Can walk,' she tried to say, but her mouth seemed to have a will of its own and didn't want to shape the words. And her back felt as though it had broken in two.

'You must have tripped,' she heard him say.

'Ground… kept moving…' At least her voice was coming back and she reached up to put her arms around Dennis's neck in an attempt to ease her weight. 'Too heavy… can walk.' As reason returned she was conscious that he was getting breathless so she wriggled to get to her feet. 'Put me down… honestly.'

He stood her on her feet, keeping his arm around her.

'Have you hurt yourself? You mustn't carry that bucket. You should call me, or get one of the boys.'

'It wasn't that.' It was no use; she couldn't hide it from him. 'It was because my back hurts. I expect everyone feels the same. It's probably just the way the baby is lying.' Sounding so strong and brave had been an enormous effort, but she couldn't keep up the pretence. 'Den, suppose something is wrong with the baby. It's…' Whatever it was was lost as she leant against him burying her face against his shoulder.

'Why didn't you tell me? One of the boys could have done the pig.' As he spoke he was holding her against him with one arm and with the other hand rubbing her back.

'It can't be the baby starting to come, can it? It's not due for more than six weeks. It can't be, can it?' He heard the fright in her voice.

'It's possible I suppose.' He made sure his voice had a ring of confidence, even though he was gripped with fear for something so far from his knowledge. 'Some people get their dates wrong, so I've heard.'

'I didn't get it wrong. My last period started on Good Friday. Oooh!' Her exclamation escaped before she could stop it.

'Arms round my neck; I'm getting you indoors. Then I'll send young Bert to bring Nurse Cox.' And with almost superhuman strength he hoisted her back into his arms and carried her to the house at what was nearly a run. Leaving her bent double in her chair he went to find Bert Delbridge and send him on his mission.

When he got back into the cottage there was no sign of Kathie.

'Kathie! Where are you? Kathie!' he yelled up the stairs then, getting no reply, took them two at a time in his quest to find her. Then downstairs again. 'Kathie! Where the hell are you, Kathie?'

That's when he noticed the door of the old earth closet was open. He found her there, leaning weakly against the wall.

'Couldn't you manage the stairs? Poor old Kathie. Come on love, I'll get you up to He on the bed. Nurse Cox will be here soon, Bert's gone to get her.' Her answer was a silent, convulsive movement she couldn't control as she retched. 'You feel sick? This place is enough to make anyone feel sick. Come on, love, let's get you upstairs.'

'…was the pigsty… the smell… it's all over my Wellies… couldn't pull them off.'

What a moment for him to remember the first time he'd seen her, a girl like no other. Slim, a picture of health, her eyes so clear and luminous, her wide bright smile. It hurt him to see what time had done to her. Even the rich chestnut of her hair seemed no more than dingy brown, her skin looked weathered and yet there was nothing to hint at a healthy outdoor life, rather it seemed yellow and tight across the bony structure of her face. There were crows' nests around her sunken eyes, eyes with dark smudges under them. And her hands! As she raised one to wipe it across her mouth it registered on him as it never had before just how work-hardened and rough they were; that happy, energetic, glorious young girl he had fallen in love with had had soft hands, he remembered clearly how she had wiped the oil off them on the rag he had given her that day when her bicycle had broken.

'Kathie, dear Kathie, what have I done to you?'

She made herself smile even though the effort made her eyes sting with hot tears. 'You've given me a baby. It must be coming early. Oh… ooh.' Frightened to breathe, she gripped his hands.

'Come out to the garden bench and I'll pull your wellies off,' he said gently. 'Then upstairs we go.'

—

By the time Nurse Cox pedalled up the track the feet of the offending wellies were standing in a bucket of water outside the back door, and Kathie was undressed and in bed, a bed in which Dennis had spread the mackintosh sheet they had in readiness. For Kathie it was hard to concentrate when she was consumed with pain, but somehow she'd managed to give Dennis instructions so that everything was ready for labour. She had no idea what to expect, but nothing less than labour could make her hurt like this. Would it get worse? She had been in the house when her mother had given birth to Algy and then to Lily, but she had had no idea that she'd been going through anything like this. And if her mother could bear it without making a fuss, then so could she. She tried to remember what the nurse had said on her one and only visit: when the contractions come, you have to push with all your might. She had imagined that when they talked about contractions it was something that came and then eased, but this just went on and on.

'Den,' she breathed holding her hand towards him, 'let me grip you.' Then when he took her hands in his, with all her might she pushed, then pushed again.

'Here's Nurse Cox,' he said, thankfully, 'I'll go and bring her in. Kathie, you'll be all right.' It was meant to boost to her confidence but it sounded more like a plea.

Kathie heard him greet the midwife.

In the village Emily Cox was always known as nurse, but in truth for all her experience of bringing local babies into the world she had no qualifications. Dr Knight trusted her, the local women had faith in her, and hearing her voice gave Kathie hope.

'This little rascal keen to get into the world, is he? Now then, Mrs Hawthorne my dear, let's take a peak at you.' With one swift movement she threw back the bed covers, then hoisted up Kathie's nightdress. 'How often are you getting the contractions?'

'The pain doesn't stop. My back… just goes on… on…' Kathie bit her lip, ashamed at how near she was to losing control.

With hands that were still cold from her cycle ride, Nurse Cox felt her patient's hugely swollen stomach. 'Um,' she grunted, an uncertain sound. 'Big load you're carrying m'dear, no wonder your poor back is letting you know about it. I'll pull the covers back over you – just want a word with your husband.'

As if by magic Dennis appeared in the doorway from where he had been listening just out of sight.

'That lad of yours, can you get him to ride out again and see if he can get Dr Knight. The baby is in no position to get born; the head isn't engaged. If it decides to try and push its way out we shall need forceps, it'll be a job for the doctor.' Then following Dennis to the head of the stairs, she said in a whisper, 'There's something here that worries me.'

Half an hour later it was apparent there was something that worried Dr Knight too. The nearest telephone was in the village street, so he reversed his motor car the length of the lane and parked by the kiosk.

'The ambulance is coming out from Deremouth. I want you to have an X-ray. I shall follow the ambulance in my motor car to be there to see the result.' he said as came back into the bedroom. His voice was big and over-cheerful.

'Why an X-ray? Is there something wrong with our baby? I can't feel it moving.' Desperately Kathie wanted to sound calm, but it was impossible to hide her terror as she waited for his reply.

'The heartbeat is strong,' he reassured her.

So why the X-ray? Kathie and Dennis looked at each other helplessly.

'Is there room in the ambulance for me?' he asked.

'It's most unusual.' For a moment the doctor hesitated as he looked from Dennis to Kathie and then back again, his mind working on the right action. 'Most unusual. But I think perhaps it might be a good thing if you were to come along. Come in the motor car with me. I'll let you know the outcome, Mrs Cox. Perhaps we'll be delivering Mrs Hawthorne home and you'll be needed after all.' He was a kindly man and he could see the fear in Kathie's eyes. In his opinion she was too old to be giving birth for the first time. A girl of twenty, now that was what he considered ideal, the body young and supple. But this one must be well into her thirties – his assumption was evidence of what her hard life had done to twenty-nine-year-old Kathie. 'Now then, my dear, can you manage the stairs or shall we see if they can get you down on a stretcher?'

Kathie took a deep breath and made sure she spoke clearly despite the dreadful feeling that she was being torn apart. 'I walked up, so I can walk down. But why do I need an X-ray?'

'I want us to be sure of the baby's position,' the doctor said with little regard to the truth. However, the answer stilled some of her fear.

For Kathie that evening was lost, but for Dennis, waiting on a hard bench, it seemed endless. They had arrived at the hospital just as the winter daylight was fading and the lamp lighter was working his way along the street. As Kathie had been carried away to where he supposed the X-ray machine was, Dennis had been told to wait and someone would come and tell him what was happening. In fact Dr Knight appeared from the sister's office after not much more than ten minutes. Immediately Dennis was on his feet.

'What's happening? Is the X-ray done? Is she in labour?'

'Mr Hawthorne, the result is much as I suspected. Your wife is already under sedation so Sister will bring the consent form for you to sign.'

'Sedation? Consent? For what?'

'The birth is not due for more than a month, but it is imperative the surgeon performs a Caesarean immediately.' Then, seeing Dennis's mystified expression, he explained, 'An operation to take the baby. Have no fear; early though it is, it appears to be a large embryo. The real cause for alarm is not the birth; it is your wife's condition. The X-ray confirms what I feared: there is a large tumour in the womb.' Whatever Dennis had braced himself to hear, the doctor's words seemed to strip him of the power to think. 'The only thing to do is to remove her womb – a total hysterectomy. How long the tumour has been developing or whether it has spread I can't tell you, but she couldn't be in better hands than Mr Freeman's. Ah, here comes Sister.'

'When?' Dennis was incapable of putting a whole sentence together.

'As I say, she is already under sedation and being taken along to the theatre. The baby will be delivered and please God it's the fine healthy specimen I anticipate. You'd better read this before you sign, although I fear there is no other way but to perform the operation.'

Dennis scanned through the words but his mind was incapable of understanding. Kathie… Kathie who had never had a day's illness… a tumour… in good hands… yes, but could even the cleverest of surgeons make her well?

'She's always been well,' he murmured more to himself than the doctor. 'If they take it all away, will she get well?'

As the sister scurried off with the signed form the doctor sat on the bench by Dennis's side.

'There is always risk with any form of surgery. But assuming that it hasn't spread into other organs we must hope and trust that she will soon be restored to her normal good health – bearing in mind, of course, that she will be unable to have more children.'

'We've been married for ten years, you know. We wanted children and I know how much she cared that she could never conceive. I wish to God she had gone on being disappointed, then this might never have happened.'

'No, my dear chap, carrying the child has been a blessing in disguise. She might have gone on far longer not knowing anything was amiss if the wretched thing had had more space to grow.'

'What are they doing to her now?' Dennis ran his fingers round the collar of his shirt. Despite not being able to stop shivering he felt a trickle of sweat run down his back. The sweat of fear; not for the first time he felt it. Memories crowded back on him. In the contentment and satisfaction of their life at Westways he had believed the past had lost its power. Then in the strange way that a mind can jump from one thing to another, he became conscious that he was still in his work clothes. 'Straight from the field,' he muttered as if he expected Dr Knight to have followed his thoughts.

'As soon as she is fully unconscious they will perform the Caesarean – indeed they are probably bringing your child into the world at this minute.'

They waited in silence. Five minutes or five hours, to Dennis it was like all eternity. Then the sister came from a double door at the far end of the corridor, hurrying toward them with a beaming smile.

'Congratulations, Mr Hawthorne. You have a beautiful daughter. She's just being got ready to face the world and then I'll let you have a quick peep. After that I'm afraid we shall have to ask you to leave.'

'And Kathie? My wife?'

'I'll make sure you have the telephone number so that you can ring us in the morning.'

'Ring? Can't I see her? Can't I wait until the operation is over? Kathie will want me. We have a daughter; we ought to see her together.'

'I'm afraid the rules don't allow anyone here waiting. There is a list of visiting hours in the reception area, you'll see it as you go out. Wednesday and Sunday from three until four in the afternoons.' Then, with a smile intended to take that frightened look from the poor man's face, she added, 'If we gave people access at other times we'd never be able to give our patients the care they deserve. Now you wait a few more minutes and I'll bend the rules and bring your new daughter out for you to see.'

Doctor Knight took his watch from the pocket of his waistcoat and checked the time. 'I can wait a few more minutes,' he said, 'then I'll drive you back to Sedgewood with me.'

Dennis' instinct was to refuse, to say that if they wouldn't let him wait on the bench in the hospital he would go to one of the shelters on the seafront. Then in the morning instead of telephoning he would call in and enquire and perhaps they'd let him have a minute or two with Kathie. But at home, there were animals to be looked after; and Kathie would need clean nightdresses brought in... please God, please make it be like that, make her need her things, don't take her away from me. Then with something like guilt he realized that as he'd tried to hold in his mind the image of being with Kathie, the operation over and she looking fresh faced, rosy cheeked, those tell-tale dark smudges gone from under her eyes, not once in those moments had he thought of the tiny person who had just been brought into the world six weeks before her time.

Soon Sister reappeared carrying a tiny bundle, wrapped so securely that the newborn could move neither hands nor feet.

'There she is. Isn't she a perfect treasure.'

'So tiny,' he murmured as he gazed in awe at the wonder of what he and Kathie had produced.

'For a seven-and-a-half-month delivery she is a bonny babe. She weighs five pounds one ounce. Another six weeks and she would have given a real problem.'

'Not much more than two bags of sugar.'

The sister saw the way his face was working as with his teeth clamped together he held his chin steady. Poor man. What was ahead of him if he had to rear this bundle of love on his own?

'And just as sweet, too,' she answered briskly, her tone doing more to help him over his bad moment than any sympathy. 'Now then, off you go. Your family will be in good hands. You may telephone any time after eight in the morning; just ask for Wyndham Ward.'

To plead or argue would be useless. There was a strange comfort in the feeling of Dr Knight's hand on his elbow as they walked down the empty corridor.

That was on Monday night, a long night of anguish he would never forget.

Gradually through the years he and Kathie had taken each other for granted, content in their shared lives. Not until that afternoon had he looked, *really looked*, and realized how changed she had become, how drained and exhausted. What sort of a night would she be enduring, frightened and alone in that cheerless hospital. When she woke from the operation – please God make it have been successful – she wouldn't know where she was. Would she be able to understand that their baby had been born? The baby, a girl so tiny she might have been a child's doll, small and vulnerable and depending on them to take care of her and love her. He felt a strange unfamiliar tenderness. What would happen to them all? If Kathie didn't… no, don't let the thought even take shape; of course Kathie will pull through and be well again. She's always been fit and full of energy. But had that really been true? She's a fighter, she would never admit to being beaten no matter how tired she was. Had he been fair in taking it for granted that working all day and every day was all she wanted? She'd seemed happy. Often enough they'd both been too tired at the end of the day for anything more than to roll into bed with a mumbled goodnight. Yet on those other nights when he'd wanted her, she had never said she was too tired; no, plenty of times he had thought it meant more to her than it did to him. Dear Kathie, he could almost hear her urgent whisper, 'Don't rush, Den. Make it last', right up to the last few weeks and even knowing how early they had to be up in the morning. Dear Kathie. Remember the day of their wedding, their honeymoon with the old zinc bath. Oh God, don't take her away. Everything was so good; all that was missing was a family. You can't give us a child and then take Kathie.

The day had taken its toll on him. When he heard a sob break in his throat he didn't care, he didn't even try to fight it. Soon after that, sleep overtook him. When he woke and reached for his torch to look at the time, it was half past five. Normally he and Kathie got up just after six o'clock but on that morning he was glad to start the day. By six o'clock he had washed and shaved and was finding a clean shirt. A clean shirt to wear to phone the hospital? To go in his work things from the previous day would have felt wrong so he took what they thought of as his 'tidy' trousers from their hanger. He would do some of Kathie's jobs early, helping the time to pass before he could make his call. So he collected the eggs, fed the chickens and replaced their bowl of water. Bertram would have to wait until later, a pigsty was no place when he was dressed like this.

Before he had married he had looked after himself quite efficiently, so it was no hardship to cook his own breakfast. At last it was ten to eight and time to drive the van to the village.

The night staff had gone off duty and the nurse who spoke to him told him, 'Mrs Hawthorne has come round from the operation and is sleeping.' And the baby? Apparently that was another ward, so he had to wait until his call was transferred. The answer was much the same: 'The baby is doing well.'

He drove home feeling strangely empty. All he knew was that Kathie and the baby were alive. He felt shut out from them and helpless. Once back at the cottage he took off his good trousers and clean shirt and put on yesterday's work things. The greatest therapy was hard work, something Westways could always supply.

By the time he was allowed to see Kathie on Wednesday from three o'clock until four she was truly back in the land of the living and she had been moved to the same ward as her baby. The curtains were pulled around her bed but the nurse ushered him in then left them alone. Propped against pillows Kathie was sitting in bed with the tiny baby at her breast. His eyes stung with tears.

'Den, just look at her.'

He nodded, frightened to trust his voice then, surprising himself and thankful for the curtains, he found himself on his knees at her bedside.

'Kathie, oh Kathie, thank God. You look fine; you look like yourself. Been so worried.'

'Worse for you than for me, I expect, Den. Most of the time I didn't know anything about it. I wanted to have her properly, I mean like nature intended. But she's so beautiful. You'd never think she came early would you?'

'But what about *you*? Is your back better? What have they told you, Kathie? They say nothing on the phone, only that the operation was satisfactory.'

'Mr Freeman, the surgeon, has been round to see me and he said it went very well and the tumour hadn't spread any further. Apparently they have to send it to be analysed or something. They want to keep me here for three weeks.' He knew from her expression that it was the cost that worried her. 'But that's ridiculous. They can't make me stay.'

'If *they* can't, then I can.' His voice was uncharacteristically masterful.

'I promise I'd rest at home. If you said I couldn't work outside, then I'd stay indoors in the warm.'

'You'll certainly do that, but not until they are happy for you to leave the hospital. Kathie, we've got a few pounds put by.'

She didn't look convinced. Every pound they had managed to save had been cause for pride and now they were expected to throw it all away when she had a perfectly good bed at home. Anyway she wanted to look after the baby herself.

'Its silly for me to lie here doing nothing while you have to do your own cooking and washing.'

'Remember, woman,' he said with an almost boyish grin, 'before you swept into my life I catered for myself most efficiently and so I am again. And when you come home don't think you're going to rule the roost, you'll do as I tell you. And that means rest.'

Kathie wriggled deeper into her pillows. With her baby nuzzling at her nipple and with Den looking at her in a way she hadn't seen for years, she felt she would burst with happiness. She wouldn't let herself consider the chance that the biopsy result would be anything but perfect.

Dennis couldn't let his thoughts go beyond the point when they would have the result from the analyst. To take it for granted that the tumour had been non-malignant would be akin to tempting fate. But today was special and precious to both of them, the first time they had been together as a proper family.

'Can I hold her?' He moved the conversation away from their meagre savings. The operation would make a huge hole in them, but none of it mattered as long as she and the baby were well. As he took the tiny form in his arms again his vision misted. 'So little,' he muttered. 'Oh Kathie, she's a miracle.'

Kathie nodded, knowing just how he was feeling for it had been the same for her the first time she had held the little bundle in her arms. 'She's tiny now,' she said, 'but she'll soon start to grow. Before I had her more than anything I worried that I wouldn't be able to feed her. I had almost no bosom – you remember. But now—' she stuck out her chest with pride— 'if all that gets full of milk she's going to grow in no time.'

He couldn't keep the smile off his face. Bosom or no, what a child she sounded.

'We can't keep calling her *she*. Which is it to be? Jessica or Miranda?' These were the two names they had selected if the baby turned out to be a girl. But in their hearts they had both been sure it would have been a boy, Conrad James.

Now they concentrated on the mite, still too young for them even to imagine what her features would be.

'She doesn't look to me like a Miranda,' Kathie said. 'She'd better be Jessica.'

'Doesn't look much like a Jessica either at the moment. We'll just call her Jess, Jessie Hawthorne.'

It was one of life's special moments.

-

Kathie stayed in hospital for three more weeks, two of them after they had been told the result they had longed to hear. The tumour had been large and fast-growing but it hadn't been malignant. Now all she had to do was get strong so that she would be ready to look after Jess. That year Christmas passed them almost unnoticed and yet had there ever been one when their hearts had been so full of thankfulness? After that afternoon halfway through

December when she had been taken into hospital, Dennis was constantly aware of her appearance and he marvelled how different she looked after these weeks of rest. The years they'd been together had transformed her from a girl to a woman, a radiant woman.

Once home she obeyed instructions and rested for two hours each afternoon, choosing her time according to when Jess, having slurped her way through her two o'clock feed, was asleep. That was in the beginning, but with each week as Jess grew bigger and Kathie grew stronger, gradually the routine changed. There was always help needed outside so with the pram close by, Kathie undertook the lighter jobs. At that stage, Stanley made himself responsible for Bertram.

By the time Kathie was once more keeper of the pigsty, Bertram had given place to Hector and Jess was taking her first staggering steps. If a Good Fairy had appeared and said she could hold time still for them, Kathie and Dennis were so aware of all they had that they might have been tempted, except for one thing: each day Jess learnt something new, each day she became more precious. And so with confidence they would have dismissed the Good Fairy's offer.

1939-1945

Three

Holding it by its two handles, Kathie picked up her basket-work container and started towards the shed. The peas had cropped well and this was her third full load that day. Glancing at her watch, she decided this must be her last. The hard work they put into Westways had ensured that it brought them a comfortable living doing what they loved best. About three years ago they had been able to afford to have electricity brought into the house and more recently a telephone too. And Kathie's natural flair had turned it into a home that radiated warmth and comfort.

'I'm going in now,' she called to Dennis. 'Only a few minutes and Jess will be home from school.'

'Right-o. I'll just finish this row of broad beans and I'll get loaded up. Kathie, get us something to eat pretty soon so that it's ready when I get back from delivering, then this evening I'll get a few more hours out here. No Terriers this evening, so I want to make the most of the long day with the weather like this.'

Dennis never missed the chance of an evening with the Territorial Army (or the Terriers as they were known). He had joined when they had started recruiting in Sedgewood about a year after Jess had been born and, although more recently a lot of volunteers years his junior had enlisted – including Stanley Stone and Bert Delbridge who, by that time, had worked for him so long that they had almost become part of the family – he enjoyed the male companionship and the half hour they spent in the Stag and Beetle after their evening sessions.

'All right, love,' Kathie answered, 'say half an hour from now. Will that do?'

'I reckon I'll last out that long. What have we got?'

'A lot of eggs. They're laying so well. We'll have cheese omelettes and I've cut you a good gammon steak to go with yours.'

'Good girl. That and a hunk of crusty bread'll do me fine.' Then he looked up from his picking, his gaze holding hers. 'Here a minute.'

How easy it had become to slip back into that easy companionship that had temporarily been lost when he'd come so close to losing her. He looked at her, remembering the nightmare of those days. There was nothing grey and drawn about her face now. She looked a picture of health, her hair glinting chestnut in the sunshine, her figure as slim as a girl's. He consciously forced himself to think that way and not face the truth that whereas when he'd first known her she had been attractively slim, now she was painfully thin. He remembered how when she had been nursing Jess she had been so proud of her shapely bosom. All that was changed; now her breasts were shrunk and shapeless beyond recognition. But she was just as full of energy as when he'd married her and, if her complexion had lost the bloom of youth, nothing altered her ready smile or the way her brown eyes looked at him carrying their own message of affection. Perhaps to the outside world Kathie wasn't seen as a beauty, but to Dennis those wide dark eyes, her short, snub nose and overlarge mouth, fitted perfectly into the woman she was.

Putting down her loaded basket she came along between the rows of broad beans.

'Yes? Do you want to show me something?'

'I was thinking – about us, Kathie. We're so damned lucky. Can it last? Not just for us, for everyone? When storm clouds build they don't just go away.'

'Hitler and all his nonsense, you mean? We must hang on to what Mr Chamberlain told us last year. Hitler has spread his wings as far as he intends.' Then with a laugh, a laugh that in truth was more bravado than mirth, 'Your trouble is that you and those chaps you march around with want to flex your muscles and frighten him. But surely everyone has too much sense to let that happen – us and the German people too.'

'Please God you're right. You know something Kathie Hawthorne? If everyone had your trust and wisdom the world would be a better place.'

'Chump.' And this time there was nothing forced in her laugh. 'Like you say, Den, we are lucky, so let's just appreciate what we have. Hark, I hear footsteps, Jess is running along the lane and here am I, still garden grimy.'

'Send her out to give me a hand. She likes picking.'

'She prefers peas; she can eat those as she goes. I'll go and say hello to her and tell her you want some help with the beans.'

'Leave your basket, I'll take it to the shed. Then when I've weighed it all up I'll run the stuff along to the shop. Jess can ride with me.'

So she left him and went towards the house where Jess was going from room to room looking for her.

'Hello love, I heard you running up the lane. I've been helping your dad with the picking. He said to tell you he could do with an extra pair of hands now that I have to start getting some food ready. Better take off your school dress first. Just your knicks will do out there; the sun is lovely.'

'I came home with Ben Williams, Mum – well, till I got to our lane I did. You know what, Mum? He skips better than I do. Isn't that funny – *better than I do* – cross hands, bumps, all of it he can do and he hasn't even got a rope of his own. I let him take mine if he promised to bring it to school in the morning.'

'That was a good idea, Jess. Arms up, while I pull off your dress and vest. There you are. Off you run.'

Yes, she thought, watching Jess dart across the small patch of lawn to the field beyond, Den's right, it's almost frightening how lucky we are. Further than that she wouldn't let her thoughts go, for surely it was nonsense to think Hitler's screaming speeches and the wonderful displays of marching youths whose pictures were so often in the newspaper would lead to war. How could they, after all the trouble Mr Chamberlain had gone to less than a year ago? If we could understand what he is shouting about it might not be so scary.

–

There were plenty of better off people in Sedgewood village, but it wouldn't have been surprising if some of them envied the Hawthornes' independent way of living. But of course that would have been seeing the picture through rose-tinted spectacles, for many a night when Dennis and Kathie went to bed they knew the sort of tiredness never experienced by those who worked regular hours.

The last of the asparagus was no more than a memory, green peas and broad beans came to an end, the crop of marrows swelled with the promise of a bumper year, the runner beans grew long and succulent. This year was no different from any other as the land brought forth its bounty. Kathie suspected there was defiance in the cheerfulness of people she met when she went shopping in the village; or did she imagine it, simply because she knew it to be the truth for herself? There were evenings when she twiddled with the tuning knob on the wireless and the screaming voice of Adolf Hitler filled the sitting room making her blood run cold. If Den had been there with her, her imagination might not have carried her into such unknown regions of horror, but by August most of his evenings were spent with the Terriers.

There was the day when Kathie and Jess went to the Old National School in the village and queued to collect their gas masks. With each breath they made a noise like a pig grunting. One little boy was crying and didn't want to put his on, but Jessie was determined to look grown up, even though hers was made to look like Mickey Mouse. She wasn't going to let anyone guess that she had a horrid pinching sort of feeling in her tummy and wished they were at home and none of this was happening.

'Remember Fred Dawkins?' Dennis greeted Kathie when, on their return, she found him picking runner beans. 'Calls himself the billeting officer apparently. He came to see what space we have. It seems they're expecting a load of London kids and are fixing up where they can be housed. Not here, I told him. Having only two bedrooms lets us off the hook.'

'Poor little souls! Imagine if it were the other way round and children from here were being sent to strangers. They've got to make plans – the same as with those horrid gas masks. But it won't happen. It won't, will it, Den?' In her heart she knew the answer as well as he did. If it didn't happen this autumn it would be next spring, next autumn, sometime. The situation was like a festering wound; it would throb and throb with no chance of healing until it was lanced. He knew she wasn't expecting an answer. 'But, if it does—' just to say it seemed like tempting fate— 'it *mustn't*, but Den, if it did and you had to go off with the Terriers, Jess and I wouldn't need a dining room. We'd eat on the little table in the "warm room". So we could always put a camp bed in there – and try and make it pretty – then we'd have room.'

'What rubbish the woman talks! If the chaps and I go marching off for King and Country, then you'll have more than enough to do here without taking other people's kids to look after. Anyway, if I have to go, I want to know that nothing is changed back here at home.'

A cold hand of fear seemed to grip her. All thought of the evacuees was forgotten.

–

By the first Sunday in September there was no way of hiding from the truth. England was at war. Jessie came indoors from playing with her ball against the side of the house to find her parents standing with their arms around each other, something so unusual that for a second or two she hesitated before she rushed at them and clasped them both around the legs.

'How long will you have?' Kathie asked as Den stooped to pick up the little girl. That was something else that set the moment apart, for Jessie's independent spirit usually kept her firmly on her own two feet. She snuggled her face against his neck instinctively knowing these seconds were special.

'No time at all, I imagine. Chaps with as much training as we have had will be wanted. Oh Christ, Kathie, that's me and the boys too. What the hell will happen to the place?'

'If you think Mr Hitler's going to get the better of this gal you can think again. If Daddy and the boys have to go away for a little while, you and I will do the work here won't we Jess?'

It had been arranged that, Sunday or no, the Terriers would meet that same evening. When they arrived at the hall they were all given their joining instructions which the captain in charge had had locked in the draw in readiness. The following afternoon they were unceremoniously conveyed in an army lorry to a base in Wiltshire to be turned into bona fide soldiers.

With Jessie sitting at her side, Kathie took the vegetables to the village, thankful that she had a full tank of petrol. For days there had been talk of rationing, rationing of petrol and of food too. There would be no allocation of fuel for pleasure, so plenty of people would have to lay up their cars and take to their bicycles. She hoped her work would be looked on as essential and she would at least be able to make the daily delivery to Jack Hopkins, the greengrocer. How strange that with Den being taken further away from them with every minute she should be planning running the market garden. When war had been no more than a fear at the back of her mind, she had imagined Den going and she left alone, broken and weeping; yet now that it was actually happening none of it seemed real, it was like sleepwalking through the hours; she felt removed from everything that was normal and familiar, even the unchanging village street became remote. This time last week, even though they had known trouble was building and couldn't be held off for long, she hadn't let herself imagine a future when Den wouldn't be with them.

Back from delivering the vegetables, that feeling of unreality lingered. The sound of the water filling the kettle, the sight of her neat rows of preserves on the shelf, all these things were so much part of her everyday life that as a rule she wasn't consciously aware of them, yet on that Monday afternoon, the 4th of September, she seemed to see it all anew.

'You know what Dad said to me?' Jessie's voice cut through Kathie's thoughts as she put the filled kettle onto the range.

She suspected Jessie was feeling as strange as she was herself – although at not yet six years old she would have no appreciation of the emptiness of the time ahead.

'What was that then, Jess?'

'When he gave me that huge hug he whispered that you and me would be fine, cos we would look after each other till he came back.'

'He said something like that to me too. And so we will.' There was no hint of the effort her bright and reassuring smile cost her.

'Course we will,' Jess agreed, clearly giving their responsibilities all her thought. 'Golly! Fancy just us having to look after all the veg and stuff. Then there's Heston,' (the latest resident pig) 'and the chickens. I'd better go and get the eggs. OK?'

'Yes, I've put the bowl ready. Make sure you latch the gate of the run carefully.'

'Course I will. And what about Heston?'

'I've done Heston. He's used to me. Even your dad never goes into the sty.' Goes? Should it have been 'went'? The question came uninvited and was immediately rejected. How strange it was that Jess appeared to find nothing different about her, while *she* felt she was only half alive. Where was he now? Where were they taking him? War – her memories of the last one were vague, one or two of her school friends had had brothers in the army, but it had been a war for men in the services; people with no one caught up in it hadn't been affected as they would be this time. Children sent away from London and from coastal ports and industrial cities to be kept safe in the country; boys – and men like Den – who had joined the Terriers already taken into the army; heavy dark curtains closed before dark so that not a chink of light showed in case Hitler sent aeroplanes to drop bombs. Ordinary people like Den and her, their lives pulled up by the roots. What had any of them done to deserve it?

'Got five eggs, Mum. While Dad's away we'll have to eat lots of eggs. Still, I don't mind, I like them.'

'Good. It'll be eggs for tea.'

'Tell you what! Laying the table can be *my* job, my 'sponsibility.'

'That's a good idea, Jess. Much better if we do regular jobs.' At her mother's words, Jess seemed visibly to puff out her chest. 'We'll manage so well your dad will be proud of us. Tomorrow I must put a notice in the paper shop asking for help to replace Stan and Bert. By Wednesday you will be back at school.'

Kathie didn't attempt to help as Jess dragged a chair to the dresser then climbed on it to unhook two cups before carefully taking down two plates and two saucers.

Change was everywhere. The normal sleepy atmosphere of Sedgewood was strangely altered; everywhere there was talk of rationing, of sons and husbands waiting for call-up papers, of children whose lives had been torn up at the roots and were frightened and unsettled.

Mr Etherington, the newsagent, pinned Kathie's card in a prominent position on the board. 'Hope there's someone here in the village to fit the bill for you,' he said as he took the two pence he charged to display notices for a week. 'Let me know if someone comes along you think might be suitable, then I'll take the card down. Otherwise I'll leave it up and add the charge to your weekly paper bill.'

Neither of them expected that even in its eye-catching position it might be spotted within the first hour. It was pinned onto the board at about ten o'clock on the Tuesday morning:

> Help wanted at Westways Market Garden.
> Experience less important than willingness to
> learn and enthusiasm for gardening.

'Mum, there's some people coming in the gate,' Jess called as she came running towards where Kathie was busy cutting spinach and filling a two-handled wickerwork container. 'Shall I tell them to come and see you here? Do you think they are going to be the ones to help?'

'Men or women?' It was silly to hope there might be able-bodied men wanting to spend their days working at Westways when, according to all the rumours she heard, there were plenty of places where they'd feel involved with the war effort and earn more than she could afford to pay.

Jessie looked doubtful. 'They're not men,' she answered. At least she could be sure of *that*. She sped back to where the visitors were waiting in the front porch, having knocked on the door.

'Mum says you can come and see her out here. We're very busy, you see, so she is getting the vegetables picked ready to take to Mr Hopkins. Come on. I'll show you.'

The two girls looked at each other enquiringly as they followed Jess between the long rows of runner beans. This wasn't a bit as they'd imagined a job interview would be.

'Hello,' Kathie greeted them, wondering if perhaps she could have been wrong in assuming they'd come in answer to her advertisement. 'Can I help you?'

'We read the card on Mr Etherington's board.' Girl No I told her. 'We left school at the end of last term. I'm Sarah Mitchell and this is Sally Brent. We're sixteen and we're both ever so fit and strong.'

'Are you both from the village?' Kathie wanted to know.

'Yes. My dad keeps the Rose and Crown. Sally lives in Rupert Street, along by the chapel. Her father often preaches there.'

Was that thrown in as a point in their favour? Kathie wondered.

Sally Brent envied her friend the easy confident way she could talk, but she was embarrassed. They had come asking for work and Sarah was chattering as if they were on a social visit.

'We are sixteen, Mrs Hawthorne.' Sally spoke the words she had been practising in her head despite the fact that Sarah had got in before her. 'We haven't been to work before, but we want to learn and we are both quite strong.'

'We haven't got a garden at the pub,' Sarah took up the story, 'so I don't know one plant from another. But, like

Sally says, we are keen to learn. And honestly we're not the sort to lean on our spades all day and just chatter.'

Kathie laughed, her initial disappointment that they weren't a pair of strapping lads disappearing by the second.

'I didn't know anything when I came here, but in the beginning that isn't as important as enjoying being in the open air and having bags of energy. It's easy enough at this time of year but not so jolly on frosty January mornings or on wet days; and we get plenty of those. The work has to be done come what may.'

'You don't mind us being girls?' Sally was still uncertain that they could be the sort of applicants Mrs Hawthorne had hoped for.

'To be honest, I had hoped for a couple of brawny lads. But the more I think about it, the more I like the idea of an all-girl team – you two, Jess and me. My husband was in the Terriers; so were the two lads who worked here – well, they were lads when they started, but that was years ago. So all of them have gone into the army and that leaves just Jess and me. It's hard work, so don't accept the job with any illusions on that score. But it's… it's… well, at any rate in my opinion, it's *great*. I can only pay you fifteen shillings a week each to start off with and you might earn more if you went into a shop or an office but this is a good life. We have to work hard but there's a feeling of freedom.'

'Sounds great to me,' Sarah said with a beaming smile. 'Better than being cooped up in a classroom – and getting a Saturday shilling from Dad for pocket money.'

'I expect we shall get pretty dirty, shan't we? I mean, we shall have to come to work in old clothes?' Sally may have been just as excited as her friend, but she was determined to be practical.

'If you take the jobs, I'll tell you what we'll do. I'll give you some money so that you can catch the bus into Deremouth in the morning and each get a pair of dungarees. Then, when you get to work each day you can change and keep your ordinary clothes tidy. How would that be?'

One look at the girls gave her their answer. So all four of them went back to the cottage, Jessie and her skipping rope bringing up the rear. Hidden behind two Christmas puddings made the previous year and kept at the end of the 'preserves shelf' (which Den had transferred to the new kitchen when the warm room became a dining room) was Kathie's emergency savings. And this came under the heading of an emergency. So she climbed on the chair and brought out her tin, carefully counting out fourteen shillings for each of them.

'That should cover your fares and the dungarees. I saw them in the window of Meakers a week or so ago at ten shillings a pair. You really ought to have two pairs each but this is all the spare cash I have in the house, so it'll have to do for a start.'

To see the girls, both so fresh from school and only used to meagre weekly pocket money, took her back to her feeling of independence when she'd gone to work for the Blackwells. Sarah appeared to be the leader of this duo, a tall, slim girl with honey gold permed hair. She was a pretty girl – and clearly she knew it and meant to make the most of her good fortune. By contrast Sally was – the word podgy came into Kathie's head, but she pushed it away – plump? No, not that either. But no one could call her slim; comfortable might be the word. Whereas Sarah's rosy cheeks were largely due to the rouge pot, Sally was a picture of health. The whites of her blue eyes were clear, her teeth would have been like an advertisement for toothpaste but for the fact that she had chipped a tiny corner off one in the front. Her bust looked heavy, but that was probably no more than puppy fat. The two girls were so unalike and yet it was apparent they were close friends.

'We'll get the five to eight bus to Deremouth and be as quick as we can,' Sally said. 'Then we'll come straight here and be ready to start work. Gosh!' Words failed her.

Watching them disappear out of the front gate and set off back along the lane Kathie imagined how they must be chattering, she knew exactly their feeling of excitement; in fact, to her surprise, some of it had rubbed off on *her*. It was still only Tuesday afternoon, only two days since they'd listened to the Prime Minister's words that had changed their world, no more than twenty-four hours since Den had been driven away from Sedgewood. An all-female establishment, and what a challenge it would be. Yet, despite the deep misery that Den had gone, she was conscious that it wasn't determination alone that made her so sure she wouldn't be beaten by what fate had thrown at her. It was enthusiasm.

'Come on, Jess,' she called to the little girl who was climbing on the front gate as she watched the departing visitors, 'we must get the rest of the spinach in the basket and then run the stuff along to Mr Hopkins. Tomorrow's a big day. Sarah and Sally will be starting work.'

'You know what, Mum? I wish school didn't start till next week so I could be here to help you show them what to do.'

The little girl's words seemed to bring Den very close. How proud he would be of her. Well, Kathie vowed silently, we'll see to it that he is proud of all of us – just like we are proud of him. But her new-found confidence took a huge knock that evening when she went up to bed. Jessie's door was always left partly open and as she came to the top of the stairs she heard the sound of muffled crying.

'Jess love, what's the matter?'

'Want Dad,' Jess gulped. 'What did he have to go away for? Don't know when he's coming back. It's horrid without Dad. Wanted to say goodnight to him.'

Perhaps there are limits to everyone's bravery. All day Jess had been bright but now the façade had fallen. Bravery? Bravado more likely, just as Kathie knew her own was no more than bravado. Sitting on the bed she held the sobbing child close. 'You know what, Jess?'

'What?'

'As soon as he can he'll phone us, so let's make a plan. We'll fix a time with him – let's say a quarter to eight every evening – and no matter where any of us are or what we're doing, that will be our special time of all being together.'

'Can't be together. He's miles and miles away.'

'Oh yes, I know. But thoughts don't get held back by distance, not even thousands of miles. If we think about him and he thinks about us, then our spirits, our souls will be together. We'll try it the first quarter to eight after we've spoken to him and we'll all get that lovely warm "know we're loved" feeling.'

'Wish we could do it tonight.'

'We could try. I bet he's thinking of us this very minute, imagining what we're doing, imagining you fast asleep.'

The final hiccup of her tears sounded almost like a chuckle.

–

Thursday teatime Jessie came home from her first day back at school full of excitement to tell Kathie that she had been put in charge of a girl she called Beth.

'She's nice, Mum. *I* know she's nice cos I share my desk with her, so I whisper things to her and she seems pleased. But she doesn't say anything to anyone, not even to Miss Brown. She sort of sits screwed up as if that way no one will see her.'

'Poor little soul. Just think if it were you, Jess. What must it be like to be taken away from your home and sent to live with strangers. Does she talk to *you*?'

Jess nodded, her serious expression assurance that she was giving it her full thought.

'Not quite *talk*. But she sort of whispers when I ask her about things. But, Mum, you know what? She's bilted – some word like that – *she* didn't say it, Miss Brown told us that the new children had been bilted on people in the village. Funny word, but it means that they've been sent to live with people. I asked Beth if the people were nice where she is bilted and she seemed to sort of shrivel up even more and her face went all twitchy. She didn't cry. I think she was too frightened even to cry.'

'Where is she billeted? Billeted, that's the word, Jess.'

'Yes, that's what it was. Anyway, about Beth. She's got to live with the people at the post office. And Mum you know they're old and sort of cross looking. Lots of people have got children to live with them. Why didn't they let us have one?'

'We don't have a spare bedroom.'

'But my bed is huge. Mum, why can't we have Beth to live with us here? Better even than a baby sister, cos she's just the same age as me. She's ever so sad. *And* she's nice; I'm sure she's nice.'

78

Kathie looked at Jessie's pleading expression and wanted to hug her. But Jess would have considered that demeaning when she was trying to hold a grown-up conversation and was waiting for an answer.

That's when common sense got the upper hand and Kathie thought of the extra hours of work she had to cram into her day already without taking on extra responsibility.

'She's bound to be sad to start with wherever she is billeted. I bet they are all sad. But Jess, she will settle and I expect she has friends amongst the other evacuees.'

That was another word for Jess to remember.

'If you'd seen her you would know, the others aren't like Beth. D'you know what? She hadn't any socks on, just heavy winter-day shoes, like Dad calls "plodabouts". And – I don't want to sound horrid cos I know it's not her fault – but her cardigan had a hole in the elbow. She's the same age as me, but she's ever so skinny and small. Mum, why can't she come here?' Then, approaching the idea from another angle, she said, 'She could help us with the jobs. Please, Mum.'

'We can't just take her away from the Bullinghams at the post office. You'd better take the basket and get the eggs, love. When you get to school tomorrow you'll find Beth has started to feel better.'

For all her cheerful reassurance to Jessie, she couldn't put the image of the waiflike child out of her mind. Long into the night sleep eluded her. By next morning her decision was made, although she gave no sign of it to Jess. After all, she still had to persuade the authorities to transfer a homesick child and it was more than likely her request would be refused. There must be thousands of homesick children.

With Jess in school and her two new helpers occupied cropping the autumn fruiting raspberries, she cycled down the lane and turned right towards the village. She had heard that the team billeting the children had worked in the village hall, but when she got there she found it was locked. Their job was finished. So her next hope was to call at Fred Dawkins' own house in Darnley Street.

'But your husband was most emphatic that you had no room. I have the list on the table here. Westways – two bedrooms, both in use.'

'And that's true. And for anyone other than the child who has been billeted at the post office I would leave it at that. At school Jessie, my daughter, has been put in charge of her. They could share a double bed. It must be so lonely for a five-year-old with Mrs Bullingham busy in the post office until it's time to lock the door.'

He didn't much care for an outsider trying to alter his arrangements, but to be honest he had felt sorry for the solitary and frightened child being put into the Bullinghams' home.

'I'll go along to the post office and have a word.' And he had no doubt just how welcome that word would be. He had been tempted to put the Bullinghams down as having no room, but she had made such a fuss trying to wriggle out of taking an evacuee that he had wanted to make her realize she was in no position to argue with authority. 'After all the work there has been in trying to sort the billets out, I don't mind telling you I could do without all this mind changing. Better leave it with me. I'll deliver her to you after school when she's had time to put her things together to bring.'

'Thank you for being understanding, Mr Dawkins.' Kathie gave him her friendliest smile which allayed some of his irritation. 'Now I'll get home and sort out the bedroom so that they can both squeeze in.'

'Nothing like a bit of company the same age to settle a child down,' he said. 'Your Jess won't mind having to share? I've had children, I know just how possessive they can be about a bit of private space.'

'Jess will be delighted; in fact it was her idea. Don't forget, she's an only child. Now I must fly. I have a market garden to run.'

The arrangements made, Fred Dawkins was ready for a chat.

'A big responsibility for a woman,' he said. 'How will you go on with your husband gone and those two lads too?'

'For the time being Sarah Mitchell, the daughter from the Rose and Crown, and Sally Brent are helping me – you may know Sally's people, you attend the chapel in Rupert Street, don't you?'

'Indeed I do. He often preaches there; a fine man.'

'They're both good girls; I'm really lucky. I must fly. See you later.'

Watching her cycle away, he thought what a lucky chap Dennis Hawthorne was to have a wife like that prepared to take on their livelihood.

–

By afternoon Kathie's good intentions had begun to give way to doubts. Normally a happy, optimistic woman, over the last seventy-two hours depression would suddenly descend on her without warning. So far there had been no telephone call from Dennis. Perhaps this evening he would have a chance to ring. If only he were here, if only she could wake up to find the horrors of the past week had been a dream. With the raspberry punnets lined up on the bench in the shed, the two girls were picking runner beans and laying them carefully in neat piles in the boxes she had put out. They had worked well, following her instructions and, as Sarah had said, never leaning on their spades while they talked. But talk they certainly did, calling to each other as they worked, competing over the length of the beans they picked, and seemingly looking on a day's hard work as a game to be enjoyed. Listening to them now as she waited for Mr Dawkins to arrive Kathie felt her own spirits bouncing back. She wished Den could see how well they were all doing.

When she heard the click of the garden gate, she looked out of the kitchen window, seeing without being seen. Fred Dawkins was holding the little girl's hand as though he was stopping her escape rather than protecting her. And the child? Smaller than Jessie, pale and thin with colourlessly fair, straight hair looking as though it had been hacked at by someone with no training and a blunt pair of scissors. Even though she was small, her faded frock was much too short and the cardigan (no doubt with a hole in the elbow) had been strained across her and done up on the wrong buttons. The sight of her gave Kathie back her resolve.

'Jess!' she called, opening the back door, 'leave the eggs till later. Beth is here. Mind you shut the gate of the chicken run.'

'Yippee!' Before the visitors reached the front door, Jess was rushing down the path at the side of the house. 'Beth. I didn't know till I got home from school. You're coming to live here with us. And Beth we're going to sleep in the same bed. It's going to be such fun. Come on, I'll show you where our room is.'

Pulling Beth away from her warder she dragged her to the back door and into the house just as Kathie opened the front door to Mr Dawkins' knock.

'A good start.' Kathie smiled at him. 'I don't think you'll have any cause to worry about her; she'll be happy here.'

'Of that I have no doubt. Now then, Mrs Hawthorne, there's just the little matter of business to transact if I may step inside. Mrs Bullingham has given me back the payment record book. Each week you take it to her at the post office and she'll pay you six shillings and four pence. You'll sign the receipt and she'll stamp the counterfoil. Another job added to the postmistress's burden, she has to keep a tally of how much she has paid out each week and send the slips to the billeting office. And then there's this – the child's ration book and a note of her parents' address.'

The formalities over, he shook her hand in farewell and departed. Kathie put the books in her handbag, and then went up to meet the new member of the family.

'Mum, I've been telling Beth about collecting the eggs. Do you know what, Mum? She doesn't know about chickens and eggs and things.'

'I don't expect you do, Beth. I didn't know much about them until I came here to live. Do you like eggs?'

Beth nodded, then, holding her head an inch higher and seeming to take a huge step into her new life, she gave Kathie what was almost a smile and answered, 'Eggs is my favourite, missus.'

Kathie laughed, reaching to lay a hand on the silky pale hair. 'That's a good thing,' she said, 'because thanks to the chickens, we have lots of them. But of course the chickens do make extra work and I've always been glad to have Jessie's help. Now that you're here, I shall have two helpers.'

Again Beth nodded, but her slim grasp on confidence had slipped from her fingers.

'Jess, take Beth and show her round outside,' Kathie said as they went downstairs. 'Not just on the grass where you play, but show her how the things are grown. And introduce her to Sarah and Sally. They help in the garden, Beth, but they're new too; they only started to work here yesterday. Coming from living in town it'll all seem very different, Beth. I know it will because I used to live in a town before I came here and I had lots to get used to. But we all help each other.'

Beth stood with her head down, making no attempt to move off with Jess. It seemed she had something else to say. Visibly she forced out the words.

'Thank you, missus, for letting me come here. I was *that* glad.'

Every impulse in Kathie made her want to hug the desolate little figure; but it was wiser to go slowly.

'It was Jessie's idea. You're friends at school so it'll be better for both of you to keep each other company. And I bet before long you'll be helping with the jobs just like she does. There's always work to be done on a place like this.'

'Cor, missus, do you reckon I'll be able to help?'

'I'd bet my last shilling on it,' Kathie answered with a laugh, just as Jess shouted for her trainee helper to buck up, they had to finish collecting the eggs. Kathie just stopped herself from calling out to say that she would finish collecting the eggs and shut the chickens up for the night herself while Jessie took Beth for a walk and showed her what was growing. A child who'd never seen a chicken-run, let alone been inside one, was more than likely to panic and drop an egg or two. But a broken egg was nothing compared with the giant step Beth's self-confidence was about to take.

Then the telephone rang and she forgot the girls as she picked up the receiver knowing even before he spoke that it would be Dennis. She had been looking forward to telling him everything that had happened.

Three minutes would go so fast, but he started by saying he had another shilling ready to feed into the pay box when the operator interrupted them.

'We're moving off first thing in the morning. I don't know where but don't panic, it can't be overseas, we still have to have more jabs. How are things going?'

When she told him she had engaged two sixteen-year-old girls for a moment his silence made her think he couldn't have heard what she'd said.

Then: 'Damn this war', almost under his breath. Something warned her it might be wiser to change the subject so she told him about the addition to the family taking it for granted he would be of the same mind as she was herself.

She was wrong.

'Kathie, oh Kathie, what the devil have you done a damn fool thing like that for? You knew I'd made it clear we couldn't have an evacuee. You've got more than enough to do with only two useless girls to help you. Why didn't you wait and get a man instead of grabbing the first to apply?' She could tell from his voice that he wanted to criticize anything that hinted at a change to the way things had been. 'I ought to be there. It's bad enough that you're having to be in charge, but at least with an experienced man I would have felt things might work out.'

'I'm not a complete fool!' There was an edge to her voice too. What was happening to them? He'd been gone only half a week, yet in those moments they were divided by something more than miles.

'I can't be sure of *that* if you can do anything as fool-hardy as land yourself with some kid we don't even know and without even asking what I thought about it. Never mind if it makes you feel stupid, I insist you're to go back to Dawkins in the morning and tell him it isn't going to work out – tell him that I object if you like – but say the child must be put somewhere else.'

'I'll do no such thing! Anyway, how can it make any difference to you if I take half a dozen poor little children into the house. You won't have to look after them.' Then quietly, she added, 'But don't talk about it now, Beth and Jess are just coming in. Listen – and this is important.' And she told him about their meeting of spirits at a quarter to eight each evening, ending with, 'Promise, Den. It's important.'

His mood changed.

'Oh Kathie, what a bloody mess it all is. Of course I promise. Is Jess there? Let me say hello to her. I've only got one more shilling to feed into the phone.'

Jess took the receiver, and Kathie moved just out of earshot holding out her hand to Beth to come with her. Obediently the uncertain child took it, taking a quick peep at her new minder.

'Were there many eggs?' Kathie asked in the same adult way she spoke to Jess.

'We got six. I never seen a chicken, not with its fevvers, only hanging up in the butcher's all white looking.'

'There will be lots of things that are new to you in the country, Beth. I remember how exciting I found it when I first came. Did you meet Sarah and Sally?'

'Yes missus.' Just two words.

'Mum, Dad wants to speak to you. It's all right about a quarter to eight. He's going to do it. Come and take the phone quickly cos his money's nearly gone.'

'Kathie… I still think you're crazy. If only I could get home for a couple of hours I'd get you out of the hole you've dug yourself into. You're all heart and no head – but I love you Kathie Hawthorne,' he said, almost shyly; face-to-face he wouldn't have said it and neither would she have wanted him too.

'And I love you, Den Hawthorne.' Then, with a laugh that seemed to bring them back to their normal day-to-day relationship: 'Just as well we do, too; we're stuck with each other.'

How many people must have been saying the same thing, even if the words were different? For them all, war was something to be lived through until life could be back in step marching towards the future they'd once taken for granted.

That evening as the three of them sat at the supper table Kathie told Beth she was going to write to her parents and suggested she might like to draw a picture to send.

'Won't be no use you writing to Tilly – that's what I call her, that's her name you see. She never learnt to read an' write. But there's Mrs Martin, she lives so that her door and Tilly's are next to each other. If anything needs reading, that's who does it.' The words had rushed out, but now she hesitated. Humiliation was written all over her. 'But, missus, it won't be no use you looking for a letter back, cos you see Tilly won't know how to do it.'

'A reply doesn't matter. But it's important for them to know what it's like for you here. So I'll write to them and hope that Mrs Martin reads it. Most important, though, what about if you draw a picture – maybe the chicken run with you and Jess collecting the eggs. Could you do that?'

The letter duly went, and with it Beth's impression of egg collecting. As expected, no reply came.

–

It was a happy working atmosphere at Westways. Sarah and Sally were keen and quick to learn and with each passing day Kathie became more certain she had done the right thing to engage them. As for the children, they both did their jobs; Beth's main responsibility being making their bed and putting their dirty clothes in the linen basket while Jess laid the breakfast table. The all-female establishment was running on oiled wheels.

'Have you heard what's happening up at the hall?' Sarah said during the second week in September.

'I thought the hall was unoccupied,' Kathie answered, trying to sound interested while her concentration was fixed on finding the best marrows to cut.

'Fancy you not knowing! I suppose tucked away down the lane here you don't hear half the goings on. We knew there was a lot of work being done. There's not much goes on that Dad doesn't get wind of in the bar and people were saying they thought Sedgewood Hall must have been sold. Well, what would a great star like Richard Marley want with living in the sticks in Devon? He's better off out there in Hollywood.'

Kathie knew something of the Marley family; it wouldn't have been possible to live fifteen years at Westways and not be aware that the woods sloping down to a gate on the opposite side of the lane belonged to the big house, which had been in the Marley family since it was built nearly two hundred years before. She knew elderly Herbert Marley had died a year or two ago and his widow had moved away; she had heard that the grandson, Richard Marley, an actor and screen idol, had inherited as his own father had been killed in the Great War. None of it had particularly interested her, but clearly Sarah had other views.

'Bang goes all our hopes that one of these days he'd come and stay in Sedgewood. Don't you think he's just gorgeous, Mrs Hawthorne? Or I suppose you never get to the flicks?'

'Not a hope,' Kathie answered with a laugh that showed she didn't consider it any great miss. 'I wonder who's bought the Hall,' she added, trying to show an interest. They really were such good girls, she thought, full of chatter and fun, but working all the time they talked.

'That's the thing,' Sarah said. 'Richard Marley hasn't sold it; he's rented it to a school, a boarding school for boys. Dad was told about it last night. The work is pretty well done and the school is moving in at the weekend. Be funny hearing a lot of noisy boys in the wood there.'

There the matter rested and as far as Kathie was concerned the conversation was soon forgotten.

–

A few days later, their breakfast eggs finished, the children were topping up with toast before going off to school when the snap of the letterbox told them the postman had brought something.

'My turn to get it,' Beth said running into the passage by the front door then returning with one envelope,

'Mur… rur. That means mister. Do you have it, Mrs Hawthorne?' In the beginning she had simply called Kathie 'missus' until she had started to feel at home with the name Hawthorne.

'You can't go on forever calling me Mrs Hawthorne. You're one of us now. How would it be if you called me Auntie Kathie?' Beth's face flushed with some sort of emotion, but Kathie wasn't sure what. 'Don't you think that's better?'

'Cor Mrs— Auntie Kathie. Cor! I never had an auntie. Aunties are people you don't just know for a little while.'

'Did neither of your parents have any sisters – or brothers?'

'Tilly don't have no one.' She couldn't cope with the bubbly excited feeling and remember how to speak at the same time. Then her thin little face broke into a beaming smile. 'But now I got an auntie, I got an Auntie Kathie.'

The letter appeared to have been forgotten, but remembering she was still holding it she passed it to Kathie then climbed back on her chair to finish her toast and marmalade.

Looking at the two girls, so different and yet already really fond of each other, Kathie felt a tug of satisfaction. Skinny little Beth might be the runt of the establishment, but she was fitting in more firmly with each passing day.

When on the following Saturday morning they asked if they could go as far as the common to play she decided it could do no harm.

'Yes, I'll trust you to be careful. Listen for the clock at the Hall to strike twelve and then start to walk home. And promise not to talk to any strangers.'

'Silly Mum,' Jess chuckled, 'there won't be anyone on the common except us.'

'Promise me, anyway.'

So they set off happily. Until that morning they had been allowed to play in the lane, but in sight of the cottage. At Westways the morning seemed to pass quickly. The sound of Sarah and Sally chatting and laughing as they worked, and the knowledge that Jess had a playmate, ought to have raised Kathie s spirits; but she felt horribly alone. Most of the hours of her working day she found satisfaction in what she did – and pride in the knowledge that she was keeping their business going – but occasionally she would be overtaken by an empty feeling bordering on despair. It must be the same for thousands of women, she told herself. In fact she was luckier than so many, for she knew that she was carrying on Den's work for him. But on that morning it was hard to feel lucky. There was only one way to win her battle and that was to work doubly hard. So that was what she did, until she heard the clock on Sedgewood Hall chime and then strike midday.

'Time to knock off, girls,' she called to them. 'Your envelopes are on the kitchen table; you can collect them when you go in to change. Leave your hoes; I'll probably do a bit this afternoon.

By a quarter past twelve they had gone, eager for their afternoon of freedom. But there was no sign of Jess and Beth. Surely it shouldn't take them all this time to get back from the common.

Four

About fifty yards from the garden gate of Westways the narrowing lane finally gave up all pretence of being anything more than a track as it rounded a bend to the right. Never before had Jess been allowed to go to the common without an adult but, playing alone, the idea had never entered her head. Kathie had been so sure that the two of them together would come to no harm. But why else would they be so late? If, from Westways, she had heard the Hall clock strike midday then Jess and Beth couldn't possibly have missed it.

Without even going back to shut the back door, she set out to look for them. As she reached the bend in the lane they came into view. Something must be wrong! Jessie's face looked flushed and, surely, Beth was crying.

'What happened? I was worried.'

'Was a horrible man, Mum, kept shouting. And he's going to beat Oliver. Wasn't Oliver's fault; he said he wasn't allowed. But I persuaded him.'

Kathie had no idea what Jess was talking about or who Oliver was – or the horrible man who shouted either – but her overwhelming emotion was relief.

'Well, I'm glad you're both OK. Now let's get home and you can tell me all about it.' With one small hand in each of hers they started back to the cottage.

'He told Oliver to go to the study and get the cane out ready, then sit and wait. Probably beating him by now. And he was so miserable,' Beth croaked.

'It was cos he was so miserable at that beastly school, Mum, that I knew we had to take him with us to play. We helped him climb back in and everything would have been all right if the horrible man hadn't been there in the woods and seen him getting back over the gate. D'you know what, Mum? Oliver looked like an animal in a cage at the zoo when we first saw him staring out through the bars of the gate. I told him that's what he looked like.'

'He didn't start to cry till you said that,' Beth voiced her opinion bravely, 'it was being in a cage like you said that made him cry. Now he's getting a whacking and the man said that afterwards he had to stay in his room all day for punishment. And we're going home to dinner and more play. It's not fair.'

'When you've washed your hands you can start at the very beginning and tell me all about it.'

And that's what they did. There was a padlocked gate from the woods of Sedgewood Hall onto the track and that's where they found their new friend. Some children might have walked on by, but not Jess. So they stopped to talk and found the boy they called Oliver was seven and miserable at boarding school. That he had no friends was something Jess couldn't understand but she wasn't going to leave him lonely and crying. So, taking control (and Kathie could clearly imagine the scene) she helped him to climb the gate and off the three went to the common where they had a lovely morning and he forgot his troubles. Then when they got back the 'horrible man' caught him and shouted at him and sent him to his study to wait to be caned.

The image triggered Kathie's anger. A man like that had no right to be in charge of young children – nor yet older ones, for what sort of an example did he set? She knew nothing about the school except that it had come from somewhere in the London area and all the boys boarded. She hated bullies and what else was he but a bully?

But the story wasn't over.

'And you know what?' Jessie's voice cut through her thoughts. 'I told him that it wasn't Oliver's fault; it was me who made him escape. His face was red as anything and his eyes sort of popped out. He shouted at us that we had no business to hang around in the lane. Didn't he, Beth?'

Beth nodded. 'He said we weren't to go there again. He said it was, what was it he called it, Jess?'

'Out of bounds. What's out of bounds, Mum? I told him it led to the common and he said I was pudent, no, *impudent*. Then he said we were to get back to the village where we belonged and not to dare to hang about in the lane again. But Mum, even if he is at the Hall, he can't boss us and say we can't go in the lane. I told him we lived here and he said I was telling lies and if we knew what was good for us we'd clear off.'

Beth added, 'Then he glared at us as cross as anything and stomped off up the track through the wood to give Oliver a thrashing. Do you think he'll make him go without any dinner?'

The ways of boarding school were unknown to all three. One thing Kathie did know was that he was a bullying newcomer and she meant to put him in his place. After lunch, leaving the girls with strict instructions that they were either to play on the grass or in the lane not too far from the house, she went to get ready for her intended outing. She ran a few inches of water in the bath, she even threw in a handful of lilac scented crystals, she scrubbed her hands in an attempt to get rid of all sign of her outdoor labours while her mind moved on to what she could wear that would make her more than a match for the man she was to confront. She indulged in imagining herself standing tall and proud in front of him, coldly bringing him down not just 'a peg or two' but so that he saw himself for the worm that he was.

With the towel wrapped around her she went to the bedroom prepared for the next stage in her transformation. Yet, once stripped of the towel, she looked in the mirror on the front of the wardrobe and felt her confidence slipping away. Gazing at her naked body she hated what she saw. At the time she and Dennis had married she had been proud of her slim straight figure, even her small, pert breasts. But slimness had become scrawniness. Her breasts were worse than small, they hung like empty envelopes! Had she not been so underdeveloped, even if they'd sagged, at least she would have looked feminine. For a moment she closed her eyes, cupping the offending appendages and caressing the low-slung nipples trying to imagine it was Dennis who was awakening this aching need.

What in the world was she doing, wasting time when there was no time to waste? The last few moments had been a sheer indulgence, something her working life didn't permit. Night after night she had climbed into bed wanting nothing but oblivion, every muscle aching and her mind going no further than the tasks that would be waiting for her in the morning. But this afternoon was different. Her reason for a midday bath certainly hadn't been to sit here daydreaming; she meant to look her best – something for which she had little hope or expectation. She would tell Mr Horrid exactly what she thought of him. It appalled her to think that parents had entrusted small boys to the care of a brute who would cane an unhappy seven-year-old.

Taking clean underwear from her drawer she started to dress. When she had the chance to get to town she would buy a better bra, but the one she put on had been bought from Miss Messer's drapery store in the village and instead of lifting the droop, it destroyed all hint of shape. She looked as straight as a lad. Fifteen years ago that shape might have been fashionable, but Hollywood with its glamorous women carrying all before them in twin peaks had changed all that. Her thoughts were tempting her where she mustn't follow; she forced herself to pull them back into line. What can I wear to face the lion in his den? It's not really high day or holiday, but I'll put my 'outfit' on anyway. Her 'outfit' was quite the most expensive thing she had ever possessed and as she took it from the wardrobe where it hung draped in an old sheet her mind carried her back to the trip she and Den (with two-year-old Jess in her pushchair) had had to Exeter. They had seen the outfit on a model in the window of a very exclusive establishment and Den had said it was absolutely made for her. Feeling wildly extravagant, they had gone in so that she could try it on without even asking the price. It was a fully lined suit of the softest tweed with a floppy-crowned cap of the same material, its exquisite autumnal shades flattering her colouring. For some three and a half years it had hung in her wardrobe, too good for ordinary wear and with special occasions few and far between. Today she would wear it to show she was a force to be reckoned with.

'I shan't be long,' she called to the girls who were occupied on the grass trying to walk on their hands – without success but with peals of laughter. 'Either stay in the garden or if you go into the lane, don't go further than just along here by the house.'

'You look ever so posh, Aunt Kathie.'

Beth's spontaneous remark was just what Kathie needed as she started on her way.

Once out of the lane she turned up the hill, anger spurring her on. Then opening the heavy wrought iron gate she walked past the lodge and on up the long straight drive. On her left was what used to be a croquet lawn but was now a rugby pitch, a background to the cheers and jeers from the boys who watched the Saturday afternoon game. The heavy front door was wide open, something she hadn't expected. Immediately opposite the entrance, across the enormous hall, was a door bearing the sign 'Headmaster'. What did visitors do? Ought she to cross the hall and knock on the door? Or would that wrong-foot her at the onset of the interview? Taking hold of the bell pull she tugged it with all her might, the clang seeming to echo through the building.

A moment later an elderly servant appeared, making no attempt to hide her displeasure.

'Wretched man,' she was muttering, talking to herself, 'Never about when you want him. Not my job to answer the door.' Then, saying nothing to the caller, she waited.

'Good afternoon,' Kathie greeted her, her manner unnaturally formal. It suited her mood well that the servant was unfriendly; it added fuel to the fire of her anger. She couldn't have resisted responding to a friendly welcome. 'I've called to speak to the headmaster if you will be so kind as to announce me. I am Mrs Hawthorne, a neighbour.'

'Step inside. I'll find out if he's free.'

And a minute later Kathie was ushered into the presence of Mr Horrid. Her immediate reaction was surprise. The man who stood up from his seat behind the large oak desk didn't look like a child beater.

'Mrs Hawthorne, I don't believe we've met.' He held out his hand. Kathie pretended not to notice it, and then felt ashamed that she could behave so childishly.

'No, we haven't. But you met my little girls this morning. That's why I'm here. Well, in part, that's why I'm here.'

'Little girls?' He frowned, obviously puzzled. But she wasn't to be put off so easily. 'Won't you sit down.' He indicated an armchair then, once she was seated, again sat in his swivel chair turning it to face her. 'That's better. Now then, what's this about your little girls?'

Jess had described him as huge and with a red, angry face. Certainly this man was tallish, but there was nothing burly either in his build or manner. He was quietly spoken; yet there was firmness in his tone that carried authority. Despite herself she felt her anger receding as she looked at him. Of course, she reminded herself, appearances can be deceptive. Jess had been quite upset – and she didn't upset easily.

'I don't understand how a grown man, a man who has the power to make or mar the lives of the pupils here, could be such a… such a…' Her anger was rising again as she imagined Jessie and Beth being at the mercy of this sly devil – as nice as pie talking to her and then terrifying the children in his charge. 'Such a *bully*. Loving parents entrust

98

their children to your care so that they will be away from war in the safety of the countryside and what do you do? To cane a seven-year-old who is homesick and unhappy, feeling as if he's in prison here! It makes my blood run cold to think of it.'

'I'm afraid you have lost me. I don't know what you have been told. But, these children of yours, does it not occur to you that they may have been misinterpreting something they heard?'

'That's a wicked thing to say! My children *don't tell lies*!'

'You misunderstand what I am suggesting. Believe me, I've had enough experience of the young to know that in the quest for excitement, adventure, they are capable of finding drama where there is none.' His voice was in unison with his unruffled manner, yet he made no attempt to smile. 'But, whatever is behind this, I do assure you that except for half an hour or so at the lodge I have been here at the Hall all the morning. Where were your daughters when they believe they heard whatever it was they believe they heard?'

Making sure her cool demeanour matched his, she replied, 'I allowed them to go by themselves along the lane to play on the common. When they reached the gate from the wood belonging to the Hall they stopped to talk to a boy called Oliver. Do you realize – or even care – what an unhappy child he is? Anyway, Jessie, my five-year-old, is a born organizer. The poor lad wouldn't have stood a chance against her and the upshot was that they helped him over the locked gate and they had a lovely morning on the common. Is that such a crime?'

'With permission it would be no crime at all.'

Kathie felt she was losing the battle.

'The rest you must know.'

'I assure you I know nothing except what you have just told me. As for caning a child of Marley's age, it's out of the question. In the senior school corporal punishment is accepted – when it is merited. And, on those rare occasions, it falls to me to handle all corporal punishment. No other member of the staff here is authorized to cane a boy. For the under-thirteens there are other ways of dealing with their misdemeanours: forfeiting Saturday morning free-time, the writing of lines, learning a poem by heart.' With a smile that seemed to start in his light blue eyes and change his solemn countenance, the headmaster continued, 'A suitable punishment to fit the crime.' For a moment neither of them spoke, each uncertain of the way forward. Then he said, 'I am glad you called to see me. I knew Oliver Marley was finding it hard to adjust to boarding; and I admit it has worried me. There are usually tears near the surface when the very young are away from home for the first time. But you think with him it goes deeper? He probably talked more openly to children from outside. He's never boarded until we moved here, but it's strange that he of all the pupils should find it hard to settle here at Sedgewood Hall.'

'You mean he is one of the Marley family who own it? He didn't tell the girls *that*. He said that his father had gone off to America and left his mother and him.'

'Yes, his parents are divorced. The call of fame, no doubt. It was Mrs Marley, Oliver's mother, who told me about the Hall being empty. At that time the boy was a day pupil and, as he was in the junior school, I saw very little of him. I dare say life had been soft for him, his parents feeling guilty as their marriage fell apart.'

'I don't know anything about that.' Kathie pulled herself back on course; she hadn't come here for friendly chatter. 'But I do know that *you*, or if I'm to believe what you say, then one of your staff, not only sent the child to his study with instructions to get the cane out ready and then wait, but also told my girls that they were not allowed in the lane. His expression was that the lane was "out of bounds" – hardly words five-year-olds would have imagined or invented.' She was like a lioness defending her young. 'That lane is public and, if you are so unfamiliar with anything outside the boundary of the Hall, I suggest you take a walk and find out for yourself. I come from Westways, the market garden fronting the lane. Beyond that point there is never any traffic, the lane peters into no more than a track leading to the common. And I shall thank you (and your staff) not to talk to my girls as if they are your prisoners just as the boys are.'

At that the headmaster's smile was overtaken by his laugh.

'Believe me, the boys are not prisoners. I have responsibility for their safety, just as I have responsibility to ensure they are confident to walk out without supervision on Saturdays. Provided that they sign the log giving details of the time of their leaving and where they are going, the seniors are allowed out in their free time. But, to go back to what you tell me of your daughters: I've already told you, whoever they encountered – if indeed what they heard wasn't just something amongst the boys themselves – it most certainly was not me. But I shall look into it.'

'Please, promise that you will. Imagine being seven years old and your life pulled up by the roots. You said just now, Mr… Mr…'

'Meredith. Bruce Meredith. Forgive me, I had assumed you knew my name.'

'Why should I? You are hardly part of the local community shut away here at the Hall.'

'Indeed.' He seemed not a jot put out by her aggressive manner; in fact she felt he was amused.

'Well, anyway,' she went on, 'you said just now that with permission Oliver would have been allowed to play on the common with the girls. Would you give your permission for him to come to Westways? Even if he's not used to being out on his own, if he came over the gate in the wood it's not far round the bend to our front gate.'

Bruce Meredith was sizing up her suggestion.

'If you care to name a day and time, then I will see he is there. But, you know, there is plenty of companionship for him amongst his peers here, if only he chose to join in.'

'We're not all joiners, Mr Meredith. Please let him come. Jess said that he had such fun with them this morning.' He was watching her closely as she talked. 'We run a market garden at Westways. Perhaps you think that letting a pupil visit what you would see as a working home isn't what the parents pay you for.'

'I have said that if you tell me when you want him to visit, I shall see he's there.'

It wasn't in Kathie's nature to feel out of her depth, but that was the effect this man had on her. She regretted what she had said, her words echoing in her head as an apology for her lack of riches. He must be looking at her and realizing she had worn her best clothes for the visit; she felt humiliated and was angry with herself.

'It will do him good. We work hard at Westways; even the children help. To my mind that's the way they should be brought up, aware that they are part of a team.'

'Indeed commendable.' Then, sitting back in his chair and crossing his knees as if he was settling for a long and comfortable chat, he added, 'And now, when shall I send him?'

'Do they have to go to church in the morning?' She knew nothing of the ways of boarding schools.

'If Sedgewood Hall had a chapel the answer would be "yes". But since it hasn't, Reverend Gilbert, a member of the staff, takes a short service in the assembly hall at nine o'clock. Any time after ten Marley can be free.'

'The girls will meet him by the locked gate at a quarter past ten. And if you say he can be free, he could stay with us until after tea. That would be long enough to let him get over any shyness. You see, I don't know him. Perhaps he isn't shy?'

'Lacking in confidence, but not shy. In fact he has an almost unnatural air of maturity for a boy of his age.' Kathie could tell he was undecided whether to say more, so she waited silently. 'Have I failed the child? Is the façade he presents no more than his wall of defence?' He might have been thinking aloud and showed no surprise that she didn't answer. 'Well then, Mrs Hawthorne—' he seemed to pull himself back in line— 'we'll say around ten o'clock tomorrow. Don't let your daughters hang about at the gate expecting to help him climb over. I shall see him through the gate and he can walk the last few steps by himself. To allow him to climb out of his cage would be tantamount to condoning it,' he added with an unexpected smile.

'The girls will be delighted. I'll go and tell them the good news and won't detain you any longer.'

'Indeed I was about to go along to the lodge when you arrived. Perhaps we might walk together as far as the gate.' She had a feeling of failure that she could find him such easy company as they walked down the long drive. Then she reminded herself that it was better to have him on side, that way he would be likely to allow Oliver to escape to Westways more often.

At the lodge they parted company. She half walked and half ran down the hill to the turning marked by the signpost pointing to the common. If she hurried to change into her working clothes she could still get a few hours outside before she had to think about supper for the children.

It was a pity she couldn't have been a fly on the wall when, after half an hour or so at the lodge, Bruce returned to school making his way to the quarters of the housemaster in charge of Oliver Marley. One man spoke with quiet authority, the other became more florid as he blustered.

Waiting a minute or two after Bruce's departure, 'Mr Horrid' went to find Oliver in the dormitory where he had been confined for the afternoon hours.

'You have been invited to spend the day tomorrow with those two infants you seemed to find such good company this morning. I have been speaking to the headmaster and he is prepared to allow you to accept the invitation. He has agreed to see you through the gate in the woods – so, just remember, there is to be no more climbing out. Understand?'

'Yes, sir. Thank you, sir.'

'Now I think you have been in here long enough. Get outside and kick a ball about with your classmates.'

Oliver went downstairs and out into the sunshine. He knew that if he walked around the back of the building there was a path that would take him away from where Saturday afternoon freedom was being marked with the sort of noise he hated. Just inside the edge of the wood there was an old tree, perfect for climbing. Even at this time of year with the leaves starting to fall, there he felt safe and out of sight.

–

Next morning, while Jessie and Beth hurried through their jobs – drying up the breakfast things and putting them away, then feeding the chickens, Kathie got ready for her morning's work outside. Den had never done much on Sundays, and the two lads hadn't worked after midday Saturday, an arrangement continued by Kathie's two helpers. But Den had been more confident with what he was doing than she was. Sometimes she felt that everything took her twice as long as it would have taken him. But she wasn't being fair on herself; then, there had been a division of labour. Pulling on Den's well-worn work trousers, she couldn't fail to compare her reflection with that of yesterday afternoon when she had been resplendent in her 'outfit'.

Well, like it or lump it, this is *me*, she told herself. Den was a slim man, but even so if she hadn't pulled the belt tight around her thin waist the trousers would have ended around her ankles. I only need a red nose and I'd look like a circus clown, she thought, taking no pleasure in her reflection. Her jumper was frayed about the cuff, the trouser legs were tucked into thick woollen socks and to crown it all she tied a scarf around her head. Stopping in the porch on the way out, she pulled on her Wellington boots. Right, she was ready. Job number one was to clean out the pigsty.

'Tell you what, Mum,' Jess shouted as she walked across the grassy patch to the shed to get her shovel and bucket, 'me and Beth, we thought we'd go to the common when Ollie (that's what we're going to call him) when Ollie comes. We can do that, can't we?'

'You can, as long as I know where you are and you listen for the hall clock like you did yesterday. But find me and tell me when you go.'

''Citing, isn't it, Mum, Ollie coming.'

The moment made a lasting impression on Kathie: the two little girls so full of life and, even after such a short time at Westways, Beth with such growing confidence. If it had done that for *her*, they had to hope it would work some sort of magic on the poor miserable lad they were expecting. Then she put them all from her mind and started to attack the least favourite of all her jobs. It was stupid to think of Horatio as anything more than tomorrow's meals, chops and bacon as Jessie said, but she had grown attached to each pig they'd kept. One more week and Horatio's life would be over. This time it had to be she who drove Horatio up the plank and into the truck. Pigs are intelligent; would he know he only had a one-way ticket? With determination she started to shovel, wishing herself faced with any task rather than this one.

'Mrs Hawthorne?' Bruce Meredith's voice caught her off guard.

Loaded shovel poised, she seemed rooted to the spot.

'I thought you were just going to unlock the gate for Oliver.' Her reply was less than welcoming. Into her mind flashed the trouble she had taken to convey the right impression the previous afternoon; if he hadn't guessed it yesterday, this morning would leave him in no doubt.

'I was tempted to come to meet the little girls.' Then with a disarming smile, he added, 'I wasn't sure that you believed what I said yesterday about not having seen them before. I thought you should see for yourself that we were meeting for the first time.'

'Well, as you can see, I'm not in a fit state for visitors.'

'A far cry from the austere lady who confronted me yesterday.'

She dumped the offering from her shovel into the huge bucket she used for the purpose. Her work attire was very different from her 'outfit', but she meant to show him that yesterday's 'austere lady' was still there below the surface.

'You'll think me very unwelcoming, but I honestly can't spare the time.'

'You have a large market garden. Is recruitment making any difference to your workforce?'

She felt he asked her for a purpose, although what business it was of his she couldn't imagine.

'Dennis, my husband, used to do most of the outside work with just two full-time helpers from the village; but September saw the end of all that. They were all in the Terriers so as soon as war was declared Westways had to fall back on me. I've been lucky and have two local girls to help.' Working with a steady rhythm she shovelled as she talked. 'They only left school in the summer, so they haven't a lot of brawn, but they make up for that with enthusiasm. They work like slaves no matter what the sky chucks at us. I think they're just hoping the war goes on long enough for them to be able to join the services. But I fear they will be tempted away long before that. You may have seen the large advert in the *Deremouth News*: workers wanted at the expanded nuts and bolts factory in town. The money will be better than I pay and they will be in the dry. I wouldn't blame them.'

She was conscious that he was giving her a hundred percent of his attention.

'If – and I repeat *if* – I were able to interest any of my sixth formers in volunteering to help at the weekends, could you use them?'

'Seventeen-and eighteen-year-old lads! You ask if I could use them! They would be a gift from heaven. But with important exams coming up, I can't imagine they'd be interested. Wages don't amount to enough to tempt boys coming from homes where parents can afford boarding school fees.' She knew she was being ungracious – just as she knew the reason for it was her clown-like garb suitable to nothing better than the job she was doing.

'I hadn't envisaged a wage. Of course I agree with you about their forthcoming examinations, but a few hours of outdoor labour could do them nothing but good.' Then, with that sudden and unexpected smile she had seen the previous day, he continued, 'This would be something they could do for the war effort. If they're worth their salt, boys of that age have high ideals; add to that their wish to be seen as men already. I can promise you nothing, but leave it with me, Mrs Hawthorne. When I take assembly tomorrow morning I shall endeavour to stir their enthusiasm. I doubt if any of them know much about growing vegetables, but I take it you would expect to give them clear instructions?' Despite the smile there was something old fashioned, even prim, in his manner. So his next remark surprised her even more than what he had suggested. 'I fear I am not conversant with the ways of you country folk but there are some jobs that I hate to see a woman doing.' He accompanied his words with a nod in the direction of the pigsty and the overloaded bucket.

She laughed outright, her mood suddenly and inexplicably lifted. 'I'm a hardened case. But just look at me! All I'm fit for at the end of this job is plunging into the bath. I'm almost at the end of the road with Horatio here; another fortnight he'll have departed this life and be what Jess refers to as bacon and chops. I'm not replacing him. Pig rearing is one job too many with Den away.'

'At least let me carry that heavy pail to where you dispose of the contents.'

'Truly I can manage. As long as we've kept a pig it has been my job to look after it.'

'I insist. Bring it out of the sty – it may be a sign of cowardice but I draw the line at trespassing uninvited into friend Horatio's domain – then let me carry it.'

What a strange man he was, A townsman indeed, for even on a Sunday morning he was dressed in a dark suit, white shirt and sober grey and blue tie. His shoes were polished to such a shine that Kathie believed any mud would slide straight off them. Looking down at her own attire and pig-stained boots, she felt even more of a mess than usual. However, she obeyed his instructions. Walking empty-handed ahead of him she found herself enjoying the unfamiliar feeling of feminine frailty. Even so, she resented what she suspected was a criticism of Dennis in this stranger's inference. She and Dennis were partners. Her mouth softened into a smile as she thought of him.

–

On that first of Oliver's regular visits he had permission to stay until teatime, but Bruce insisted that in future he must return to school for his midday meal. Already this new war was making its mark and it was recognized that hospitality had to be more measured than pre-September. So autumn progressed: Beth became ever more one of the family and the magic of Westways rubbed off on Oliver just as Kathie had hoped.

'You know what, Mum?' Jess said as the two girls were jostling for place at the kitchen sink to wash their hands before coming to the table at lunchtime one Sunday in November. 'Well, two things. I'll tell you. Jack Dench from the next class up at school was on the common this morning with two squidgy little puppies and their mother – the dogs' mother I mean, not Jack's. And do you know, it's awful what's going to happen. One of the puppies has been found a home but the other one is going to be drowned when his dad – Jack's dad I mean – when he has his next day off from the factory where he works. Jack says they do it when the cat has kittens too; his dad ties them up in a sack with a brick in it then throws them in the river. Mum, listen Mum, please, *please*, say yes Mum. Can we have him? He's a little boy puppy and he is like a beautiful cuddly bundle of fur just the colour of fudge. We could call him Fudge, Mum. Please. Beth and me've both got birthdays soon. We could share him. Just think of him all by himself with a brick in the sack... *please* Mum.'

It would have taken a hard heart to turn the request down without even considering it, and a hard heart had never been part of Kathie's nature. Even so, hadn't she enough to do without adding an unhouse-trained dog to her burden?

'We've got such a lot to do, Jess. He'd have to be taught to be clean in the house; then he'd have to be taken for walks.'

'We'd do all that, Mum. Beth and me. Wouldn't we, Beth?'

'Honest we would, Auntie Kathie,' Beth said solemnly.

'I'll have a word with your father when he next phones.' And that was as far as Kathie would promise. But fate played into the hands of the children when, on his way back to Westways that afternoon, Oliver met Jack taking the two mongrel puppies for a walk. That's how it was that when the girls heard the click of the garden gate they ran to the small front garden to find not only Oliver there but also Jack and the puppies.

'Look Mum. Do come out and just look.' Did Jess really think that Kathie would be able to 'just look' – two tiny dogs, one with a home to go to and the other with the prospect of sharing a sack with a brick. Fudge endeared himself to her just as he had to the girls.

'Dad called at the pet shop in Deremouth, but the man there said that they couldn't sell the dogs they already had – because of the war, he said. People aren't spending and anyway they were frightened about having to feed them. In the shop they were charging five shillings for theirs. Dad's off tomorrow, so I expect this will be this one's last walk. Bonzo, he's the one with the white on his face, he's not going to his new home for another week or two but Dad says if they have to be drowned you want to get on with it when they're young.'

Kathie picked up the furry bundle that was Fudge and was rewarded by having her face licked.

'We could save him, Mum. I promise Beth and I would look after him, we'd see he had water and take him to the common.'

'We could brush him too,' Beth put in for good measure.

'Do you think Dad will phone this evening? You said you'd ask him. You can't let Fudge be killed, Mum.' She didn't actually know the expression 'below the belt'.

'If I give you five shillings, Jack, will you give it to your father? And will you throw in his lead?'

So the deal was done. Probably Jessie's reminder that if she didn't say 'yes' she would be as good as signing Fudge's death warrant had something to do with her decision; or was it that she expected a call from Dennis that evening and, when she kept her promise and asked him, she knew what his answer would be. It was wiser to present Fudge as a fait accompli.

When Jack and Bonzo had gone, Jess, Beth, Oliver and Fudge walked the entire length of the lane twice, taking turns in holding Fudge's lead. Kathie told herself she must be crazy; yet when the little party returned and the puppy strained at his lead to get to her, his tail trembling with excitement, she scooped him up into her arms. He seemed to know she was his saviour.

Just as she had anticipated, Den was not pleased.

'Kathie, I don't understand you. When I was home that land took the chaps and me all our time to keep as it should be kept. Now there's just you and those two chits of girls you were foolhardy enough to waste good money employing, yet you seem intent on spending your time caring for other people's kids and animals.'

'Fudge isn't other people's anything; he's ours. You'll love him, Den. You won't be able to stop yourself.'

'Can't stand little yappers. If you must have a dog why couldn't you have got a Labrador – something big and sensible? But we didn't want a dog. In fact it's a liability in an establishment where we grow crops for sale.'

That thought had already occurred to her so she was ready with her answer.

'I'm putting fencing so that he won't be able to get onto the growing area.'

'And I suppose that won't cost money we can't afford.' She heard the sarcasm in his voice.

'Oh Den, don't be a grouch. If you'd been here and heard the way Jess pleaded you would have done just the same. And what sort of an example would it have been if I'd said "no" when the alternative was that he was going to be put in the river tomorrow. You wouldn't have let that happen; you're a bigger softie than I am.'

'Humph.' And she knew from the tone of his grunt that his mood was softening. 'It's just that I worry about the gardens. It's not women's work. I ought to be there.'

'What rubbish the man talks. Den—'

'Not something else you have to confess?'

'Nothing wicked – nothing you don't know, I expect – just, Den, I miss you.'

'Me too, Kathie. I miss you more than I thought possible. Bloody war.'

So Fudge was forgotten. Den liked to think of Westways just as he had left it and had no wish to let either an unknown child or an untrained puppy spoil the image.

–

December meant birthdays for both the girls, Beth on the 7th and Jess three days later on the 10th. So a few days beforehand Kathie left Sarah and Sally picking sprouts and set off to Deremouth to buy their surprise presents. With no male assistance she and the girls – with the help of Jess and Beth – had erected the netting fence so, with the front gate firmly closed, Fudge had been left with the run of the garden where the children usually played.

Kathie meant to catch the five past two bus from opposite the post office. That would get her to Deremouth at about half past and give her time to go to do her shopping before catching the three fifteen bus home.

Five minutes past two, six minutes past two, seven… it was coming up to ten minutes past the hour when a car drew up by the bus stop.

'Mrs Hawthorne, I'm on my way to Deremouth. May I give you a lift?' Bruce Meredith offered, leaning to open the passenger door.

'I really am grateful. The buses are usually so punctual, but I was here long before time so I know I didn't miss it.' Kathie got in and slammed the door shut. 'I daren't take the van or the petrol won't last out for deliveries.'

'And this will be my last trip for a while. I get a very limited ration, simply for school use. So let's enjoy the luxury of our own transport. Have you a lot to do in town? I have an appointment at the bank, but I shan't be there many minutes. Can I wait and bring you home?'

'That would be wonderful. You see, Jessie and Beth don't know about the trip and I want to be home and get my shopping hidden away before they get in from school. It's all a big secret. They're both of them coming up to six.'

'So I understand. You are working wonders on young Oliver. I had a long chat with him on Sunday when he came back from you; the difference in the child is quite remarkable. He tells me you have a puppy. You don't believe in making life easy for yourself, do you,' he added with a laugh.

Memories crowded back to Kathie; she seemed to hear Dennis's voice. 'I had a dog when I was a child,' she said. 'I know just what it means.'

'I do agree with you. And perhaps because Jess and the other one know you have taken on so much more with your husband away, they will want to be responsible for the pup. I don't imagine that will let you off the hook, but it will be good for them. Oliver tells me the other child, the little fair one, is an evacuee. They get on well?'

And so the ride to Deremouth passed with amiable even if superficial chat. When he drew up outside the toyshop he came around the front of the car to open her door.

'I'll be no more than five minutes in the bank. How would it be if whichever of us is first goes to the tea shop across the road and orders – well, I leave it to you to decide if you get there before I do. A pot of tea, scones, cakes, whatever you fancy – or should I say, whatever they can offer. If we're a little later than you anticipated I could always take your shopping home with me and bring it down to Westways when they're at school tomorrow.'

The afternoon was fast turning into a treat. Kathie ought to want to rush back to Westways so that she could change into her work clothes and give the girls a hand with the sprouts; but she pushed the thought to the back of her mind. After all, if Bruce Meredith was driving her back it was up to him to say when they went.

He was easy company and all too soon they were driving home.

'I must thank you, Mrs Hawthorne, for your kindness to Oliver Marley. I believe he will always be a loner, but I find him much more amenable to his surroundings; you have given him the stability he needed. And I believe he told you that his mother is about to move into the village.'

'Yes, he did. He's very excited.'

'And was your impression the same as mine? With two parents, a child has a balanced approach, but with only one the balance is thrown. I fear Marley holds his mother on an unnaturally high pedestal.'

'And yet she sent him to boarding school at only seven.'

'Your Beth came as an evacuee before she was even six. For him to board was perfectly natural; many day students did the same as London saw the general exodus.'

'Well, now with her close by he'll have all the stability he needs. He is a delightful little boy. It might be better for him if he rebelled a bit against the way Jess organizes both Beth and him too—' the affection in her voice took the sting out of her words— 'but he seems happy to follow her lead.'

'And Beth?'

'Oh, Jess can do no wrong as far as Beth is concerned. Life can be so unjust, you know. She has had no chance at all – no real home life. Yet she is incredibly quick to learn. One term at the local school – and living with Jess has helped because they share everything they do – but already she has caught up with her reading and writing. And she never has to be told anything more than once.'

'So this war has done her a favour, given her an opportunity she wouldn't have had. And speaking of the war, are you expecting your husband home for the festival?'

'For Christmas? No, apparently not. The highlight of Christmas Day for the men seems to be that the officers serve them their lunch. Who would have thought this time last year that we could have been having a conversation like this?'

'Indeed. And please God by next year this mad world will have come to its senses.'

'Are we even in sight of victory? Den is itching to get overseas and play a proper role. It's so awful.'

'Indeed,' he said again in what she thought of as his old-fashioned manner. 'My senior boys can't wait to get into uniform. But they don't know… how can they know?'

'Were you in the last one the same as Den? He put his age up to get in.'

'Ah, well I must be a few years ahead of him. I was seventeen and just leaving school when it began and so I went right through. War to end wars... dear God, what fools men are.'

'Do you think Mr Chamberlain was wrong to declare war? Surely not. If you have a bully in your school I bet you'd soon have him in your study to give him six of the best.'

Bruce laughed. 'I bet I would too. Bullying has to be stopped. It's sometimes difficult to define the line between tolerance and cowardice. These days I do very little classroom teaching; my job is mostly administration. But as headmaster my responsibility is to see that children who enter the school young and impressionable leave it at seventeen or eighteen as men of courage and self-confidence. To my mind that is of even more import-ance than their examination results. And I fear that in the beginning I made no headway at all with young Marley. I couldn't even begin to understand what went on in his mind.'

'I had the advantage over you there,' she said as they approached Sedgewood village, 'Jess and Beth broke through the barriers. If Ollie carries a torch for anyone, it's his mother. And that's right and normal, except that in his case I think he holds her on such a high pedestal that she remains just out of his reach. And that's where the trouble lies. Once she gets to Sedgewood things will be much better.'

Bruce circled his right arm out of the window to indicate that he meant to turn left into the lane to the common.

'I'll hop out here—' she started to say, but he was already bumping his way along the lane to Westways. 'I'll open the double gate so that you can turn the car,' she said as she reached for the latch to open the gate.

'No need, I'll reverse. Thank you for a pleasant afternoon, Mrs Hawthorne.'

–

As is so often the way with dogs of no fixed ancestry, Fudge was quick to learn. And the two little girls took their responsibility seriously. Keeping him on his lead, they walked him along the lane to the common, stopping and waiting patiently each time he found something that required sniffing. They changed the water in his bowl and scraped the leavings from the plates into his bowl. They even imagined he was making progress in his attempt to stand on his hind legs when he was told to stand up and beg.

Despite the mishaps that had to be cleared up, Kathie was thankful to have him. Christmas had loomed in front of her like a black cloud; she was haunted by memories of previous years. Yet as the days of December raced towards the 25th, she found herself with a new mission: if she and Jessie had been alone, memories would have killed the joy. But they weren't alone, this year there was Beth whom Kathie suspected had never experienced a proper Christmas, and there was Fudge.

She knew just where to find holly and greenery on the common and it was impossible not to be infected by the children's excitement as they helped her collect enough to bedeck the downstairs rooms. Even Fudge seemed to know the outing was something special. In previous years, since Jess had been old enough to take part in the gathering of the greenery, she and her father had gone on their own. For Kathie this was a new experience, one that was enhanced by the sight of Beth's face.

'Cor, Auntie Kathie, its like as if there's something magic everywhere.' Then, almost shyly tugging at Kathie's hand, 'Sniff as hard as you can, you can smell it all different today, sort of… sort of… dunno what it is – but you can feel it, can't you?' She looked up at her adopted aunt, wishing with all her might that she knew more words and could describe what she could sense in the atmosphere.

'That's right, Beth love. For these last days before Christmas everything is different. The holly bush has a sort of magic about it. If you come back next week it will be just an ordinary holly bush – but not now. The spirit of Christmas is everywhere.'

'Cor. But it must be just here where it's all trees and grass and that, cos back in Merchant Buildings where I was for other Christmases the days were just the same as always. No, not just the same: the chestnut man used to get his fire going in our street; I remember the smell of it. And after Tilly got all dressed up and went out in the evenings I used to watch out of the window and see the people getting their cooked nuts. Do you reckon they're nice, Aunt Kathie? Have you ever tasted any?'

'Yes, they're lovely. But here in the country we don't get men cooking them in the street. We'll buy some and cook them ourselves on the fire. How would that be?'

'Cor…' Clearly it would be good beyond words.

With the girls dragging the sack containing the holly, ivy and sprigs of fir tree while Kathie took Fudge's lead, the raiding party returned home where they found the tree Kathie had ordered in the village was waiting for them in the porch. Work was in full swing when they heard someone walking up the path to the front door.

Recognizing Bruce, Kathie opened the window and called, 'The door's on the latch, you can come straight in. We're doing the decorations.' It must have been that spirit of Christmas that gave her this relaxed acceptance of such an unexpected caller; and perhaps that same spirit was responsible for Bruce's offer of assistance.

'Have you any steps? I was thinking we might fix some of the greenery to the ceiling beams. What do you think?'

'Cor, it looks like fairyland,' Beth said in a whisper that spoke volumes of her awe for the magic of it all. Just for a brief second Kathie and Bruce let their eyes meet, the message passing between them encompassing the importance of keeping the wonder of it alive for her. 'Is it cos of that spirit of Christmas you told me about, Auntie Kathie?'

Kathie nodded. 'Oh yes. And you wait until it gets dark tonight, then look up at the stars,' she said, thankful that the day had been cold and clear, 'you'll feel the wonder of it all around you.'

Bruce moved the steps to where Kathie had already secured the tree firmly in a large bucket of soil.

'What's for the top? A fairy? An angel?'

'We always have this big star,' Kathie said, trying not to let her mind dwell on all the other years when it had been Dennis who had mounted the steps to fix it. Would he be imagining them today, the Sunday before Christmas, carrying out the annual ritual? Or would he assume that without him there would be no real Christmas at Westways? No, of course he wouldn't. He would want everything to carry on as it always had for Jessie's sake.

'What next, while I'm up here?' Bruce's voice cut through her thoughts.

And so the winter afternoon progressed, the children unwrapping the stored and fragile baubles with exaggerated and unnatural care – something else Kathie silently attributed to the influence the spirit of Christmas was having on them.

Walking back up the hill to the main gate of the hall, Bruce's mind was on the hour he had spent in the little sitting room of Westways. No wonder Oliver Marley wanted to spend every free hour there at the weekends. And yet was it any different from family homes up and down the land, homes where this year people were fighting to cling to a way of life that had been overshadowed by what was going on in Europe? He wasn't prepared to dig too deeply for an answer to his silent question. Instead, reaching the lodge, he unlocked the front door and went inside.

–

It was much later. Bruce had gone back to the school that was empty except for one or two kitchen staff. At Westways the children were in bed, and Kathie tried to stir a last gasp of life into the dying embers of the fire. All day she had managed to keep up a show of high spirits, but now she felt like a popped balloon. She knew Dennis would want everything to go on as normal at home, but there was nothing normal about anything while he wasn't there to be part of it. The room was getting cold; the greenery festooned with silver 'icicles' held no magic. Kneeling on the rug she bent nearer the dying fire, but it wasn't physical warmth she craved. When she felt the sting of tears burning her eyes she made no effort to stem them. What was the point? No one could see her; no one would care whether she laughed or cried; all that mattered was that she was strong enough to work like a slave in the garden, come wind or rain, doing Den's work through the hours of daylight until, when it was too dark to see, she was here to cook and clean in the house.

She heard her stifled sob, then realized she wasn't alone. Pushing the door open with his tiny paw Fudge came to her, standing against her on his hind legs and trying to reach to lick her ear.

–

Far away in his army base, Dennis lay awake, his imagination winging him southwards to Westways. Kathie had told him she had bought the tree. Securing it in its tub of soil was *his* job; it always had been. How was she managing? She ought to have bought a small one to put on the table. But no, Kathie never let herself be beaten.

Staring at the ceiling he listened to the sounds from the other beds: some of the chaps were sleeping, the chorus of gentle snores told him so. From a bed opposite his in the long hut came disturbingly obvious grunts from its occupant, Harry Brooks, a young Devon man whose bawdy conversation touched a raw nerve in Dennis, emphasizing to him that, no matter how closely men had to live together, there was no automatic meeting of spirit. He disliked the man's coarse language and he disliked his nightly performances. As the seconds passed in the otherwise quiet hut and Brooks' excitement mounted, so he grew louder. Did the others who may still be awake find it as offensive as Dennis did? He turned on his side and pulled the blankets over his head, trying not to hear. Think of something else – imagine Jess and her excitement as they did the tree, think of Kathie out there in all weathers working on the land. Oh damn it, what the hell am I doing here when I ought to be home with her?

Five

Christmas saw Kathie taking on yet another job which had always been Den's: while the children were walking Fudge on the common she caught one of the chickens then, with her eyes tightly closed, she gripped its neck and with one swift movement stretched and twisted it, hearing the click as the bone broke. Her hands were clammy, she felt slightly sick as she looked down at the bird. It twitched and fluttered as if it still had the life she had taken from it. Then taking it to the shed she hung it on a hook in the ceiling. Later that evening she brought it indoors to pluck and dress it, feeling better as it took on the shape of 'Christmas dinner'.

Another Westways tradition was to play a gramophone record she and Dennis had bought the first year after they were married. Custom had it that the first hearing was at teatime on the 24th, following the Kings College Choir from Cambridge on the wireless. Kathie wound up the old gramophone, fitted a new needle and the cottage was filled with the sound of carols; the tone was poor, the recording old and scratchy, but the festival had started! Beth listened in wonder; the spirit of Christmas was all around her. It was the first time she had heard a carol, so Jess was able to show off her superior knowledge and 'la-la' the tune even if she'd forgotten the words. It was just coming to the end, the sound of 'Hark the Herald Angels

Sing' reverberating through the cottage, when there was a knock at the front door.

Kathie opened it to find Bruce Meredith in the porch. He was holding a parcel not very elegantly wrapped in a sheet of garish paper she recognized as coming from the village stores, and held together more by luck than by the yellow ribbon tied around it.

'I've just done the unforgivable,' he greeted her. 'I've climbed over the gate for a short cut. Oliver Marley left this with me, with the request to bring it to you and the girls on Christmas Eve. My word, but don't you sound Christmassy!'

'Tradition has to be upheld, war or no war. Won't you come in? That was very kind of Ollie. Let's drop it off in the sitting room so that the girls won't see it until the morning. When is his mother moving down from London?'

'The first week in January, I believe.'

She hid the package under a cushion on the sofa just as Jess ran from the warm room.

'Mum, it's still going round and round. Can you put it on again so Beth can learn the songs?'

'Jess, where are your manners? Say hello to Mr Meredith and perhaps I'll see what I can do.'

So it was that a minute or two later she and Bruce were alone in the seldom used sitting room where the fire was laid ready to be lit the next morning while, from the warm room came the haunting sound of the treble voices of the boys of Winchester Cathedral choir.

'Have you staff at the hall to prepare your meal tomorrow?'

'I may go to the lodge. It depends how things are with Elspeth, my wife.'

That a wife was the reason for his frequent visits to the lodge had never entered her head.

'Your wife?' She spoke before she could stop herself. If he was so secretive about his wife perhaps it was tactless to ask about her. 'I didn't know you were married.'

'Indeed I am. I know you're busy now, but when the holidays are over perhaps you would allow me to take you to visit her.' His reply went no way towards explaining why he had never previously spoken of her. And yet why should he? Kathie asked herself. They were comparative strangers, why should he have felt impelled to talk of his marriage? And yet there was something strange about keeping his domestic life so separate from his position at the hall. After a few seconds' hesitation, he went on, 'We were married nearly seventeen years ago, she was just twenty and the loveliest creature you could see, and with a nature to match.'

'Is she ill?' Kathie asked tentatively. There was something unnatural in the way he spoke of her, 'she was' not 'she is'. At thirty-seven, or thereabouts, she might have lost the innocent beauty of those early days, but changes come so gradually they are scarcely perceptible in someone you love.

He nodded. 'We had a happy year. There was only one problem: her mother's deteriorating mental state, even though she was only in her forties. Then my father-in-law had a huge stroke and died within hours. It tipped the scales. She was a lost soul. Each time we visited she had slipped further away. We think of dementia as belonging to old age, but she was a beautiful, middle-aged woman. As a child Elspeth had had a nanny and, when she outgrew the need, Nanny Giles stayed on in the house, a sort of companion helper for my mother-in-law. But it wasn't many months after her husband's sudden death that it became obvious she needed more care than Nanny Giles could give. She became violent, wild, her whole character changed. She would look at Elspeth, her own daughter, and have no idea who she was. And it was just about at the same time that Elspeth was thrown from her horse when we were riding. The injury was to her head. In hospital she was in a coma; no one thought she would come out of it.' He looked at Kathie as if he had forgotten she was there as he let his mind slip back down the years. She read anguish in his eyes as she held his gaze.

'Go on,' she whispered. 'Elspeth came out of the coma?'

'Do you believe in prayer? I prayed. God, how I prayed. First as she lay helpless, I prayed that she would wake and come back to me. She woke but she was lost to me, lost to everyone. Their doctor said it was in the family, for three generations the strain of dementia had been passed. The fall, the brain damage, perhaps they only speeded up what would ultimately have happened. In body and in spirit she was the loveliest person I'd ever known, and for a year or so we had shared complete happiness. On the first of January it will be sixteen years since the accident. In the beginning I watched for some sign of recognition. I was consumed by terror and misery. My prayer wasn't answered in the way I wanted. And yet, Kathie—' for the first time he called her by her Christian name, neither of them so much as noticing— 'some sort of strength came, strength to face what our future was to be.'

'And now?' She was frightened of what he'd tell her.

'I don't know. She smiles at me; when I sit with her she never pulls away when I take her hand. Sometimes if I say something she will repeat a word or two. Whether she knows who I am, who *she* is, I don't know. Her manner is as gentle and sweet as it always was. I don't know—' he ran his hand through his hair, his tight control threatening to break – 'I don't know. If I didn't see her each day, would she notice?' Kathie put out a hand and laid it on his arm. They were little more than strangers and yet she was moved beyond words.

'Perhaps your prayers have been answered. Perhaps the answer is there in her contentment.'

'I try to believe that. She is like a contented baby, warm, well fed and loved. It breaks my heart to see her and yet I am thankful and – can you understand this, I wonder? – sometimes just sitting with her, feeling her hand holding mine with such trust, some of that peace and contentment rubs off onto me. Is that crazy?'

Kathie shook her head. 'I think it's beautiful; it's a sort of pure, honest love that's not tainted by the mess of the world.' He nodded.

'That about says just what she is: pure, untainted by the mess of the world. She has no visitors, but if you could spare the time I would be grateful. Perhaps she won't even notice that you are from outside her normal world but, if she does, surely it would be good for her.'

'Of course I'll come. The girls start back to school before you do, I expect, so the first day of their term I'll come with you to the lodge. Does Elspeth get taken for walks? If she isn't frightened off because I'm strange to her, I was thinking perhaps she could be brought down to Westways. There's something very, very…' She hesitated, groping for the right word. 'Sort of full of *goodness* about outside work, nurturing plants.'

He gazed at her steadily and for a moment she was disconcerted by his unfathomable expression.

'How could she be frightened off? My belief, indeed my hope and my reason for suggesting you let me take you to her, is that because she isn't like the rest of us, she will see beyond an unfamiliar stranger and know you for the person you are.'

'Mum!' Jessie called as she rushed into the room, 'come quick, Mum. It's gone all funny.'

Kathie listened. '...bleak midwinter, stormy winds did... bleak midwinter, stormy winds did...'

'Nothing serious, love. The needle is stuck. I'll do it.'

'Didn't I tell you, Beth? Mum knows what's happened; she's coming to put it right.'

Jess climbed on a chair so that she could see Kathie lightly touch the head of the gramophone, setting the stormy winds on their way. If it happened again she would be able to do it herself, she decided. There was much of her mother in Jess; she wasn't prepared to be beaten.

Those days of Christmas and New Year needed every ounce of Kathie's strength of character. Her salvation came from the two little girls and her determination to give them happy and lasting memories.

They returned to school on the first Thursday in January and so at mid-morning of that day Bruce called for her and together they walked up the hill to the main gate of the hall. Another morning and the earth might be rock hard and white with frost, but that Thursday the air was soft and the birds seemed to believe nature's call of spring had arrived. As soon as Kathie had set Sally and Sarah to work she had gone indoors to dress for her outing. Her wardrobe held nothing to inspire her, nothing except her 'outfit' so, smiling to herself as she remembered the last time she had worn it, she had taken it off its hanger. January demanded a thick jumper under the jacket.

Immediately, Bruce recognized the effort she had made.

'You look extremely smart,' he said, a twinkle in his eyes as he raised his brows.

Just weeks ago Kathie would have been annoyed and embarrassed. Now, though, she surprised herself by laughing.

'I know what you're thinking, and you're right. I *did* make a supreme effort when I came to the hall to take you down a peg or two. Today is different. I put on what we call my outfit because I wanted to do my best for Elspeth.'

'You look delightful, then and now. But, if I'm honest, I prefer you in those ghastly clown-like trousers and Wellington boots.'

'Hardly the right attire for going a-visiting.'

'Will she so much as notice? Perhaps the idea of taking you there is crazy, but there seems to be a magic healing power in Westways – and it must stem from *you*. You worked something of a miracle with young Marley; and have you any idea what it has meant to me to be accepted in your home?'

This time his remark deprived her of words; she could respond to playful banter, but there was a depth of seriousness in his voice that made her uneasy. It was a relief when he held open the wrought iron gate of the hall and, opening the door of the lodge with his key, ushered her inside.

'Look, Elspeth my pet,' Nanny Giles said to her charge as Bruce and Kathie came into the sitting room, 'here's Mr Bruce and he's brought you a visitor.'

The woman seated on the sofa in front of the fire nodded, her mouth opening in a smile. Kathie couldn't let herself look towards Bruce; she was moved with sympathy that physically ached.

'Hello my dear,' he said, stooping to kiss his wife's forehead as he sat down by her side and indicated to Kathie to take the nearby armchair. His words brought a nod of Elspeth's head, in fact more than a nod, it continued at the same momentum as she looked past him to Kathie.

'I live just down the road,' Kathie said. 'Bruce and I walked here together. It's such a perfect morning. Just look at that glorious blue sky.' She pointed to the window and was rewarded by Elspeth turning her nodding head to admire the day. 'Where I live we have a field full of things we grow – vegetables, I mean. Perhaps you would like to come and see me when you and Nanny go for a walk?' She addressed the invitation to Elspeth, but looked to Nanny Giles for approval.

'Why now, Elspeth my pet, wouldn't that be just champion.'

But Elspeth s attention was lost. As Bruce had sat by her, so he had automatically taken her hand feeling her fingers entwine themselves with his. Kathie tried not to look at them as he raised their clasped hands to move against his cheek. Make her show some sort of response, she begged silently, surprising herself that it should matter so much to her. She hardly knew him at all and his poor 'lost' wife was a complete stranger, but she couldn't bear to remember how he had exposed his heart to her when he'd talked on Christmas Eve. We're so lucky, Den and me. Even though he's away we are never separated, not as these two are as they sit holding hands. What sort of hell has Bruce lived through during the years that have brought them to this?

Ten minutes later she and Bruce were on their way back down the hill. Their previous easy bantering conversation had gone and yet neither of them was ready to talk about the still beautiful, but 'empty' woman they had just left.

That same afternoon while Kathie was putting every ounce of her energy into turning the soil which had been ploughed in her first effort to master the motorized digger, Elspeth and Nanny Giles arrived. Nothing could ever really break through the fog that was Elspeth's mind, but her first visit to Westways came nearer than anything had for a very long time. She must have been aware of her surroundings, for when the nurse tried to lead her to the gate she pulled back, not wanting to leave.

'Nice warm fire at home, my pet,' the nurse said encouragingly. 'Give Nanny your hand like a good girl.'

The good girl let her hand be taken, she walked by the nurse's side, but time and again she turned her head to look at what they were leaving.

'Poor woman,' Sarah said as she and Sally watched the couple depart. 'Gosh, but doesn't it make you count your blessings when you think of your own family. I bet she's not as old as our mums are.'

'Why do you reckon he married her?' Sally wondered. 'I bet back in those days, when they got hitched, I mean, I bet he was a real dish.'

'And so must she have been. She's good looking now, except that her face is sort of blank. Fancy, he keeps her there in the lodge and no one, not even the locals who come in to the pub, chaps who never miss a trick, none of them have an inkling that the headmaster has a wife. Don't let's say anything, Sal. Be rotten for him to have the village talking.' It wasn't said lightly. Sarah's conscience had to battle, for it would have been a great talking point in the bar. 'I expect they gossip just as much at that chapel your dad's so tied up with as they do in the pubs.'

'I expect they do. But they might want to show Mr What's-his-name, her husband, that they were sorry for him.'

'Bet he'd hate that. Well, anyway, I know I would if I were in his shoes. Have you filled your box of parsnips yet? My turnips are about ready. It'd save Mrs Hawthorne having to stop the digging if we suggested taking the old cart to the village. What do you say?'

So, ten minutes or so later the old hand cart was loaded with the day's delivery and they set off to the village. In the four months they had been at Westways they had forgotten all about looking for work in more comfortable surroundings and relished the challenge of keeping the all-female market garden as productive as it ever had been.

That afternoon was the first of Elspeth's frequent visits. It became an almost daily habit if the weather was fine. There was no doubt she enjoyed walking between the rows of vegetables, the smile never leaving her face. But as to recognition, it was as if each visit was her first.

–

It was the week following Kathie s visit to the lodge, in the early hours of Wednesday morning when Kathie half woke. She'd gone to sleep indulging the same picture in her mind as she so often did: the sound of familiar footsteps and she would look out of the window and see Den. So, half stirring, she knew she must have been dreaming when she heard someone coming up the garden path. But hark, what was that click? No, it must have been imagination; there was no other sound. Lying perfectly still, she strained her ears to listen She climbed out of bed and switched on the light, only then remembering to close the heavy blackout curtains.

That's when, almost frightened to death, she heard the bedroom door open.

This was no dream. Den was home. Wordlessly they moved to each other. His arms were strong, his mouth on hers banishing everything from her mind except pure joy. Neither the scratchy material of his uniform nor its unpleasantly disinfectant smell could mar the moment.

'Fourteen days,' he whispered, 'fourteen whole days.'

'I would have waited up. Oh Den, you're real. I've dreamt it so often; but this isn't a dream. We'll creep downstairs and I'll find you some food.'

'No, we'll just stay here. Is Jess OK?'

She nodded, unbuttoning his battledress top.

'Just wait till she sees you! And Beth. Beth's a dear.'

His only answer to that was a grunt that spoke as clearly as any words.

'Let's get to bed. I want to hear about everything,' he said, speaking in a whisper and starting to take off his uniform. 'Hell of a journey. Crowded like sardines on the train; I sat on my kitbag in the corridor right from Paddington to Exeter. Blinds down, only that dim blue light lost in a fog of cigarette smoke. They've cut the evening country route bus or I would have been home hours ago. Got the local train to Deremouth. I thought, hang the expense, I'll get the station cab. But there wasn't one.'

'Who brought you?'

'Shanks's pony. Walked the whole ruddy way. Damned war!' Then, his tone changing as with his hands on her shoulders he held her at arm's-length, looking at her, 'Kathie, oh Kathie, you don't know what it's like to come home. Everything I want is here.' He looked remarkably manly despite being stripped to his army issue vest and underpants which defied any man other than one with a perfect physique to appear attractive and which smelt of the same disinfectant as his battledress.

Surprising herself as much as she surprised him, she tore off her nightgown as he divested himself of the offending undergarments. How often she'd dreamed of this; now he was here, he was real. She raised her hand to his naked shoulder. For four months while he'd gone through initial training he'd had no leave, they had come no nearer than voices on the telephone; surely he was as hungry for love as she was herself.

'Kathie, oh God, Kathie, you don't know how much I've missed you – you, Jess, everything here. I'll turn the light out while you pull those beastly curtains back.'

A minute later, despite it being mid-January, he pushed the bottom window up and leant far out taking in great gulps of the crisp, night air.

'Sniff the air, Kathie. Home. Tomorrow you'll know what it's like to have a man out there working.'

She came to stand behind him, holding her arms around him.

'Tonight I want to know what it's like to have that man in here with me.'

Laughing softly he turned back into the room and drew her into his arms.

'Fourteen whole days – and fourteen whole nights.' Then, after a brief pause and speaking softly, he added. 'Kathie, the waiting's over. This is embarkation leave.'

'No,' she whispered in disbelief, 'not so soon. This is the first leave you've had. They can't send you abroad—'

His mouth covered hers, then still clinging to each other and she walking backwards, they moved towards the bed. That night their emotions were heightened by the thought of a separation so much more final than a posting to a camp somewhere in the same country. The future loomed before them, unknown and unimaginable. Only the present was real, familiar and precious.

–

Jess was beside herself with excitement when it was Dennis who woke her next morning. Standing up in bed she hurled herself into his open arms.

'Dad's come home. Look Beth, this is Dad.'

'Let's look at you, kiddo. My word, but you've grown. It must be because you're six.'

Jess giggled, nuzzling her face against his neck.

'Silly Dad. Dad, this is Beth. She's never had a dad of her own, so she's going to share with me. Stand up Beth; come and let's all have a squeeze together.' Said with such certainty that the other two would be as pleased as she was with the situation, that she was at a loss to understand why neither of them made a move.

'Hello, Beth.' Den forced a note of heartiness into his voice. 'You're settling in, are you? I expect you're like me, looking forward to the day this bl—' He quickly substituted a different adjective from the one that came naturally to his lips. 'Blessed war is over and we can all get back home.'

Beth shook her head. 'I like being here with Auntie Kathie and Jess.'

'And Fudge,' Jess threw in for good measure. 'Did Fudge bark when you got here, Dad?'

'I remembered in time and left my boots in the porch. He seems a nice enough puppy.'

Jess and Beth exchanged a look of satisfaction. At the back of their minds and never put into words had been the fear that he might say there was too much to do at Westways to keep a dog.

The breakfast fare was the same as any other morning: a bowl of porridge, a boiled egg, then toast and either jam or marmalade from the jar of preserves made before there was any thought of shortages. Yet, it struck Kathie that there was an underlying feeling of festivity. Only three weeks ago it had been Christmas, a time when she had been determined the house would be filled with that elusive spirit of joy; but being determined was a far cry from letting it happen naturally as it did that morning.

'You know what, Dad?' Jess held her stubby first finger up in the way that told them she had had a bright idea. 'Beth can't call you Dad if she calls Mum, Auntie Kathie. So, tell you what, Beth – you call him Uncle Den. OK? OK Dad?'

Looking uncertain Beth nodded. Kathie had come to know her well and she recognized just how much the little girl wanted a sign of approval.

'That's a good idea, Jess love,' she spoke before Dennis even had a chance to make a grunt of acceptance. He knew he was being unfair, but it was beyond him to stamp out his niggling resentment that a fourth person at their table spoilt the image he cherished.

The morning ritual got back on track. The children were sent to rinse their hands after their meal, and then put on their coats, berets and scarves. Then, as every other day, at exactly twenty-five to nine they promised Fudge a walked as soon as they got home and were off to school. From the window of the kitchen extension Den and Kathie watched them scurrying along the lane, their pace never slackening despite the fact they were obviously deep in conversation.

'She's a great kid,' Den mused. 'The other one seems a bit slow.'

'Slow she most certainly isn't. In four months she has come on in leaps and bounds. She didn't even know her letters—'

'There you are then! It must be hard for teachers to have backward kids put in their classes. But Jess will help her.'

'She reads as well as Jess does now and writes well too. She'd had no chance, poor mite. She and Jess are such – such *mates*!'

'While you wash these dishes I'll take this tripe-hound up to the common. Then, just think, Kathie, a whole day out there getting my hands dirty in God's good earth.'

A whole day, then there would be another and another, but so soon they would all melt away. To shake off the devil of gloom and fear that threatened, she planted a quick kiss on his cheek and started to stack the plates. No shadow must be allowed to fall over the gift of a fourteen-day leave – not yet, not until the dreaded day when he had to put on that smelly uniform, not until all this was no more than a memory they must cling to until he came home from this nameless 'overseas', home not just for leave but to slip back into the life he loved.

By the time Sally and Sarah leant their bikes against the shed just as the clock on the stable at the hall struck nine, Fudge had answered the call of nature and immediately been made to retrace his steps. Den was tinkering with the motorized digger and an oil can, and Kathie was pulling on her Wellington boots. The working day at Westways had started.

On their way to school the girls had had to pass the greengrocer's shop where Jack Hopkins was bringing his boxes of vegetables to prop against a frame he had made for the purpose outside the front window.

'D'you know what, Mr Hopkins? No, course you can't do. My dad has come home. He's home for a whole two weeks. I bet he'll bring the veg himself today.'

'Well, Jessie m'dear, that's a bit of good news if ever I heard one.'

Jess nodded her head in a way that was almost regal, believing it conveyed to him how grown up she was. Then tugging at Beth's hand she started to run. 'Come on, Beth, or we'll be late. Don't spect we'd be grumbled at, though, not when we told them about Dad.'

Jack Hopkins had been established at the greengrocery shop before Dennis turned his first sod of earth at Westways, and after twenty years he still thought of him as the young man he had been, just home from that other war. So, an hour or so later he called up the stairs to his wife, 'Any chance you can hold the fort here for half an hour or so, Mabs, I hear young Dennis Hawthorne has got some leave. I'd like just to have the chance to shake him by the hand and ask him how he's been doing.'

'Bet you he'll be here with the veg this afternoon. Can't see him making a holiday of a bit of leave.'

'Ah, I dare say he'll bring the stuff. But there are usually people to be served at that time of day; there would be no chance for a chat. He's got nothing but women for company at his garden. That little lass of his ought to have been a boy, darned if she didn't. Got the makings of a real little tomboy if ever a child had.'

'I'll see to the customers. Off you go.'

'I'll go on my grid, so I shan't be above half an hour or so.'

–

If Dennis had been living at home when Fudge had joined the family, he would have been more careful. For the first few days when the children set off for school Kathie had reminded them to be sure the gate was properly fastened, just as she always reminded Nanny Giles. But all of them were careful and Fudge spent most of his time with his nose in the mesh of the netting that kept him shut away from the growing area.

'There's Mr Hopkins from the veg shop coming up the path,' Sarah called to Dennis. 'I bet word has got round already that you're home. Shall I let him through?'

So a minute or two later, sitting on a plank held between two upturned empty oil drums, the two men were soon lost in conversation. As Dennis listened to the familiar voice he thought as he had a hundred times in these last few hours just how much all this meant to him – the cottage, the smell of the earth, the challenge that had become part of his life, Kathie, Jess, all of it. If he felt that these things were the reason for his fighting, then there was no dragon he wouldn't have challenged. But what had the way he had spent the last months got to do with the things that really mattered? He held his packet of Gold Flake for Jack Hopkins to take one, then put one between his own lips and felt for his matches.

'Your young Jess stopped on her way to school and told me you were here. Growing up fast is Jess. That skinny little evacuee kid hangs on her every word; I've watched them together. Your little lassie is a real leader.'

'Being an only one, I dare say she's grown up faster than some. I hope always being with Beth won't hold her back.' The words were out before he could stop himself.

'Likely it'll work the other way round. No sharper knife in the drawer than your Jessie. I shouldn't be smoking your fags. They're getting as hard to find as gold dust, and here we are only four months into the war. What do you reckon? Do you think we're going to beat bloody Adolf in quick time? Me, I'm frightened to look to the future.'

'God knows how long it'll take. But rest assured we'll not give up till we've got him grovelling. I'm just thankful I'm being sent overseas at the end of my fourteen days, at last I'm going to have a chance to do what I've been training for.'

'One war is enough for any man and you did your bit last time round.'

'It was the silly sods who carved up the peace that caused much of the trouble.'

Puffing peacefully at their cigarettes the two men believed theirs was the wisdom. So the minutes passed until Jack Hopkins' conscience reminded him he had a business to run. Dennis walked with him to the gate and even then they seemed loath to put an end to the visit, but at last the greengrocer pedalled off down the lane while Den came back to pick up the thread of his morning's work.

'Where's Fudge?' Kathie asked as she ladled the lunch-time soup from the saucepan.

'What does he usually do when you're working?' Den asked. 'The last I saw of him he walked off in a huff because I wouldn't let him follow me through that gate you put up in that "Charlie Harvey" net fence you ladies erected. And, by the way, that gate needs stronger hinges than those little things you put on it. I'll get some when I take the stuff into Hopkins later on.' He was looking forward to the afternoon trip to the village; often enough he'd imagined it. New to the task of keeping an eye on the puppy, he didn't consider it any cause for concern that the little creature wasn't watching Kathie's every movement as she passed soup bowls to Sally and Sarah. In truth he was put out by the fact that the midday break he and Kathie had always shared by themselves were invaded, as he thought of it, by a couple of girls from the village.

'I'll take a look outside for him,' Sally said, getting up from the table.

'And I'll check upstairs,' Kathie answered.

Den laughed as he took a spoonful of vegetable soup. 'Leave him be,' he said. 'Once he smells food he'll show up.'

'You're sure you shut the gate, Den?'

'I told you. That's when he sloped off in a huff. I've dreamt of your soup for months, Kathie, I'm not having it spoilt by a puppy with the sulks.'

But Kathie was gone. She hadn't been talking about the gate in the netting fence, she had meant the one onto the lane. As soon as she saw it was open she knew Fudge had escaped. He must have gone to the common, that's where the girls always took him. So she turned left and hurried along the narrowing track, calling his name as she went.

Once on the common the calling went on, 'Fudge! Come on, boy! Fudge!' Please don't let him be lost; this is the only place he knows his way to. 'Fudge!'

Perhaps he'd got into the wood of the hall, he could easily have got between the wooden bars of the gate. The pupils had returned the previous day, but they would have been in class. 'Fudge!' But she called more quietly, sure that if he was there he would hear her walking on the carpet of dead leaves and come to her. She stood still and listened, hoping to rear a rustle in the leaves and see him bounding towards her. Yes, listen!

'Kathie! What are you doing here all by yourself? Is everything all right?'

In her relief at hearing the concern in his voice, she turned to Bruce and told him the story.

'We're all used to making sure the gate is latched properly, but you see Den has come on leave.'

'Your husband? That's wonderful. I hope I get a chance to meet him. These grounds are vast, Kathie. Before the boys are excused from the dining room I'll tell them about Fudge. Some of the older ones know him, of course. They have half an hour free time before afternoon classes, so they'll have a good hunt.'

'He must have come this way. The girls always take him to the common so he wouldn't have gone towards the village.'

'When you get home you may find he's arrived first. Dogs have an instinct for retracing their steps.'

She nodded. Talking to him had chased away the vision of having to break it to the girls that Fudge was lost.

It occurred to her that it was a strange place for them to meet in the middle of a school day. 'I was trespassing,' she said, her eyes seeming to smile as she asked, 'but what was the headmaster doing lurking in the woods?'

'Guilty as charged,' he laughed. 'I often escape down here. The perfect place for a quiet cigarette and solitude.'

'Then along I come and spoil it all.'

He shook his head. 'On the contrary. I often lean on that gate and look along the lane towards Westways. The house is out of sight, but I can just see the bottom part of your land and I like to imagine you out there.'

Surely it was the sort of remark any friend might make and yet she found herself looking anywhere rather than meet his gaze.

'Imagine the girls and me working away while you're skiving with nothing better to do than lean on the gate, smoking,' she bantered.

'It must be a great relief to you to have your husband home.'

She nodded. 'It's embarkation leave.' There! She'd actually made herself put it into words. So far they hadn't even told Jess and, although there was no sense in it, she had felt that as long as it wasn't spoken she could hold it off. 'Fourteen days. Don't know where he'll be sent. Perhaps it won't be France. He should never have joined the Terriers, he's too old to get called up.'

Hearing the fear in her voice, Bruce's first feeling was that her husband was a lucky man: imagine if it were *he* just home for fourteen days embarkation leave. What difference would it make to anyone if he went to war? He thought of Elspeth, her never failing smile, the emptiness in her eyes.

'It's because of men like that, men who choose to serve even though they wouldn't have been called, that we shall win this war. You must be very proud.' Then, with a shrug that seemed to imply his uselessness, he continued, 'And me, with time on my hands to lean on a five-bar gate listening to the silence.'

144

'I must go and see if Fudge has come home. And thanks, Bruce, for saying you'd get the boys to look in the grounds.'

He went with her to the gate ready to give her a hand as she climbed over, but she was nimble and it presented no problem.

'If we find him, I'll bring him home this afternoon. If we don't I'd like to look in after school to make sure you've got him back – and to meet your husband.'

Kathie arrived home to find no sign of the puppy. The two girls returned to work, but their hearts weren't in it. Fudge had wormed his way into everyone's affection and at the back of all their minds was the thought that before four o'clock Jess and Beth would be home.

'It was my fault, I couldn't have thought to shut it after I stood outside talking to Jack Hopkins,' Den said as he carried the tray of bowls to the kitchen. No one had had any appetite; even he who had thought so often of Kathie's cauldron of home-made vegetable soup, had found it was spoilt by his feeling of guilt. It was that guilt which put the bluster in his voice as he went on, 'When we find him I must see there is a notice on the gate reminding people to latch it properly. I wonder you hadn't had the forethought to do that from the start – there are always callers, the postman, the milkman, anyone might leave it open if they're not reminded.'

'Rubbish! People don't need reminding to close gates behind them.' Her tone carried criticism. Would they have spoken to each other like this six months ago? They weren't the only couple whose roles had been changed by the war. He was pulled in two directions: partly he was proud – and relieved – at the capable way Kathie was running Westways; but he harboured an underlying feeling of resentment of her cheerful efficiency. And her sentiments were as undecided as his: it was wonderful to have him home but there was something in his manner as he inspected how she, Sally and Sarah had been caring for 'his' market garden that she found patronizing. For a moment silence hung between them.

It was his sense of guilt that made him pump up the tyres of his bicycle and set off to ride round the village looking for a sign of the escapee. Fudge was a pretty puppy, wasn't it quite likely that someone had seen him out without a collar and had taken a fancy to him. The village was small, he went a mile or so on along the Deremouth road, then in the other direction on the road towards Exeter. After more than an hour he returned home hoping, just as Kathie had earlier, that Fudge would be there before him.

—

The village school was in Highbury Lane, a turning off the main street just past the shops. Most of the houses were beyond the turning, so as the children bundled out into the freedom of the afternoon the majority went back to the corner then turned to the right. Two or three lived above the shops, but Jess and Beth were the only ones to head towards the lane to the common. On that afternoon, just as they usually did, they climbed a stile into a meadow belonging to Merrydown Farm. Some of the grazing cows looked up at them in an uninterested way as they kept to the edge of the grass before climbing another stile into a cutting that took them to the village street between Jack Hopkins' greengrocery store and the fish and chip shop. They never dawdled, especially since the advent of Fudge who would be waiting for his walk before it got too near dusk for them to be allowed to take him.

Heads together they chattered as they scurried along, then Beth suddenly noticed something that cut her off midsentence.

'Look Jess! Over the road, just coming under the gate of Colebrook Field!'

'It's Fudge!'

The bus from Deremouth was stationary as the local passengers climbed out by the fish and chip shop so, calling Fudge, Jess ran onto the road just behind it. She had been taught to look both ways before crossing a road and she made sure there was nothing following after the bus.

'Fudge, come on Fudge,' she yelled, rushing towards him just as he heard her voice and bounded to meet her. Never cross a road in front of a parked car, she had been told, in case there's something coming. But in her excitement at seeing the little dog she forgot to look to the left. The driver of the white van stamped hard on his brake pedal; there was a screech of tyres, a thud, then a deadly hush.

'Poor little mite. Wretched dog out by itself. Don't touch her, she must have broken bones. Lucky if it's no worse than that. Oh dear God, someone's little girl… The dog's a goner, that's for sure.' Then noticing Beth: 'Don't hang about here, dear, just you run along home.'

Two minutes ago the street had been quiet, yet suddenly there was a crowd. Where do people come from, like a colony of ants on a drip of honey? Jack Hopkins himself pushed his way to the front of the group.

'That's the kiddie from the market garden. I was with her dad only this morning – home on embarkation leave. Someone run to the call box and ring for an ambulance, it's no use any of us trying to move her.' Then to the driver of the van who was leaning against the vehicle for support, he added, 'Here, old man, let me give you a hand into my shop. You all right? My missus'll give you a cup of tea. We'll have to get the police along, but it wasn't your fault, I'll vouch for that. The kiddie just ran out without looking. When we get in the shop I'll look up the number of the little one's parents. Poor buggers. What a start to her dad's leave.'

Beth half heard the remarks. She tried to push through the group so that she could reach Jess – Jess and Fudge.

'Run along home, there's a good girl,' a woman said to her in an authoritative voice, 'it's no place for children.' Others round her backed her remark. They meant kindly, but how could Beth 'run along home' and leave Jess lying hurt? Beth moved away from the group of spectators and out of sight in the cutting from the stile into the meadow. They'd said an ambulance would come; did that mean Jess would be taken to hospital? When Auntie Kathie got here it would start to get better and perhaps the men with the ambulance would say she could take Jess home. But those people had said that Fudge was a goner; that meant he had been killed. Beth pushed her small body against the hedge that bordered the cutting as if that way she would be invisible. But no one was interested in what had happened to her. As if they were watching a play unfold, they were anxiously awaiting the arrival of the next characters. Who would get there first? Would it be the ambulance or the child's parents?

At Westways, with a hand that felt weak and clammy Kathie put down the telephone receiver. An accident outside Jack Hopkins' shop! Jess hurt and an ambulance on its way!

'Den,' she called as she ran outside to find him. 'Den!' But her mouth was so dry it didn't want to form the word. She found him loading the afternoon delivery into the van and somehow managed to tell him what she knew.

'Get in the van. Leave everything. Christ! What was she doing crossing the road?' He asked it with no hope of an answer for, after all, how would Kathie know?

'She saw Fudge. Fudge has been killed.' It was like living a nightmare. They didn't speak again as the van raced down the lane at a speed that nearly threw them from their seats, and then took the right-hand turn with screeching tyres. Immediately they could see the gathered crowd and the stationary van. How had they managed to get an ambulance so quickly? Already it was there and the doors closed ready for its journey to Deremouth.

'They're taking her to hospital,' Kathie made a supreme effort to speak clearly and with a confidence she was far from feeling.

'We'll follow it and get there at the same time. She'll want us. Thank God I'm home. Bloody dog.' What a moment for Kathie to realize that until he went away in the army she had probably never heard him swear; often on the phone it would be 'bloody war', 'bloody army' and now it was 'bloody dog'. Poor little Fudge, such a bundle of love, now he was dead. If only they could turn back the clock and not leave the gate open, the girls would be home from school and taking him for a run on the common. She felt a sob catch her breath.

'You should never have let them have the animal,' Den's voice cut across her thoughts. 'Well at least we can get rid of that dreadful netting you and those girls put up. We shall be hours at the hospital, you know; you've not left anything cooking have you? If the poor kid has broken anything they will have to X-ray her and then set it.'

His words were a pointer to the future, a future with Jess at home to be cared for. Her confidence took a step towards recovery.

'No, it was too early to be cooking. I even remembered to lock the door and call to the girls not to worry if we weren't back when they went. I'm glad they aren't ringing the bell on the ambulance; that would frighten her. I wish there was some way of letting her know we are right behind them.'

By that time they were crossing Picton Heath. It wasn't far now to the main Exeter road where they would turn left until they reached a right turn to Deremouth railway station. Then down Station Hill and they would be at the hospital.

'Sorry mister, you can't leave the van there,' someone called to Den as he pulled up by the side of the ambulance. 'Only ambulances here. Drive on round to the side and you'll find plenty of space.'

'I must park here. It's my daughter just going to be brought out of the ambulance.'

'Sorry. The other ambulance will be back and there's only room for the two. Go round the side and by the time you get back they'll have your daughter inside.'

Kathie started to undo the door to get out, but Dennis stopped her.

'Stay where you are! We'll go in together.'

By the time they got rid of the van and ran back to the Casualty entrance, there was no sign of Jess. They expected to find her on the stretcher waiting for a doctor to see her, but there was only an elderly man with his arm in a sling.

'Which way did they take the stretcher? Did you notice?'

'Ah, that I did? Just a youngster so the men were saying. Down that corridor you'll find someone. Is she your kiddie?'

'Yes,' Kathie answered. 'She'll be so frightened. We must find her.'

'Don't waste time talking,' Den called as he hurried down the corridor.

The elderly patient, speaking more to himself than to Kathie who was already following Den, said, 'Oh my dear, and here's me moaning about a broken arm.'

Kathie told herself she had misheard him or misunderstood the implication behind the words. But a minute later the sister was ushering them into her room, her face solemn.

'Sit down, both of you. Were neither of you with the child when the accident occurred?'

'No,' Kathie answered. 'She has always come home from school alone. There are no roads to cross.'

'Children are impetuous,' was Sister's opinion.

'We want to see her. Please, let us see her. She'll be so frightened.' Kathie begged, suspecting that this sister valued efficiency above compassion.

'It's too late for fear; her life was over by the time she reached the hospital. In fact, even when it happened, I doubt if she felt fear or even shock. It must have been too sudden for her to have known what was happening; the injury to her head must immediately have knocked her unconscious. There were many other injuries, a post-mortem will identify the exact cause of death.'

'No, no, she can't be...' But Kathie couldn't even say the word.

She was held in the grip of a sensation such as she had never experienced. It was as if something of herself had been stripped from her. For a second she glanced at Dennis, aware of a nervous tic at the corner of his mouth, something she had never seen before. How his hands shook as he gripped the edge of the sister's desk as if for support. She saw these things and yet she was removed from them. Jess... Jess can't be gone. She knew she ought to reach out and cover Den's hand with hers, but she couldn't. Jess... the tiny baby gazing at her and sucking hard on her breast... the strong little girl always so anxious not to be looked on as a baby... Jess so proud of her 'sponsibilities' as they took care of each other. Westways without her, without that happy, determined voice... with no Jess there was nothing.

Kathie felt she was looking at life through the wrong end of a telescope.

–

Throughout it all, neither Kathie nor Dennis had given a thought to Beth who was waiting too far from the village street to see what was going on. The little girl was aware that things were happening – and then all sound faded into silence. She had pressed her body so far into the hedge that something prickly had got stuck in the material of her coat, a coat that used to belong to Jess until she grew out of it. Beth loved it; not so much for the coat itself as for feeling that it meant she was part of the family. Carefully unhooking the thorn, she cautiously moved towards the street. Everything was quiet, the van had gone, all the people had gone, and the place was deserted. She must go home, it wasn't actually getting dark so much as there was a difference in the light. It was the hour when she and Jess would know they must hurry if Fudge was to have time for a game on the common. And that's when she noticed him in the gutter on the other side of the road. They'd said he was dead, a goner; but he looked just like he did at home when he stretched out on the rug in front of the fire. Careful to look both ways before she stepped off the path, she went across to him.

'Fudge! Come on, boy, wake up.' But he wasn't asleep; his eyes were wide open and his mouth too. Very gently she picked him up and cradling him to her set out for home. Sarah and Sally were still working, she could hear them talking as they hoed. So she made sure she shut the gate quietly and walked right round the cottage to get to the back door. It was locked. But, of course, Auntie Kathie and – and him – she couldn't quite bring herself to think of him as Uncle Den – had gone to the hospital. They might be ages, for they wouldn't want to come home until they could bring Jess.

There was a bucket outside the back door, so laying Fudge carefully on the ground she carried it to the front garden where she turned it upside down to make a seat, then she went back for the puppy. By that time it really was getting dark and she could hear the girls putting their tools away. In a minute they'd wheel their bicycles down the path and Beth's instinct was to hide so that they wouldn't ask questions about what had happened – and they wouldn't put into words what she knew to be the truth: Fudge wasn't going to wake up anymore. So she again moved her bucket, this time into the far corner of the porch and once more took up position with Fudge on her lap.

By the time she heard footsteps in the lane and then the click of the gate it was quite dark. But there had been no van. Who could be coming? Despite being shy, she had never been a cowardly child, but now she could feel her heart beating. Even leaning hard against the wall of the porch there was no escape.

'He's come home then,' Bruce said as by the light of his pocket torch he saw them. 'What are you doing out here with him?'

Through the horror of the last hours Beth hadn't cried, but now in her relief at the sound of his familiar voice, the tears came. Hearing her, seeing the stillness of the puppy the truth dawned on him, or at least the partial truth.

''e's a goner, that's what they said. Don't know how he got out; we shut the gate, honest we did. Was over the road when we were coming home from school.' The relief of being held close to Bruce was almost too much to bear. 'Jess gave him a call and quick as anything he ran to get to her, just like she did to him. Didn't see it coming, the van, didn't know cos the bus was in the way.'

'And Jess?' he asked gently.

'Been took off to 'ospital. Aunt Kathie and – and *him*. Mr Hopkins, him from the veg shop, he was phoning to tell them so they could follow the ambulance. 'Spect that's what they did. But I got sent off, so I hid up the cutting till everyone had gone. Then I found Fudge and brought 'im home.'

'They've been gone a long time?'

She nodded. 'Since just after school.'

Bruce felt in his pocket for a notepad. 'Can you shine the torch for me so that I can write them a note, and then you can come back to the hall with me. We'll find Oliver and you can have supper with him and the boys.'

'What about Fudge? Please, I can't leave Fudge all by himself. Me and Jess are in charge of him.' Then with a huge and uncontrollable sob, she added, 'Now he's dead and Jess is hurt, I know she is. She just lay there. I heard people saying she must have got bones all broken. So it's *me* what has to look to Fudge.'

'Yes, of course, I understand that, Beth' he answered her, speaking with the sort of respect in his voice he might use to the parents of his pupils. 'We'll walk the road way to the hall, it's too dark in the wood. But if I carry Fudge for you, can you take charge of the torch. Make sure you shine it on the ground not upwards. Now, just aim it at my notebook and I'll scribble a message to put through the letterbox for when they get home so that they won't worry that you aren't here waiting. If they don't get home until really late you can stay at the hall for the night.'

'But you only got boys at that school?'

'We have a spare room, I promise you.' The note written, he put it through the letterbox then took the small, stiff form of the puppy from her, resting it on his left forearm so that his right hand was free to take her small hand in his. His thoughts were in Deremouth with Kathie. Accident or illness, the anxiety is the same, but the suddenness of an accident seems to strip one of the ability to accept how a life can change in less than a minute. Sixteen years had gone by since Elspeth had been thrown, hitting her head on a milestone of all things. It had been a milestone in her life and in his too; it only took an event like this evening's to bring back the anguish of those days. But he was being maudlin; perhaps once Jess regained consciousness she would have nothing worse than a broken leg or arm. She was a brave little girl; she would soon bounce back.

'When we get to the hall, we'll send for Oliver Marley. He'll take you in to supper with the juniors. I expect you're hungry, aren't you?'

'I 'spect I am. Ollie didn't know Fudge very well cos of the Christmas school holiday, but when he saw him they really took to each other. What should I do about Fudge, Mr Meredith? I can't keep him like he is. If he was a person he'd have a grave, wouldn't he? But supposing *he* – not Fudge – I mean Jessie's dad, suppose he says we've got to just put him in the bin like we do if there's a dead bird or mouse or something? We can't do that to Fudge.'

'Of course we can't. Fudge shall have a grave, I promise you. But first of all, when we get to the hall I'll lay him in the old stable.'

'It's got a clock, the stable I mean, hasn't it? When me and Jess go to the common Auntie Kathie always makes us listen for the clock to strike so we know it's time to come home. 'Spect Fudge has heard it too. That'll make him feel sort of safe, won't it?'

Bruce tightened his hold on the small hand, moved by the child's thinking.

–

From Deremouth to the turning into the lane to the common, neither Kathie nor Den spoke a word; they were cocooned in their own memories, frightened that to talk would strip them of moments that were their own, their own and Jessie's. They'd been gone nearly four hours but time had ceased to have a meaning; four hours, four years, a lifetime, it was as if the past was stripped away and the future had no ray of hope. But as the van bumped over the ruts the outline of the cottage could be seen through the darkness and Dennis pulled up by the garden gate. That's when for the first time in all those hours Kathie remembered Beth.

'Beth! She must be so frightened.' Hardly waiting for the van to stop, she threw open the door and stumbled out. This time she was the one to leave the gate open, the knowledge that it no longer mattered adding to her misery. She didn't stop to analyse why it was that that was misery she could accept. Later she would remember and realize how dwelling on a lesser pain can help to make a greater one bearable. 'Beth! Beth. We're back. Where are you, Beth?'

While she went to the garden, Dennis found his key and went indoors. He didn't switch on the light and in the darkness he seemed to hear Jess running down the stairs at the sound of his voice. 'Jess,' his throat contracted so that even a whisper was barely audible, 'Jess, kiddo.' He felt dizzy, and gripped the newel post. 'Oh God, why Jess?' He heard someone sobbing and realized it was him. He wanted just to get away, to be by himself. Outside darkness was his friend; out here he could feel she was close.

'Beth's not here,' Kathie said as she came into the dark house. 'Beth isn't here. Den, where are you?' Then as she closed the front door and switched on the light she saw the piece of paper. Relief flooded through her, or as near to relief as she was capable of feeling. It was a quarter to eight, she must phone Bruce. He would ask her how badly Jess had been hurt, she would tell him. She would have to hear herself say it. For a moment she stood with her hand on the instrument trying to force herself to speak to him. It was kind of him to have looked after Beth; he was a good friend; he had suffered a blow as bad as this, in some ways worse, so he would understand. Then, just as Dennis had believed he heard the rush of Jessie's tread on the stairs, so Kathie seemed to hear her voice, a voice so bright, so full of hope and determination. She closed her eyes to escape the emptiness of the room.

'Tell you what, Mum. Me and Fudge saw each other at the same time and we ran to meet fast as anything. I expect he thought he was meeting us from school, don't you, Mum?'

Kathie wanted to answer or to hear the voice again, but she knew if she spoke her words would be met with silence.

Picking up the phone she asked for Sedgewood 172, the number that would take her directly to Bruce's rooms.

'Kathie?' Something in the way he spoke seemed to tell her that he was expecting the news to be bad.

'Yes, we've just got back. I'm ashamed; I didn't give Beth a thought. I am so grateful to you for rescuing her.' It surprised her that she could talk so rationally, as if her voice had nothing to do with the aching emptiness she felt.

'Tell me, Kathie.'

'We were too late. It was all over.' Silence. 'Bruce? Did you hear?'

'Yes. I don't know what to say to you; there are no words…'

'I know. Don't say anything. But I know you understand.'

'Jess was a child, full of life, full of hope and love. Kathie my dear, you must be feeling you can't bear it. But from somewhere your strength will come. And even if tonight you aren't ready to believe it, you and your husband will grow even closer because of sharing your misery.' This was the Bruce who had talked to her just before Christmas, allowing her to see the sadness he always kept hidden. She wished he were here with her instead of just a voice on the telephone. But perhaps this was easier because if he were here and she could see the sorrow and sympathy in his eyes she was frightened she wouldn't be able to act out this charade of acceptance.

'You have been so kind to take Beth home and feed her. I'll walk up and get her.'

'She had her supper with the boys; Oliver took good care of her. But a late night won't hurt her for once, will you give me half an hour or so with her and then I'll walk her down, Don't ask me in – not tonight.'

'No. Not tonight. But aren't Ollie and the others in bed?'

'Yes, they are. Will you allow me to tell her about Jess? I believe I know how best to help her.'

Six

Bruce chose a spot beyond the lake, at the far side of the lawn that sloped to the wood. If Jess had been coming home, he would have left Dennis to bury the puppy at Westways but, as Beth had said 'me and Jess are in charge of him' and Bruce feared from reading between the lines that Fudge wouldn't have been dealt with with the reverence he deserved.

Before he could bury the puppy he had to break the news to Beth that Jessie wouldn't be coming home; she and Fudge had died together.

'Think I knew really. Didn't want to know.'

He ached with pity for the waiflike child who, despite the good home cooking she was fed at Westways and despite Jessie's outgrown clothes from last year, a waif was what she still looked. To see sadness in the eyes of an adult is hard, but when a child looked at him with misery combined with fear, uncertainty and trust, he wanted to hold her in his arms, to break the barrier that held back her tears.

But there was something Beth wanted to tell him and listening to the words pouring out of her he was thankful; what she said gave him a hint as to how to approach the next few minutes. The only evidence of Beth's bottled up emotion was that the recent improvement in her speech was forgotten.

'When Jess ran into the road and Fudge saw her and came dashing to meet 'er, she was so happy. It was like she'd seen something sort of wonderful – and she had of course cos she'd seen Fudge. What am I going to do with Fudge? If I ask them, after school tomorrow – I don't want to go to school, not without Jess…'

'After school…?' he prompted.

'I' been thinking the girls might help me dig a place for him. But I gotta hide him for tonight, cos you see Jessie's dad wasn't pleased about us having him and 'e might just throw him away like he was rubbish. Not Fudge… 'e was such a nice puppy, him and me and Jess, we sort of belonged like.' And with that her battle was lost. As her face crumpled she found herself lifted in his arms and held close.

As her uncontrolled sobbing grew quieter he passed her a handkerchief that he unfailingly wore in his breast pocket to match his tie. 'Blow your nose and wipe your face and then I'll tell you what I think we should do.'

So it was that a minute or two later she gave Fudge a final stroke and goodbye kiss, then they reverently put him in the pillowcase Bruce had found in readiness and went off with a shovel.

–

Some days go like a flash, some seemed never to end. This one was one of the latter. When Kathie heard the click of the gate she ran out to meet Beth and already Bruce was starting back along the lane.

'Bruce,' she called in a stage whisper as she ran to catch up with him, leaving Beth standing in the dark front garden. 'Bruce, thank you. I forgot her. So ashamed.

Didn't think of *her* – or Fudge. Do you know what's happened to him? We just drove straight past where Jess had – had been – hit by the van, just followed the ambulance.'

Her voice was tight; he knew the effort it cost her.

'Fudge and Jess were hit at the same time. Beth and I have given him a grave in the grounds at the Hall.'

His hand was on her shoulder, the pressure of it saying more than any words. She longed for the comfort of it and yet it brought her near to the edge of her own control. Better by far to shut her mind and like a zombie to follow her nightly routine of jobs.

'Beth's waiting for you,' he said softly. 'She's very lost, frightened. But she tries hard not to let it show; there's a steely streak in her. Goodnight, my dear.' Perhaps it was the silent emotion finding an outlet, or perhaps it was the comfort of the moonless night shutting them away from their surroundings; whatever prompted him, he bent towards her and gently kissed her forehead before turning and walking away, immediately swallowed in the darkness, even the sound of his footsteps on the unmade lane soon lost.

That night she went up to the bedroom with Beth, neither of them speaking about the day that had changed their lives or about anything else. But Beth was glad to have her there and when Kathie bent to kiss her goodnight, just for a brief moment the child clung to her.

Downstairs she was again in zombie mode as she put into the oven the vegetable pie she had made in the morning. She tried not to think about how her world was when she was making it: Den sitting out there talking to Jack Hopkins, Fudge, as he spent hours every day, sprawled on the ground with his nose poking into the mesh of the netting that kept the market garden out of bounds. It had been one of those mornings that painted an image on her mind that would last forever, but an image that on that night she was frightened to see.

With the pie cooking, she laid the table in the warm room. She gave no thought to what she did; to give coherent thought to anything was beyond her. Den came in from his solitary and private retreat to the winter chill of the garden.

'Don't give me anything to eat,' he said as she brought the golden-crusted dish to the table. 'I feel as sick as a dog.'

'We should eat. You'll feel better with food inside you.'

'I said, I don't want it.' As if to prove his point he belched. Then, drumming his fingers on the mantelpiece above the old kitchen range he turned to look at her as he said, 'You must see the billeting people in the morning and say that child must be found somewhere else.'

For a moment Kathie was pulled out of zombie mode.

'I most certainly won't! Den, however *we* feel, it's not right to take it out on Beth. She was Jessie's friend. You don't understand; you never saw them together. They loved each other like sisters.'

'She's not staying here!' In his misery he sounded cornered, frightened. 'That's my last word.'

'Good. Because there's no point in discussing it. This is Beth's home until her mother wants her back in London.' They glared at each other, needing to hit out, needing to find something less important than the true reason for their misery. 'Anyway it's not for you to say who stays here; what difference can it make to you? You won't be here.' Was she trying to hurt him or herself? If only one of them could have reached out to the other, in sharing their anguish they might have found a way through it.

Instead, they were as far apart as strangers, each cocooned in misery too achingly deep to find expression. Turning away from her, he went outside leaving her looking at the two plates of untouched food. First hers and then his, she carried them to the waiting bucket and scraped the food onto the bit already there to add to the chickens' corn in the morning.

She washed up; she took Fudge's bowls, one for food and one for water, and scoured them well before putting them on a high shelf in the kitchen cupboard; she put out the milk bottle. It was after that, she was standing alone in the warm room she had the strangest feeling. Her mind carried her back four months to the day Den had left home and, knowing the days ahead would be hard for the little girl who so adored her father, she had tried to give a shape to the new pattern of their days.

'We've got 'sponsibilities, Mum,' she seemed to hear the voice she knew so well. 'Tell you what, Mum, I'll be the one who lays the table.' Then, only weeks ago: 'Me and Beth are just going to take Fudge to the common. All right, Mum?' How could she never hear that happy, excited voice again? She wouldn't look ahead, not a day, not an hour. Live each minute, do the things that have to be done... And following her newly laid rule she went out to the coalhouse to fill the hod with coke so that she could bank up the range for the night.

Glancing at the clock she was surprised to see it was a quarter to eleven. So leaving the back door unlocked and the light still on, she went up to bed. Not for a second did she consider going outside to look for Dennis, to throw herself into his arms and let them share their anguish. She wanted just to be alone.

But once in bed and lying in the silent darkness, she wished she had stayed up. Now there were no jobs to do, nowhere to hide. The memory flashed into her mind of what Bruce had told her about the time of Elspeth's accident. 'I prayed. God, how I prayed...' And had he been wasting his time and emotion? He'd prayed that she would come back to him; well, at least physically his prayer had been answered. And Elspeth was content; surely that was what he had wanted for her? Kathie closed her eyes tightly as if the tighter shut they were, the more ardent her own prayer. But it was no use. She hadn't prayed for years except for the occasional plea as she went about her daily business; and she'd never asked herself whether they were prayers to a divine Godhead or simply something to boost her confidence when she was faced with a task that hadn't previously come her way.

Now she found that wanting to pray and actually giving her whole mind to it were two different things. She had never felt so alone as she did lying there gazing into the darkness.

Since arriving home, Den had spent most of his time sitting alone on the upturned oil drum in the garden, smoking one cigarette after another, frightened to let himself open his heart to Jess. Angry at the world, he needed someone to vent his spite on – and who better than Kathie who had been so remote from him through the last hours. How could she want to cook supper as if their lives hadn't been torn apart? Or perhaps hers hadn't been, not as his was. He pictured the golden crust of the pie and the very thought of it made him retch emptily. Since breakfast all he had eaten was a bowl of soup. He heard the clock on the stables at the Hall strike eleven. He must go in. Kathie would be asleep by now, she wouldn't want to talk about… about Jess, about the moment they had been told. Imagine the relief of losing himself in sleep. But sleep comes from a contented mind – either that or physical exhaustion. Standing up he felt dizzy.

Why Jess? Why not that other kid? If she went, no one's life would be wrecked. Or why not *him*? Jess had been the future, now there was nothing, nothing except the prospect of going to fight some poor devil probably with a wife and kids. Don't think about it.

If Kathie was asleep he'd wake her up. All his emotions were heightened on that January night and the desires of his body responded. He couldn't analyse why it was he felt as he did, he didn't even try.

When Kathie heard him coming up the stairs she turned on her side pretending to be asleep. Could it be less than twenty-four hours ago that he had come unexpectedly into their room? It was like looking back at another life, at two different people. The images in her memory only made her feel more isolated.

She heard him stripping off his clothes and waited expecting him to reach in the dark for his pyjamas. Instead he climbed naked into bed. She didn't move; he lay on his back moving his head restlessly. With a sudden movement he sat up, then pulled her to lie on her back, climbing above her. He'd never been a man with a high sex drive, so what he was doing drove the wedge further between them.

'No, Den! You *can't* want that! Not tonight, not with—' But she couldn't say it, she couldn't say Jessie's name. Her sentence hung between them, unfinished.

'I must. Can't you see, I must.' He was pushing her legs apart with uncharacteristic roughness; another second and he would have forced himself into her. It was the only way to reach the exhaustion that would let him escape into sleep. 'You've got to let me.'

'No, damn you! Get away from me!' With more strength than she knew she possessed, taking his full weight she wrenched him off her then, as he lay breathless at her side, turned her back on him.

In the stillness of the room she heard the quickening of his panting, and lying perfectly still she could feel the jerky movement from his side of the bed. Never in all the years they had been together had she felt about him as she did in those moments. That he could have come expecting them to find pleasure in sex disgusted her. But this was even worse. He must have known she could hear and recognize what he was doing, it was almost as if he was glorying in it. What a moment for half remembered words to come to her, come from where? Perhaps heard on one of the rare occasions she and her mother had gone to church? 'Could you not watch with me one brief hour?' Tonight belonged to Jess, to Jess who was part of them and yet was wholly herself, her precious, glorious self. His movement grew faster, his breathing a series of grunts as he brought himself to a climax. She felt he wanted her to hear and to know that he managed well without her. Normally she could never have harboured such thoughts; no matter how tired she had been, at the slightest hint that he wanted them to make love she had always been wide awake and ready to respond. Now he was still, it was all over and she knew from experience that he would immediately lose himself in sleep. But what was that? Burrowing his head into the pillow in an attempt to muffle the sound, he sobbed.

Why was it she couldn't reach out to him? What had happened to them that they couldn't share their despair? Then another sound, surely it was real or was it just in her imagination? Clearly she heard Jess laugh. 'You know what, Mum? I've got Fudge with me. Mum, keep on loving Beth. She doesn't want the war ever to end cos she likes it with us and never wants to go back to that London place.' By then Kathie knew she heard it in her imagination, but even so she nodded, mouthing the words, 'I promise you, Jess.'

Her suffering was like a heavy weight, sapping her of energy and even of interest. She heard Den's muffled crying but felt isolated from his pain. This is Den, she told herself, he is your life, and you love him – so why can't you turn round and hold him close? There was no answer or, if there was, she hadn't the energy to look for it. The thought of lying where she was through the long hours of the night was unbearable. Trying to move without disturbing the covers, she got her feet on the cold linoleum floor covering. Her dressing gown was in the wardrobe, so she'd have to manage without. Once she got down to the 'warm room' she'd sit close to the fire. But she didn't get even as far as the head of the steep, narrow stairs for escaping from the sound of Dennis's crying she heard Jess's. 'Keep on loving Beth.' There was no sound of that familiar voice but as clearly as if the words had been spoken, Kathie felt the nearness of Jessie's spirit. 'Loving Beth… loving you…' she answered silently. Standing in the dark passage just for a moment she was held by a feeling of peace. 'As long as I have her to love, I shall still have you.' It made no sense and the moment passed as she crept into the bedroom.

Without a word she slipped into the bed and drew the trembling little figure into her arms.

'Won't never see her no more,' Beth sobbed. 'She liked being alive – more than anyone she liked it – made everything sort of warm and good and exciting.'

'I know, sweetheart. Don't know how we're going to bear it.'

She felt the thin little arms come round her neck and one leg hook itself across her body. Was that the moment her own floodgates opened or had she been crying when she'd come into the bedroom?

'What about Jess's dad? Didn't you ought to be in there with him?'

'I think he needs to be on his own.'

'Do you want to be on your o—' The last word was lost in a sob she couldn't control.

'No. Just for tonight, Beth, can I stay in here with you?'

She felt the movement of Beth's head against her shoulder as she nodded. 'Bet Jess'd like that. Wish we could speak to her, Auntie Kathie, tell her things – things like that.'

'Tell her with your heart, your spirit, and she'll know.' Probably beyond a six-year-old's understanding. Or was it? Somehow Kathie believed that what Beth was too young to understand, she would take on trust.

'Then she'll know about Fudge and where me and Mr Meredith made his grave. He made doing it sort of *important;* didn't say about Fudge, "just a dog" nor noffing like that. He's a nice man. You like him, Auntie Kathie?'

'Of course.'

'But *really*, I mean?' Beth was quieter now, her small body not trembling and she wasn't going to be fobbed off with just 'of course' for an answer as if she was too young to be taken seriously.

'I've only met him a few times – yet I feel I know him well. And, yes, Beth, I do like him.'

'So do I. He sort of understands things without being told.'

–

'You weren't in bed when I woke up in the night?' By which Dennis actually meant 'Where were you?'

'I was with Beth.' There was unexpected comfort in remembering.

'You told her she was to be found a new billet?'

'Oh, Den don't start that again. She was – is – Jess's dearest friend. This is the first time she has known a proper, happy home. You don't really want to break faith with Jess and send her away, you know you don't.'

'To be honest I don't care about anything. What's the point? Another three weeks, and a bullet might get me.'

'Then you just be sure you keep out of the way of the bullets.' Kathie managed to instil more warmth in her tone that she was capable of feeling. The emotion of the night had left her drained and numb. He must feel much the same, and poor little Beth too. What a lonely little figure she had looked as she went off to school.

'We have things to do, Den. If you want to work outside, do you want me to go to Warbeck and Giles?' She named the Deremouth undertakers. 'Not sure what we have to do, but they'll tell me.'

'You'll stay here. It's my place to make the arrangements.' Just for a second he looked at her directly, his misery not hidden in his words but clear to be seen in his eyes. 'The last thing I can do for her. Why? Why? Why *her*?'

'Not the last thing. People don't just drop out of your life like that. Here, or wherever they send you, and later when you come home and it's all over, Den, we haven't lost her, we must never lose her.'

'Emotional claptrap, that's all that is. Her life was snuffed out – and all for that bloody dog you ought never to have taken on.'

Pulling on her wellingtons, then reaching for the old coat she kept on the back of the kitchen door, Kathie didn't answer. Why did he have to talk like that? Was he frightened that he'd call out to Jess and she wouldn't answer.

'Her body might have lost its life, but Den, listen with your heart. We haven't lost her, we must never lose her.'

There was bewilderment in his expression. He looked at her as though she were a stranger, someone who spoke a foreign language.

'We shan't forget her, if that's what you're trying to say. Anything else is rubbish and you'll have to face up to it,' he told her.

Slamming the door behind her, she left him.

–

Work was a help as the days of his leave went by. On the Monday after the accident, at half past eleven in the morning, Jess's small, white coffin was lowered into the ground in the village churchyard. Beth had gone to school as usual. As the single bell tolled, Kathie knew she would be listening. It might have been kinder to bring her, but Dennis wouldn't hear of it. What neither of them had expected was that the church would be so full. All these people hadn't known Jess, so why were they there? Perhaps it stemmed from the feeling of community brought about by the war. She didn't know and wasn't interested enough in them to give the question any intelligent thought. The one person she was glad to see as she and Dennis followed the coffin from the church was Bruce. He was sitting in the back pew amongst villagers neither of them knew.

Somehow the days were passing. In their raw misery they hadn't been able to reach out to each other, but there is nothing like work to help habit overcome emotion, and there was certainly more than enough work to keep them occupied. On the Friday of Den's second week the two one-time lads – Stanley Stone and Bert Delbridge, both on embarkation leave just as Dennis was – came to Westways at the beginning of the afternoon and within ten minutes had joined the workforce as if they'd never been away.

'What do you think of them, Sal?' Sarah whispered to her friend as they carefully washed carrots and tied them in bundles. 'The tall one, that's Stan, his dad comes to the pub and he says he's buying a ring for his girl before he goes back. Don't know who she is, but Dad looked a bit sniffy about it. He reckons because of the war – romance, drama, the sort of emotion he turns his nose up at and calls Hollywood rubbish – he reckons that because of all that, people are too keen to get tied up. Stan looks a nice chap, doesn't he? Well, they both do. It'd be all right if after the war all of us could work here together. Wish this war would buck up and get finished.'

'Don't want it to finish yet, not the way it's going. Reckon it'll take another year or two before we can get them beaten. But, like you say they're nice chaps. Awful having to go off, never knowing if you're going to get home again.'

Sarah nodded. 'Don't need to go to war for that though. Jess only went to school.'

The thought sobered them and they finished the carrots in silence.

Having the lads working alongside him it was almost possible for Dennis to imagine things were like they used to be. But the afternoon was soon over and the solitary child coming slowly up the lane wasn't Jess. If he closed his eyes he could almost hear the familiar sound of the homecomings as they used to be: Jess's feet pounding on the rough ground as she raced up the lane. He wasn't even conscious of the unwelcoming expression on his face as Beth, seeing where Kathie was busy digging parsnips, ran straight to her. It was Friday afternoon; school was finished for the week. Last Saturday Mr Meredith had invited her to the Hall and she and Ollie had made a wooden sign to put on Fudge's grave. She would like to have gone there again this Saturday but no one had suggested it. Ollie was going to the house in the village where his mother had come to live. She hoped he wouldn't want to go there every week. Beth didn't like the picture she'd built in her imagination of Ollie's mother, but that was partly because he kept saying how pretty she was, how much fun she was, how clever she was. Was he meaning that he hadn't really thought it was wonderful here at Westways, just him, Jess, Fudge and her? She didn't want to think about it, just thinking gave her a nasty tight feeling in her throat and made her eyes sting. Well, tomorrow she would have to see if the girls could give her a job. The time would pass, *he* would soon be gone – and perhaps after a while Ollie would want to come back. His rotten Mum couldn't be as much fun as they had here.

Soon tiring of watching grown-ups working and not being given a job to do, she went off to feed the chickens and collect the eggs. But the responsibility she and Jess had enjoyed didn't hold excitement on her own like it had when they had been together vying to pick up the most eggs. Everything would be better once *he* was gone. Friday would soon be over and he was leaving on Tuesday so there were only three whole days. Was it wicked of her to want him gone? She told herself that Jess had loved him so he must really be all right; but when he looked at her she *knew* he was thinking horrid things about her and wanting her not to be there.

The evenings were the most difficult times. No one talked as they ate their supper, but there was nothing comfortable about the silence. Usually before sending Beth to get ready for bed, Kathie suggested they play a game. That's what they used to do when Jess was there.

'Games aren't for me,' or words to that effect from Dennis, meant that Kathie and Beth played while he sat by the range reading the paper. Beth didn't think he was really reading it at all, just staring at it; but she was glad he didn't want to play. Snap, Ludo, Happy Families, Beat your Neighbour Out of Doors, Draughts, all the time-honoured games took their turn. Kathie wasn't sure whether it became easier or harder once Beth was in bed and she and Dennis were left alone. They talked about the work they had been doing during the day, one evening they went over the account book and he actually told her he was impressed with the way she was coping. If only they could talk about Jess, about the years they had waited for her and been disappointed, about the joy of her birth

– in truth joy that had been overshadowed by fear for Kathie, but that was all in the past and their memories were of joy and relief. But to talk about her would be as dangerous as walking on melting ice. And so they acted as if their world hadn't fallen apart.

At the sound of the shrill bell of the telephone attached to the wall just inside the warm room door, Dennis stood up to answer it. Kathie listened to the one-sided conversation.

'Of course I remember you… No I don't know their routine…' Then with a humourless laugh: 'I'm just a visitor in my own home these days… That's extremely kind of you… yes, yes much better for them… Last Saturday? I can't remember… ah, yes, that was it… Well, it's different for your son, he's at the school but why this evacuee child was included I don't know… To be truthful I didn't notice her absence. Working outside no doubt… No, I know where the house is; let me walk down with them. I'd be interested to see the alterations you spoke about… About half past ten, then. And thank you. I find it difficult having her here… I know and I appreciate what you're saying. Until tomorrow…'

'Who was that?' Kathie asked as he replaced the receiver. The call had brought them nearer to awakening natural curiosity than anything that had gone before.

'Claudia Marley. I had a long talk with her when I took today's crops to Jack. He introduced us. I wonder she went out of my mind. What a creature! I dare say we're not accustomed to London fashion down here in the sticks. But she's a real cracker. Fancy that husband of hers going off and leaving her. Jack told me about them. Her ex owns the Hall.'

'I know. Ollie talks about her. Anyway, what did she want?'

'She is having the pair of them, Oliver and young Beth, for the day tomorrow. He'll call here and I'll walk them down.'

'He must know where the house is. They're quite capable of going on their own.'

'I said I'd take them; you heard me tell her so. Don't forget she comes from London with its busy streets.'

'So does Beth, but she's safe to go anywhere around here on her own.'

She expected a cutting remark and he looked as though he was ready with one but instead, he once again picked up the newspaper.

—

Next morning the threesome set out, the children both slightly ill-at-ease and making sure they were on their best behaviour. Then Kathie concentrated her efforts on cleaning out the hen house. Saturday was always an extra cheery day, with the advent and enthusiasm of the sixth formers, although on that Saturday they were very aware of the tragedy that had struck Westways and kept their voices subdued. Kathie wished they would act normally. What had softly spoken words and fear of laughing to do with Jess? She glanced across at where the work party were intent on proving their manhood to impress Sarah and Sally. She wanted to hear the normal sound of their banter, she wanted to smile as she listened just as she always had. Oh Jess, why can't they understand you'd hate them to be solemn and buttoned up? Yet was she any different? And was she being loyal to Jess by being afraid to find happiness where she could? Imagine if Jess were here helping with the henhouse. A smile tugged at the corners of Kathie's mouth even though her eyes smarted with tears she blinked away. She seemed to hear that chuckle that was so much part of the little girl's character. Leaning on her shovel she closed her eyes.

–

'The old major was a sort of hermit, the place was a complete tip when the agent took her to see it the first time,' Den said when he returned, 'but she showed me the drawings she'd had done of the improvements and, give it a few months, it's going to be a real corker. Claudia Marley, living in the village in the shadow of the Hall. What a hoot – her words not mine. She's going to find it hard to make friends in the village; she comes from a different world. I told her you'd always make her welcome here. Well, she must have known you would. I'm told you've made this a second home to that queer egg of a kid of hers.'

'Nothing queer about Ollie. Not that it would be surprising if there were, with a father deserting them and a mother who shipped him off to boarding school at just seven.'

'Well, you have your opinion and I have mine. Anyway Claudia's taking him back to school after tea and says she'll see your Beth on her way up the lane. I imagine she and the headmaster are quite close.'

'I wouldn't know. I'm just one of the village women.'

With a sigh he turned and left her. It would have been so easy to quarrel, time and again they came to the edge of it and then either one or the other drew back.

Neither of them referred to the incident in bed on the night Jess had died, yet it was there in both their minds when, as if it were an ordained part of their routine, each night Dennis moved towards her and she drew him close. Making love? There was little passion or urgency in their nightly ritual even as the time of his going drew closer; the even rhythm of his movements didn't vary, there was no wild abandonment, no demanding desire with excitement mounting until he attained his climax. She might remember how she'd compared love making with climbing a mountain, striving to reach the summit. Now, though, she was stranded in the foothills, she didn't even connect with what was happening, it had no more meaning than the hundred and one tasks which helped her through her days and hours. Did he realize how distant from him she was? Or perhaps it was the same for him and he was following the route expected. All the years they had been together and in so few days he would be gone. Six months, a year, eighteen months, when would he be home? Most separations, however long, have a set time giving a framework to build on. Not everyone will come home, suppose one day the dreaded telegram was brought to Westways. Kathie tried to imagine the scene, desperately trying to bring sensation to her numbed mind, but she could feel nothing; her emotions were dormant. So her mind wandered as with steady rhythm he moved on her, whether from duty, convention or desire they neither of them asked. At last she felt his movements quicken, one or two more thrusts and it was over. As he rolled off her she suspected that he was satisfied he'd done his duty.

'I expect you were tired.' He made excuses for her as he settled for sleep (please God, let me sleep, let me escape the long, empty hours). ''Night love,' he muttered, to be answered by her unfailing ''night dear'. After that they would settle for sleep or, at least, pretence of sleep.

The locals who had been on embarkation leave were to meet at Deremouth station at three thirty on the Tuesday afternoon, but as the bus service seemed to be taking advantage of the excuse of wartime conditions and had become less dependable, those from Sedgewood decided to catch the five past two. If it was late or had been cut then there would still be time if they went on the next. After twenty years of being his own master – albeit hard working and often impecunious – Dennis had never been more aware of his new status.

'I'd better be off,' he said to Kathie as complete with the kitbag bearing his name and service number he appeared in the doorway of the extension kitchen.

'That bag looks heavy, I wish we had the petrol to take you to the station.'

'No, the lads are getting on the same bus. The bag will be easy enough on my shoulder. It holds all my worldly goods, right down to knife, fork, spoon, metal plate, darning kit, clean shirt and underwear. You name it, I have it.' He made a supreme effort to keep his voice cheerful.

Coming across the room she put her arms around him, willing him to meet her gaze.

'Oh Den, all these days gone. We wasted them, hiding from each other. Now it's too late.'

'I carried a picture of this place in my mind when I joined up, I wanted – I expected – it to stay the same. But nothing's the same, nothing ever can be.'

'We're the same. When you come home I promise you I won't have let you down. One thing is sure, people are going to want vegetables even more than they used to.'

'There you go! You see, now it's *you* who's hiding from what really matters. If there's a god, then why did he let it happen? She didn't deserve it; *we* didn't deserve it.'

She heard the ominous crack in his voice and buried her face against the rough material of his battledress tunic as she said, 'Somehow we have to remember every precious day and be grateful.'

'Words! Just empty words! How can you lose anyone you love and learn to be grateful for what you've had? I can't do it. I'm too full of resentment that other kids, kids like Beth, still have a life ahead of them and Jess gone.' She nodded, but still she didn't look at him. 'And there's something else, Kathie. I'm frightened right to the pit of my stomach. Imagine coming face to face with a German, having to shoot before he does – or even worse imagine running a bayonet into him.'

'Can't imagine it,' she shivered and felt his hold tighten. 'Den, we think we know what's ahead of us, but we none of us do. Whatever is ahead, we have memories to treasure – and when you come home again, we've got the rest of our lives.' This time she raised her head and looked directly at him, her lips opening as his mouth covered hers.

'This is it. Don't come down the lane, Kathie, I want to leave you right here. We'll be all right, won't we, when this lot's over we'll make something of what's left.'

'She'll always be with us. Please, just open your heart and let her in. A quarter to eight – she always watched the hands of the clock. All of us together, Den.'

His expression changed, she could feel the tenseness in him as he answered, 'Why can't you understand? You like to imagine her; you believe she can see you. It's rubbish, I tell you! What happens as the years go on, as all the other kids grow up? Do you imagine she'll still be there for you then? Jess is gone.' He took hold of her shoulders and for a second she thought he was going to shake her. 'Jess is *dead*, and if you try to believe anything different it's because you haven't the courage to face the truth.'

'Don't...'

'If I get back from this bloody war, we have to make something of what's left to us.'

'Don't Den. You have to go. We can't say goodbye like this.' She clamped the corners of her trembling mouth between her teeth. He saw and pulled her into a tight embrace.

'No,' he whispered, rubbing his chin against her head. He regretted the way he'd spoken. If Kathie found comfort in her damn fool ideas then he must leave her with her illusions. He forced a note of cheerfulness into his tone; these were their final seconds. 'Once the lads and I get out there, we'll sort Adolf out. I'll be home before you've had time to miss me.' Then, unable to stop himself: 'And you've got Beth for company.' A last crushing hug and he shouldered his kit bag.

'All you need for an army life.' She tried to put a smile in her voice. 'Don't try and be a hero, Den, just concentrate on coming home safely.'

A few seconds later she was watching him striding away down the lane, one arm swinging as he walked and the other balancing his kit bag on his shoulder. Her mind jumped back six months: summertime, Den and the lads working outside, she putting up her bottles of peas and beans, making jam, believing life would go on without change. It would have been easy to let herself sink into self-pity as she remembered those days when there had been three of them. But work had ever been her salvation, so taking her laundry basket she went out to the paved patch between the cottage and the shed and started to unpeg the washing from the line. The sight of Beth's small garments helped restore her optimism. Wars don't last forever. Den would come home. Then there would be another heart-wrenching parting for, with the end of the war, Beth would have to return to her mother.

–

He'd been gone no more than two hours when the new regime started to take shape, for it had to be a new one, it could never be the same as it had before his leave. Kathie was determined to use the rest of the daylight working outside and determined too that when Beth arrived back from school she would be included and made to feel part of the team.

'Poor little sausage. And she's not the sort to be able to talk about it if she's down in the dumps; she's the sort to bottle things up.' Young and inexperienced though she was, Sarah showed surprising perception. 'We mustn't let her think we want to find her jobs because we're sorry for her, though. She'd be embarrassed, don't you reckon?'

'Yes, I'm sure she would,' Kathie agreed. 'Den gave the far end a second digging, so can you two prepare the new rhubarb bed for the normal outdoor crop. Den has put a stake into the ground where each crown is to be planted. With our mild winters, we ought to be able to get them in at the beginning of February. That'll give us a head start. What you need to do today is take out a stake – take a patch each – then dig really deep. About twice as deep as we do for most things. Then into each hole, shovel a bucket of manure from the load in the corner down there. That has to be dug in, really amalgamated with the soil at the bottom of the hole. Then a second bucketful has to be spread on top before you fill the hole in with the topsoil. Get that done and we shall be ready to plant the crowns at the end of the month. OK?'

'But what about Beth? She's not big enough to dig. Can she help you?'

'No,' Kathie answered, 'I shall be using the digger, giving the soil its second turning. Anyway, I think it's important she does something on her own. Den collected the seed potatoes for the first earlies. He opened the bags and left them in the greenhouse. I'll show Beth how to lay them out with the shoots uppermost and she can make it her job.'

This was Afternoon No 1. Tonight there would be no phone call from Dennis and, although she wasn't prepared to admit it even to herself, now that he'd been home and seen for himself that she could manage, she didn't want to make her report on the events of the day.

'Look Mrs H,' Sally cut into her thoughts, 'look who's coming. It's Mrs Meredith and her nurse. They didn't come while Mr H was home.'

'Nanny Giles could have brought her just the same, I told her so when I called in last week. But she refused; she said it would be an intrusion. Funny old stick; Den would have made them very welcome.'

'She can bring her down to watch us digging, it'll be quieter than where you'll be working with that machine.'

Not for the first time Kathie felt her spirit lift when she talked to the girls. She waved at Elspeth and was answered with that blank, open-mouthed smile.

'You sure we shan't be in anyone's way? Oh but you should have seen her face when we turned into the lane. Beamed, she did, and I could hardly keep up with her, so keen she was to get here. And they say she doesn't understand and know things. We'll just take a wee walk around. Come on, Elspeth my pet, let's just you and me have a look around.'

But they hadn't got far when Beth appeared and, snatching her hand away from her nurse, Elspeth held it out towards Beth. So no mention was made of the seed potatoes.

'Here then, ducky,' Nanny Giles relinquished her post, 'how about if you walk with Mrs Meredith.'

Beth's thin face didn't attempt to hide its pride. The pretty lady had actually chosen her. Taking Elspeth's hand she said, 'Let's go for our walk this way, I can hear Sally and Sarah somewhere. We'll find them. OK?'

Elspeth might not have understood the meaning of her words, but she knew the little girl was pleased to be with her. Always content in her comfortable and well cared-for life, she knew that walking with Beth was something special. In the confusion of her mind was an image of another child, Jess. She looked back over her shoulder. No, she wasn't here today. She might not have been able to untangle her thoughts enough to realize that she had been uneasy with Jess; she hadn't been comfortable with her forceful personality. This one was pleased to take her for a walk. She made a strange noise in her throat, half sigh and half grunt; if a human being knew how to purr that's how Elspeth Meredith would have expressed her pleasure.

Sarah and Sally went home much earlier in the winter than they would when the days grew longer. So it was that at about half past four they put away their shovels, washed the bucket they had used for the manure and were ready to go home. Nanny Giles had already taken Elspeth, she could never be sure how long the walk home would take them and she liked to be indoors before the light went so that she could see to the blackout curtains.

'You've got a visitor, Mrs H. I don't know who it is: a lady on a bicycle.'

'I know who it is, Aunt Kathie. It's Ollie's mum.'

Immediately Kathie was on the defensive. She looked at her work hardened hands, she glanced in the mirror over the mantelpiece in the warm room and what she saw did nothing for her confidence. Den seldom noticed a woman's appearance, but Claudia Marley had certainly made her mark. At a glance Kathie took in her visitor's lovely face, glamorous figure and expensive attire and wasn't surprised at the impression she had made on Den. Clearly she was everything that Kathie wasn't. On top of those thoughts came his open invitation for the newcomer to visit Westways where Kathie would be ready to be her friend, and it didn't make for a promising start to their association.

'Gosh, I wonder I didn't break my neck on the bike in that rutted lane,' Claudia said as Kathie opened the front door to her. 'I haven't cycled for years.' It was impossible not to smile at her. 'Do you mind me coming to see you? Dennis said you would take pity on my lonely state. Oh, sorry, I didn't tell you who I am—'

'You're Ollie's mother. Mrs Marley. Of course we're pleased to see you.' Could she really be saying it – not only saying it but meaning it too?

'Thanks. I hoped you'd say that. I wanted to come earlier but I knew he was going today so I waited until after that and then I thought the last thing you would want was a visitor while it was light enough to be working.'

'Hello, Mrs Meredith,' Beth said in her best behaviour voice as Kathie ushered their visitor into the warm room.

'I expect Aunt Kathie would have found you a job if you'd come while they were working. We all do jobs, don't we, Auntie Kathie?'

Kathie laughed. 'We certainly do. There's no such thing as a free ride at Westways. Anyway this is a good time for you to come, this is when we stop work and get something to eat. We usually have a proper meal early in the evening, but with Den leaving he and I ate at midday.' She heard herself say it: 'with Den leaving'. Where would he be now? Back in the company of other men may help him. It all seems like a dream: here I am, with a woman I don't even know, just Beth and me and a stranger. And this is my life, our lives, him going to God knows where, me here. What's it all for? Jess's life snuffed out, that's what he said. He's wrong, he must be wrong. Somehow we do the things we have to do: working outside, talking, smiling and now making this stranger welcome.

'If it's mealtime, I shouldn't hinder you. But, can I come sometimes, I don't know anything about growing things but I'm a willing worker.'

The suggestion came as a total surprise. What would a gorgeous, sophisticated creature like Claudia Marley want with working on the land?

'That's the sort we like, isn't it, Beth love?' Kathie answered, giving no indication of the way her mind was turning. Beth had no such inhibitions.

'Yes, but – well, it's dirty out there. It's lovely,' she added hastily in case her words had been badly chosen, 'but Mrs Marley has posh red nails and that.'

'Beth, you're a real treasure,' Claudia laughed, resting her elegant hand on Beth's pale fair hair. 'In the shops in the village I get eyed as if I'm some sort of a woman of the night, but no one says what's in their mind. Actually, though, Beth, the coloured varnish does help protect my nails so I really wouldn't be frightened of work.'

'The village people don't mean to be unkind, honestly they don't,' Kathie said earnestly, 'but I expect they feel uncomfortable. We're a pretty workaday lot.'

'Oh well, I don't give a damn what they think of me anyway. One is awfully stuck; the bus service to Exeter is almost non-existent and there's no chance of having petrol. Was I stupid to come, do you think?'

'I don't know enough about you to be able to answer that. I do know, though, that Ollie will love having you near the school.'

'That's what Bruce said when he told me about the house. But when it comes down to it, I really don't think Oliver needs me here. When he was in London for Christmas – well, I didn't see a lot of him, Christmas is party time isn't it – but all he talked about was this place and Jess and Beth.' Then, as if she realized what she'd said, 'Gosh, I'm sorry. Sorry for talking about her casually – and truly desperately sorry for all that's happened.'

'Yes. We all are, desperately sorry. But it was so good to hear her mentioned, spoken of in an ordinary voice, part of ordinary living. She and Beth and Ollie were great friends. He was very patient, he never objected when she organized them all.'

Claudia laughed. 'Not Oliver. He'll never be a leader of men.'

'Are you planning anything special to eat this evening? I mean, if not you can stay and have pot luck with Beth and me.'

'But I can't eat your rations.'

Kathie was surprised that her glamorous visitor should think of anything as mundane as rations.

'We're not eating rations. What you can smell cooking are roast vegetables from the garden and I'm going to make omelettes with eggs from our own hens. Are you any good at beating eggs?'

'You bet! I've been given a job. And it won't hurt my nail varnish either, Beth my friend.' Claudia surprised Kathie more by the minute.

Beth chuckled. This was turning into a really jolly evening.

And so it continued. The meal over, Kathie washed up, Claudia dried the dishes and Beth put them away, then they played Ludo. It was a far cry from the club Claudia often went to in London where she wasted time and money on roulette, but she enjoyed herself enormously.

Beth went to bed and after Kathie had been up to see she was settled and kiss her good night, the two women drew dining chairs nearer to the old kitchen range.

'Cigarette?' Claudia offered her gold case.

'Thanks.' The situation was unlike anything Kathie had ever experienced. Often on winter evenings she and Den had sat close to the range, chattering about the day's work, sharing a crossword puzzle or, in more recent years, sharing their pride in Jess's progress. But to spend an idle hour with another woman was something she hadn't done since she'd been a schoolgirl, living alone with her mother. And, because it was so different, it helped her through this first evening of the hundreds that must follow it. Only a fool would think there was hope of the war soon being over and Kathie was no fool.

As they sat in comfortable silence, she looked more closely at her visitor. In repose she was utterly lovely; the perfect symmetry of her face, the gloss of her dark hair, hair she wore pulled off her face and knotted in a bun in the nape of her neck. Kathie had noticed as they played Ludo that when she laughed a dimple appeared near either corner of her mouth. And there was something else that was out of keeping with her appearance, something which at that moment Kathie couldn't quite grasp. It was only later that she realized what it was.

For a while they sat in comfortable silence, then Claudia said, 'Funny being here. I wonder if he'll ever come back to the Hall.' For a second Kathie didn't follow her train of thought, then she realized it was Richard Marley Claudia was talking about. 'I was crazy about him, you know. He joined the company where I was in rep and it seemed like destiny. We were married within a couple of months. His only family were his grandparents, but they made an excuse not to come to the wedding. He'd never talked about them, so I had no idea what sort of people they were or that he was heir to Sedgewood Hall – or, as the old buffer used to put it, they none of them *owned* the place, they were custodians. Did you know the old couple?'

Kathie shook her head. 'Only by sight. They used to be driven through the village in their carriage—'

'Typical!' Claudia interjected. 'Why couldn't they travel in a motor car? Oh no, a carriage and coachmen implied they were part of some ancient line. But they were no different from anyone else; go back a hundred or maybe a hundred and fifty years and the first Marley to make his mark was a tailor. But he must have had a nose for success. He was a well-trained bespoke tailor so Richard told me later on, but did he follow the herd and make suits for anyone with the money to pay? You bet he didn't. He specialized in clothes for country gentlemen and spent every penny he could afford on advertising so that his custom came from far and wide. After that the bespoke bit was more or less dropped and articles were sold ready-made. But the standard never dropped – and you may bet your bottom dollar, neither did the price. But to meet him and that stuck-up little madam he was married to, you'd think their roots went back to the Norman conquest.' The outburst seemed out of character with Claudia's highly groomed and glamorous appearance, even her voice had a rougher edge to it. Kathie suspected there was more to this young lady than met the eye 'Sorry, I butted in. You were describing how they swanned it round the village.'

'I never thought of it like that. The village folk always seemed so proud of them and I only saw them a few times so I had no opinion one way or another. I remember how local men. doffed their hats to them and the women performed a sort of bob-cum-curtsey as the carriage went by.'

'Gordon Bennett!' Claudia exclaimed with a hearty chuckle. 'Proof they never really knew them. They were a right pair of miseries. The first time Richard took me to meet them was just after we were married, and I could feel them weighing me up and not caring for what they saw. I bet they took it for granted he must have married me because he'd put me in the club. But he hadn't. Some of our friends in the rep shacked up together but we didn't. Richard was different from the others. I was pretty ordinary. Oh, I was lucky, I'd been handed out good looks and I'd learned to make the best of myself. As for family, I'd been brought up in an orphanage then turned loose when I was fifteen. A job in service, that's what the home found for me. I only stayed a fortnight.'

'How did you manage?' Kathie looked back to when *she'd* been fifteen and remembered it as a happy, carefree time, a time when the home belonged just to her mother and her.

'Best way I could,' Claudia answered vaguely. 'I used to busk outside theatres – a sad ballad sung by a ragged looking girl with a pretty face. It was as good a living as I had with the rep. But that's how I came to be taken on by The Thespians, as the company optimistically called itself. And later on that's how I met Richard.' The way she said his name suggested that his one-time wife still carried a torch for him. 'He's a *real* actor, one who gets under the skin of the character he plays. Like I told you, I didn't go to bed with him until after we were married. Yes, I was crazy about him. And I'm sure it could have worked if he hadn't been a better actor than I was. I was useless really, I only got taken on because I'd been blessed with good looks and a better than average figure. I guess that's what he saw in me too. Anyway he was much too good for rep and was spotted for something better. And quite right too. He was given a West End lead. I was expecting Oliver by then. How any woman can say she feels *good* being pregnant, I'll never know. I had a rotten pregnancy, looked like death and felt like it too. Lost my looks and my figure, was clumsy as an elephant. God, how I hated it! It took all the wonder out of marriage. No man wants to make love to a woman who spends half her time vomiting with her head down the lavatory. Better after the first three months, that's what people say. I was like it right to the end. And by the time I went into labour Richard was making his first film. Thank God we had enough money coming in for us to engage a nurse for Oliver. But Richard was on location in Ireland, he seldom came back to London and when he did there was always the fear that I'd get preggie again; he didn't like having to be careful. I found friends of my own. You'd think I ought to have been the happiest woman alive, the wife of the wonderful Richard Marley. Oh well, life goes on.'

'Are you actually divorced?' Kathie asked, feeling she had to say something and yet wondering how Claudia could talk so freely to a stranger.

'Gosh yes. And a good job for me he can demand the sort of money he gets. He has to pay me good alimony – and he pays for Oliver's education. Oh well, he can afford it. But one thing I vowed, after I'd looked so awful when I was pregnant, and that was that I'd never let myself go to seed. What's the good of money if you can't pretty yourself up with it?'

Kathie laughed. 'I'm not the one to ask. I've never had money and as for prettying myself, something about silk purses and sow's ears comes to mind.'

'That's not actually true. Well, the money part may be, but not the sow's ear. You're a good-looking woman, really good bone structure. You're slim, a bit shapeless perhaps but that's better than being wobbly and hard to control. Most important, you look *real*! She lit a cigarette from the stub end of her first, and then held the case towards Kathie. 'Gosh! I don't know when I've talked so much – really talked I mean. I'm sorry, Kathie; you ought to have shut me up. And tonight you can't really have felt in the mood for a visitor, especially one who likes the sound of her own voice.'

'You know what? You've been a blessing. Den's been gone since the beginning of September, but this time it's different. The first evening with just Beth and me; I'd tried not to think about it. This really has been a first for me: I've never sat chatting with another woman. You're not a bit what I expected.'

'You are – what I expected, I mean. You know what Dennis said about you, about your home? He said if I felt lonely in Sedgewood, come here and see you. He said you gave a magic quality to your home. It was a shelter for lame ducks.'

Kathie gave an inelegant guffaw, a sound that belied the warm glow Claudia's words gave her.

'You hardly come under that category! A son who absolutely adores you; a new home and the money to have it made as you want; you are beautiful; you are charming and most certainly not a lame duck.'

'I've never thought of myself as one but it was your Dennis who said it, so he must have seen through the shining veneer I try and present.' Then, with that disarming smile that produced the two dimples, she continued, 'And, thanks to Richard, even a shining veneer is a lot easier if you have the cash to get your face pampered and indulge in nice clothes.'

'You'll be hard pushed to find anywhere around here to get your face pampered. But, give you six months down here, and you possibly won't even mind.' Kathie surprised herself by saying it. The lovely Claudia probably did little else with her life but indulge in pampering herself. But what else was there? By her own admission she had fallen violently in love with Richard Marley. That was nearly a decade ago; but what about now? If Kathie had learnt one thing from the evening, it was that you should never have preconceived opinions about people. All Claudia needed was love, real love.

Seven

Each morning Kathie listened for the click of the letterbox. Sometimes she was lucky and Beth went to pick up any envelopes from the doormat, but nothing came from Dennis. Despite having no letter to answer she often wrote when she was alone in the evenings even though her long epistle, under various date headings, couldn't be posted until she had an address. Perhaps she was using Dennis as a diary, trying to record her days as if any of it really mattered.

'You suggested to Claudia Marley that she should come to Westways. Before I met her I had made up my mind about her, disliking everything I knew. But, you know Den, even though she and I are poles apart, we have struck up a real friendship.' Then a few days later: 'High heels don't fit with helping in the garden, so Claudia decided to invest in a pair of wellies. Have you ever seen red wellies? I hadn't. I expect the assistant wouldn't have thought of showing them to folk like me. What a surprising person she is. Looks like a film star and wears gloves to protect her hands, but works as hard as any of us and seems to look on it all as a bit of fun.'

A day or two later: 'Bruce Meredith, you remember he is headmaster of the school evacuated to the Hall and organizes the teams of sixth-formers to help here at the weekends, he often finds time to drop in now that Claudia is here so much. She must be so used to having men hanging around her and I expect she knows what she's doing when she encourages him. But it worries me; he has a wife who is no wife; poor soul she is out of this world. The weather has been milder this week and Nanny Giles brings her most afternoons. It's so sad, even if she and Bruce are both here at the same time she doesn't realize he is someone special. But she loves Beth and as soon as she sees her she holds out her hand so that Beth can walk her around the place. Like I said, she is out of this world. But she is his wife for all that and I'm afraid Claudia is riding for a fall. She is so lovely, such fun and a really nice person, but I believe deep down she still hankers for her ex-husband.'

Then, about three weeks after Dennis had gone: 'The bursar from the school has been to see me with a request that we supply them with vegetables. Its a Godsend as it means I shan't have to use petrol taking stuff to Dere-mouth so often – at least not until the more exotic things (asparagus, etc) come along. Can't spoil schoolboys with luxuries like that.'

If only she could tell him of her misery, of how some-times as she climbed into bed it would flood over her, misery that even when the war was over and Den home again, nothing could ever be as it had been before they had lost Jess. Instead of their love for her drawing them together, it built a silent barrier between them. How could she tell him of those nights when it seemed nothing could stem her tears, nights when her spirit called out to the little girl and, silently, she beseeched to be given some sign, to hear that merry laugh or the familiar 'Tell you what, Mum!'. Sometimes nothing happened, the silence mocked her. But other times the voice was as real as if Jess were in the house. Den wouldn't understand; worse, he would worry about her and believe the events of the last months had unhinged her. So anyone reading her letters would find no mention of the little girl who had been their world, and the very omission held them apart.

It was March when his first letter arrived. It told her nothing of his surroundings, nothing of the routine of his days. But it gave her his field address, the means of getting her mail to him. They might have been on separate planets.

In Sedgewood village and in towns and villages across the country people were avoiding saying what was at the back of their minds: things were going badly, there were even whispers that some sort of a truce might be reached. But that could never happen, it *must* never happen! None of that could be put in their letters and the shadow cast by his leave made it impossible to write the sort of letters to each other they could have written before they had been torn apart by tragedy.

When, only weeks after she posted her first long epistle to him, German troops marched into Norway and Denmark, the future was lost in a fog of uncertainty. Something had to be done to set a new course. Everyone knew it, yet no one had any power. Then early in May the Prime Minister, Neville Chamberlain, resigned. But who would fill the void? There were plenty in the country who for years had seen Winston Churchill as a warmonger, but when he was appointed Prime Minister of the new National Government it was as if the country let out a great sigh of relief. Here was a man who would never give in to appeasement, who would stir patriotism in the hearts of the people, who would lead from the front until they achieved victory. On the Continent the situation was going from bad to worse as German troops poured into Belgium and the Netherlands and the Dutch queen with her court took refuge in England. One disaster – or triumph, according to whose banner one waved – followed another as the Germans took Holland and Allied troops were pushed back towards the north coast of France. Was Den one of that bedraggled army? England was never beaten; wasn't that what was taught to every schoolchild?

But there was nothing victorious in the bedraggled British Expeditionary Force as it was forced towards the channel. Although Dennis had been in the same unit as Stanley Stone and Bert Delbridge, in the retreat they had lost contact with each other. In England, with a new government and a new leader, hope stirred. But it couldn't last. The lives of the people were coloured by the bulletins they listened to on the wireless, and surely the colours of such hopelessness must be grey or black. Less than three weeks after the advent of the new prime minister came the event that would live in the nation's memory: the commencement of the evacuation of British troops – and many French too – from France.

'Can't sort of take it in, can you?' Claudia spoke in a hushed voice. 'Imagine being chased away with nowhere to go but the sea. They say naval boats are going to get them off, but it's too awful to imagine.'

Kathie shook her head, her mind was in such turmoil she was frightened to think at all. For days the news had been bad but somehow she, like thousands of others, had expected a miracle. In the finality of this latest news her emotions had come back to life, come back to life with force that was almost too much to bear. Den was there, forced towards the sea – but not everyone would be there, there would be those wounded and unable to make the distance, there would be those lying lifeless as their comrades retreated. Den – don't let him be one of those, bring him home, let him know that nothing has changed for him and me. Bring him home.

Coming in with a bowl of eggs Beth was aware of the atmosphere and her excited cry of, 'We got five today and look at this whopper. Bet it's got two yolks', died on her lips before it was spoken. Very carefully she took her bowl to the kitchen then came back into the warm room (the too-warm room at that time of year as the fire was kept in for the sake of hot water) and picked up her school satchel. This term she had started to have homework and on that evening she was glad of it.

'Coming near the shore to pick them up, the naval boats will be sitting ducks.' Kathie turned her head away, frightened to trust her voice to say any more.

'Do you want me to clear off home?' Claudia asked. 'Yes, of course you do.'

'No, no, don't go. Please.' Then, seeming to notice Beth for the first time, she said to her, 'Homework time, love?'

'Got two sums, adding up ones. Then I've got to read from this piece of paper and answer questions, yes or no sort of answers.'

The normality of her answer was balm to the chaos in Kathie's mind.

'When you've finished we'll have a game. How about draughts for a change?'

Beth seemed to relax, there was relief in her eyes as she promised she'd hurry.

'Don't rush so fast you can't add up right,' Claudia laughed. And if the laugh was forced Beth didn't notice, which was probably due to Claudia's years with the repertory company.

'Not one packet, but two!' Taking her cue from Claudia's assumed cheerfulness, Kathie dug into her shopping basket and pulled out two packets of cigarettes. 'Only Woodbines so a couple of puffs and they're gone, but they're better than nothing.' Then, pretence slipping: 'What a crazy upside-down world we live in. You know the one lesson we ought to learn from all this is never to take anything for granted, not a single day. The trouble with happiness is that it turns into habit and then you don't realize it's there.'

'So we'll take a deep drag on our slim ciggies and appreciate them. But what you say isn't quite true, Kathie. I did appreciate the time I was happy, I was almost drunk with joy.'

'Do you have any contact with him now? Don't you write about...' Kathie hesitated, conscious of Beth. 'His son?'

'No. He's been advised of my new address through the solicitor. If he wanted to know about anything he could contact me. But he doesn't. I was just a temporary hiccup, a physical temptation he couldn't resist. I always knew he thought he'd stooped and picked up nothing when he married me, but in the beginning what we had was more important. I told you what I was like carrying the fruits of our lust – because that's what it was. I think I always knew it, but I didn't care. I was even stupid enough to believe we would grow together. Silly, wasn't it? Gosh, you're right about these ciggies, three puffs and they're gone. Shall we check your sums, Beth?'

Watching them Kathie's mind was on the beaches of northern France. Perhaps he was already aboard a ship, perhaps they had started back across the channel, perhaps tomorrow or the next day she would hear his familiar tread. If only the door would open and he'd walk in, she could almost smell that revolting disinfectant of his uniform. But would it be like that now or filthy with mud and dirt, just as he would be dirty, unshaven, dishevelled? Den, she begged, Den come home, let's love each other so that we still share all those wonderful years and the preciousness of Jess. It was easy to forget how through those 'wonderful years' when month after month had come disappointment, excitement had given way to habit, the colours of life had dimmed. Once Jess arrived they saw each other afresh, their days had found a new meaning.

Later, with Beth in bed and Claudia gone home, she sat by the wireless waiting for the late night news. But it was only a repeat of what she'd listened to earlier. Yet for those soldiers on the beaches each hour must be like a lifetime. Would they be shot at as they were trying to escape? Would they be rounded up and taken as prisoners? Would the boats be bombed? How could she go to her comfortable bed and find relief in sleep when she didn't know where he was, whether he was alive or – no, she wouldn't even think it. He *must* be alive. He *must* come home.

The next day she heard the appeal for people with seaworthy craft to help with the evacuation. How strange it was that fresh hope could come from such a request when really it must mean that without the help of people volunteering to cross the Channel in boats they had simply used around the coasts at weekends the remains of the Expeditionary Force couldn't be repatriated. Or did that fresh hope come from the knowledge that the nation was in this together, that other lives would be risked in the rescue operation, civilian lives? This wasn't a war just for men and women in uniform, it was a fight for every man and woman in the country. They may not all be occupied in making guns or growing food, but they were all united.

It was announced that the Prime Minister was to make a broadcast. Kathie sat alone to listen, her heart swelling with pride. His words turned defeat into victory. As she listened she imagined those small craft, pleasure steamers, fishing boats, motor boats which had never gone more than a couple of miles off shore, plying backwards and forwards as they brought the men home. Yes, it was a victory, a victory for the invincible courage of an island race. Surely that ought to tell the world that no power on earth was strong enough to break their spirit. 'We will fight them on the beaches... We will *never* surrender.' Sitting alone by the wireless, Kathie found the tears running down her face. If the Prime Minister could have looked into that cottage set in its market garden he would surely have been satisfied that his rallying cry had touched the heart and soul of the nation.

—

On the other side of the Channel, bedraggled soldiers, hungry, footsore, some needing help, were wading the final few yards towards the boats. Dusk was falling, there was something nightmarishly unreal, made worse by the fact that they hadn't slept for what seemed like weeks. Dennis had lost track of Stanley and Bert and it worried him. There was no logic in his feeling responsible for them, but he'd known them since they'd first left school twelve years ago and he had a fatherly feeling for them.

Now he was about to wade into the water and he didn't know whether they'd gone ahead of him, whether they'd been wounded and had to give themselves up, whether – he tried to close his mind to the other alternative. But as he stepped into the water he took one last look at the country he was leaving, and that's when he heard his name being shouted and he recognized Bert Delbridge limping towards him.

'Thank God,' he greeted him, his voice sounding tight and strained to his own ears. 'Been looking for you. Where's Stan?'

Bert opened his mouth to reply, but his mud-stained face was working out of control.

'Copped it… couple of miles back. Plane swooped down, fired along the line. Went down like ninepins. Tried to carry him. Couldn't.' Passed caring, Bert's face crumpled as he sobbed.

Dennis held his arm around the shaking shoulders.

'Bloody war,' he mumbled. 'Poor young bugger. Come on, lad, be our turn to be picked up in a minute, better get out to the boats.' It took him all his strength of will to force even a hint of confidence in his voice. The two boys (for that's how he still thought of them) had been such a close part of his life, he felt they were almost family. Imagining Stanley lying lifeless as they were rescued he felt physically sick. But how much worse it was for Bert. They had been inseparable since their first day at school, more like brothers than friends. The nightmare of trying to carry the tall figure, realizing he was dead and having to rest him back on the roadside, would surely haunt Bert for the rest of his days. Unable to stop his loud uncontrollable crying, exhausted and trembling, Bert needed Dennis's help as the walked from the shore to the first ripples of water. Being depended on helped Dennis hang on to what courage was left to him. And so they walked into the water, feeling their boots fill, their thick scratchy trousers cling to their legs, then the water was to their waists, their shoulders, until they had to start swimming. The shock of the cold water helped restore Bert. Overhead a plane swooped, just as one had a couple of miles back. Aiming at the men climbing onto the flotilla of small boats, some of the shots went astray.

Dennis felt a sharp pain in his back, he tried to kick his legs – heavy legs with water-laden boots and clothes – legs that had no power.

'You go on,' he tried to say the words, but he didn't seem to know what was happening. Water over his face, over his head. He was going down. This is it! 'Kathie! Jess!' He believed he was shouting their names but how could he be when he couldn't breathe and his lungs were filling with water. Someone was dragging him – where to? Consciousness finally left him.

—

Ambulances were waiting on the quayside. The walking wounded were loaded aboard, as many as could be carried safely in each vehicle. For those who were more fortunate, army lorries were lined up to take them to the station for rail travel by special trains to the base where they would be medically checked, then issued with fresh uniforms heavily impregnated with the hated disinfectant, given ration slips and passes for fourteen days' leave. As the open-backed lorry drove away from the quayside, the first of the stretchers was being carried ashore. How else could casualties be offloaded, some conscious and thankful to be on home soil, others who had breathed their last as the little boat had chugged its way across the Channel.

And still there would be hundreds on the beaches waiting, ducking for cover, praying not to lose the freedom that was so close. With their human cargo all delivered to English soil the little boats refuelled and set out again.

As each special train travelled, at any vantage point where the railway line ran alongside a road, there were people waiting and watching, men waving their hats, women their hankies and children small Union Jacks. Dirty, exhausted, weak beyond imagination, the troops waved back to the welcome parties. If there were a few who weren't aware just how near the surface tears threatened, Bert wasn't one of them.

Could this be the defeat Hitler broadcast about to his people? Rather, this was a family welcoming home its sons. Pride had never been higher.

–

'Bert Delbridge came in the pub last night,' Sarah said a couple of days later. 'He'd not been hurt, but Mrs H he looked really rotten. Dad said he had to be careful not to push him with questions. But it's awful, he said Stanley Stone had been shot dead. Stanley! He was here working when they were on leave, remember?'

Oh yes, Kathie remembered. She remembered all the years he had been one of them. How many times had she heard Den's heartfelt, 'bloody war'? Stan not coming home, not going to marry the girl he had got engaged to before he went away. There were no words. How could she say 'I'm so sorry', or 'How dreadful'? She looked at Sarah in silence.

'Did he say anything about Den?' It took all her courage to ask. Her mouth felt dry and stiff; she had to force the words. 'I've not heard a thing.'

'I thought you would have heard from him by this morning. Bert said he helped get him onto a boat, but it was too full to take anyone else. So Bert got picked up by a different one. But Mr H was definitely on board and the boat got across OK. Bert said he saw that much. But his lot was offloaded first. Mr H had to be lifted aboard because he was wounded, but it can't be anything too serious or he wouldn't have been able to swim to the boat. Him being older than Bert, I expect he was exhausted with the swim.'

Kathie nodded, thankfulness seeming to deprive her of speech. Thank God, Den is safely back in England. Perhaps he wants to surprise me, just arrive like I've been dreaming. She leant on her hoe letting her mind run wild while, her news both bad and good told, Sarah went to the shed to fetch her tools ready to set to work.

Over the last few days, at some stage during each morning Bruce had walked through the wood to the lane, not climbing the gate but using the key and undoing the padlock, then those few steps more and he was at Westways. More often than not Claudia would be there and would see him, hailing him with a wave. The magic of this place never failed. That glamorous and worldly Claudia should have been drawn to it was the biggest surprise of all. He could understand what had attracted Oliver, and certainly Elspeth who would have responded by instinct rather than design, but it seemed to have touched a chord he had never suspected in Claudia.

That morning, arriving unnoticed, he stopped just inside the gate to take in the scene. There had been rain in the night and even though it had soon dried away, Claudia was wearing the red wellingtons to which she seemed very attached. To protect her hands as she picked broad beans she wore the same gardening gloves he had seen on previous visits. Where did she manage to find these things? They were gauntlets, as red as her boots, not thick heavy gloves as most people wore for gardening (at least, those who wore gloves at all, he thought, a smile tugging the corner of his mouth as he thought of Kathie), but made of strong rubber, with an artificial white rose on the back of each wrist.

Seeing him she raised one elegantly clad hand in a wave just as she always did. As a rule that drew him to stop and talk to her, but on that day he acknowledged her greeting and walked on down the field to where he could see Kathie checking the progress of the outdoor tomato plants and tying them to the poles as they grew. He watched unseen for a moment as she gave her concentration to examining each plant, pricking out any young shoot that grew in the leaf joints. In those old working trousers of Dennis's she so often wore – and from the look of her, an old shirt of his too on that morning – and with a scarf covering her hair and tied like a turban, it was impossible not to find himself comparing her appearance with Claudia's. His Adam's apple seemed to fill his throat. At that moment she sensed that someone was watching her and turned around.

'Bruce! How long have you been standing there? I was just finishing checking the tommies. They're coming on well. What's that in your hand?'

'I met the post-lady at the gate. She broke the rules and let me have it to give you.'

The buff envelope looked ominously official. Don't let it be bad news for her, he begged silently. She hurried towards him with her hand out, but one look at the typed envelope and hope faded.

'I thought it might be from Den.' She tore the envelope open and took out a single typed sheet. 'Wounded,' she murmured as she read. 'It's his spine. Operating… until after the operation they won't know how fully he will recover.'

He had never seen that lost, frightened look in her eyes before.

'Where is he?'

Kathie passed him the letter, a letter that told so much and yet so little. At least he was alive – and surely before any operation the medical people had to give that warning. That's what Bruce tried to make her believe as taking back the sheet of paper she reread the message.

'There's a telephone number. You must ring them, Kathie, find out if you can see him.'

Biting hard on her bottom lip, she cast a glance at the field that surrounded them. She felt trapped. The hospital was miles away. She had a child to care for; she had a business to run. The girls worked hard but they only obeyed instructions, she couldn't possible leave them. Anyway, what about Beth? She felt Bruce's firm touch on her shoulder.

'I'd never do it in a day. His spine. That sounds… sounds…' But the words died before she could speak them. It was probably something minor _ yet in her heart she knew it wasn't.

'We'll go indoors and you telephone the hospital. The letter was sent yesterday. Perhaps he's already had the operation and they'll be able to give you good news.'

She nodded. Brave words, but she wouldn't look him in the eyes.

Ten minutes later they were back outside. He would be out of the theatre within the next hour. It would be evening before he was recovered sufficiently to know she was there, and even then he would be under heavy sedation. The sister she spoke to was sensitive and helpful. 'If you can make the journey to be here tomorrow, I believe that would be best. But I do suggest you telephone again this evening.' The reason for calling again remained unspoken.

'There's Beth… there's this place… regular orders to be filled…'

'I believe, Kathie, you are hiding behind excuses. But you are strong. Whatever has to be faced you will find the courage. As for leaving Westways, you have all day today to arrange with the girls what must be cut – dug, or whatever you do with things – and I am offering you my services to make the delivery round. Unless Claudia sees that as an intrusion and wants to do it.'

But when the idea was put to Claudia it was clear that much as she enjoyed herself at Westways she had no ambition in the direction of delivering the packed boxes. Right from the day of her arrival she had stood apart from the villagers and that was the way she meant to continue.

'There are the chickens to be looked after – and, more importantly, there's Beth.'

'Beth is welcome to spend the night at the school. It won't be a hardship for her, I promise.'

'And I'll do the chickens. You can let me take a couple of eggs for my breakfast,' Claudia said with a smile that dug those dimples deep. 'Beth can take me on as an apprentice when she does them after school today so that I know what they expect of me. There now,' she beamed with satisfaction, 'all your problems are taken care of.'

Not for the first time Kathie brought to mind the image of the elderly Marleys and imagined their reaction when their beloved grandson produced over-glamorous and down-to-earth Claudia. It was apparent from Bruce's expression as he watched the young woman who had been rejected that his understanding of her went deeper.

–

Late that afternoon, the deliveries made and Beth put in Oliver's care at the school, Bruce dipped into his meagre petrol allowance and drove Kathie to Exeter. From there she travelled eastward and by dusk she arrived at the hospital. She had been told she couldn't see Den until after the surgeon's ward round in the morning, but she had to be reassured that he was out of theatre and had regained consciousness. More than that the nurse she spoke to could tell her nothing except that he was under heavy sedation and could have no visitors that evening.

After a night at a nearby bed and breakfast establishment, she returned to the hospital where, before she was allowed into the ward, she was taken to the sister's office.

'Sit down, Mrs Hawthorne. I spoke to you when you called by telephone yesterday and it's because you have come so far and for such a short time that you are to be allowed to visit out of normal hours. Five until six in the evening is usual, but I believe you will be well on the way home before that.'

'Yes, I can't be away long. I run our market garden until Den can be home to do it himself.'

'I see.'

'I was told last night that the operation was over,' Kathie prompted; but why was her heart beating so hard? She must keep that hopeful smile on her face, she mustn't let the kindly sister know how frightened she was.

'There will be many jobs he can undertake, but working a market garden won't be possible. What a mercy you are so capable. There is more to running an establishment than doing the hands-on work.'

'What are you trying to tell me?'

'Yesterday's operation was to remove shots from his back and to examine his spine. There were three shots, one of which had severed his spinal cord low in his back. You understand what that must mean?'

'Severed his spinal cord? He won't walk?'

'He will learn to get around. Wheelchairs are very different from what they used to be. And he will learn to use crutches, even without putting one foot in front of the other, this war is showing us that planting the crutches, swinging the body, its amazing the independence that can be achieved. More than amazing, it is truly humbling to see some of the lads we have had in here. But gardening, even simply *getting around* on land that is dug and cultivated...' She shook her head helplessly.

'Does he know?' Kathie asked in a voice that seemed trapped in her dry throat.

'Colonel Fulbrook, the surgeon, saw him this morning. I told him you were coming in after he left and I hoped he would let your husband hear it from you. But he said he would tell him himself; the sooner he knew the better. And perhaps he was right, perhaps too it was easier to take from a senior officer. I've seen so many times over these last months just how much it means to a man to be one of that band of servicemen. Each is isolated in his own tragedy and yet they are one small part of... of a brotherhood.'

But had Den ever felt himself to be that? 'Bloody war', she seemed to hear him say.

'Now I'll take you to the ward. This way.' It was like a living nightmare, and what a moment for Kathie to remember how she had imagined Den would return unexpected to surprise her. 'Here we are. You'll find him at the end of the ward in a bed with the curtains closed around him.'

'Thank you.' Kathie remembered her manners and added, 'You have been kind.'

The sister bustled away and if Kathie had been able to read her thoughts she would have found they were similar to Dennis's.

All eyes were on her as she walked the length of the ward. In a second she would see him. He was home, for him the war was over; wasn't that cause for thankfulness? Through recent weeks she had, if not forgotten, at any rate ceased to be haunted by the memory of how distant they had become when last he was home, but now without warning it flooded her mind. With her hand on the curtain she found herself hesitating, then as suddenly as it had come so the memory faded and she was filled with certainty. However difficult he found the adjustments he would have to make, they would share the problems; that wedge of ice that held them apart had melted under this new challenge. Losing their precious Jess would never grow less painful but surely as they made a new future – for it must be a new future, nothing could ever be as it was in the past – they would be able to reach out to each other and share their sadness. Almost timidly she pulled the curtain aside and stepped into the enclosed space.

She'd lived with Dennis years enough to know when he was genuinely asleep. Now he was lying propped up with pillows with his eyes closed, the pallor of his skin giving the tan gained under French skies an unhealthy yellowish tinge. He probably imagined it was a nurse who had just moved into his limited privacy.

'Den,' Kathie whispered, leaning over him, 'you don't need to act asleep, it's me.'

His eyes shot open and his mouth too. She bent over him, moving her face against his. He raised his arms and pulled her close, so close that she couldn't move her head away from his. Then she heard the sob he couldn't hold back. In the hour since the surgeon had given him a truthful account of the hopelessness of his case, fear, misery, even self-pity had combined and time and again it had taken all his willpower not to give way. But that was when he'd been on his own. Once Kathie was with him he could fight no longer. She cradled him in her arms holding his head against her.

'No bloody use to anyone. I'd rather have been killed.' His words were muffled as she held him against her, but she heard them clearly and dug desperately for something to say that would help him. But what could there be? Of course he felt he was 'no bloody use to anyone', but they had to fight their way through and build something new.

'*You* might wish it, but I certainly don't.' She ached with compassion for him, but there was no sign of it in her voice. 'Den, wallowing in misery won't help either of us. We've been chucked a challenge and we're going to beat it. Right?'

'We? It's *me* who's got the prospect of life in a wheelchair. You? You'll be all right; you and those girls will go from strength to strength. Stan's gone. He'd almost got to the coast and a plane came out of the sky. Machine gunned the line as they tried to get to the beaches. Bert started to carry him, but he'd gone. Stan gone, me useless,

Bert's war isn't over yet, and God knows what's in store for him.'

'We none of us ever know what's in store, what any day might throw at us.'

For the first time, they looked directly at each other. Jess seemed very close.

'Tell you what, Dad!' Kathie found comfort in using the child's expression. In her mind she seemed to hear Jess's voice, surely Den would open his heart and feel her spirit to be there with them as he heard the words: 'You and Mum are going to sort it all out. When you get home you'll feel better.'

He shook his head and leant back on the piled pillows.

'How long do you think it'll be before they send you home?' Kathie asked him, this time in a voice that was just her own.

'God knows. What's the difference?'

'Look here, my fine fellow,' she tried another tactic, 'I've come a long way and spent a night on a lumpy mattress in a B and B so that I could come a-visiting.'

'I'm sorry. But you shouldn't have left the gardens. Everything depends on you.'

'The gardens are in good hands. The girls know exactly what they have to do and Bruce has promised to do the deliveries – just Jack Hopkins and the school. And as for the chickens, Claudia is seeing to them and earning herself eggs for breakfast.'

'And the waif?'

She looked at Den with grudging affection. He might resent Beth being in their home, but he was conscious that she would need someone to look after her.

'No need to worry about Beth. She's living it up tonight, staying at the Hall. "Bloody war" it might be but there is a new feeling of kindness, of camaraderie, you can feel it amongst people. Rich and poor, we're all alike. People queue with their ration books, all in it together.'

'What am I going to do, Kathie? The future – it's just… just nothing.'

'It's only nothing if that's what we allow it to be,' she answered.

He was quite composed when he spoke again.

'It's easy for you,' he said, his voice distant. 'You can walk, you can dig, you can drive, you ca—' He couldn't trust his voice. She saw how tightly he set his jaw.

'Den,' she whispered, dropping to her knees by the side of his bed and gripping both his hands in hers, 'I know it's easier for me. But surely we've been a team so many years that we can face this together.'

'I'm just a bloody encumbrance. You know what?'

'There you go! Now it's you who sounds like Jess.'

'Don't!' he snapped. Then, going back to what he wanted to say, he continued, 'I remember it happening, I was almost to the boat and the plane swooped down with its gun blazing. Just one searing sharp pain, then nothing. Then I couldn't feel my legs, couldn't swim. I felt the water closing over my head. But, damn him, Bert dragged me up. The rest is just a blank. So it all could have been a blank, it would have been over, if only he'd let me drown. Why? Why in God's name couldn't he have let me sink to the bottom? Better than this, better for both of us after that swine in the plane had done for me. What can I do? Oh God, what can I do?' Was he even aware that she was with him or was he blind to everything but fear and despair? He wasn't just crying, he was bellowing. She imagined the patients in the other beds in the long ward looking at the closed curtains in sympathy.

It wasn't surprising that Kathie didn't hear a nurse approach. The first she knew was the swish of the curtain rings on the rail.

'I'm sorry, Mrs Hawthorne, I'm afraid I have to ask you to leave him. I'm going to give him an injection and then he'll sleep. If you come at visiting time this evening you will find an improvement.'

The arrangements at home had been for one day. Would Bruce keep Beth for a second night, would he be prepared to continue acting as delivery boy and what about Claudia? She could see it was useless to try to talk to Dennis, sunk deep in an abyss of misery he seemed unaware of his surroundings or of the noise of his crying either. So she walked the length of the long ward, conscious of the sympathetic glances from the other patients. Walking down a corridor she read a sign pointing to the Rehabilitation Department and looking through an open door she stopped to watch men out in the sunshine in wheelchairs propelling themselves with growing confidence. Once Den could get amongst them some of his natural optimism would return.

She had noticed a telephone box near the hospital so the first thing was to put through a call to Westways. She imagined how the outside bell would shatter the midday silence and knew she would have to wait while Claudia got back to the house and indoors to the telephone.

'Westways Market Garden,' the voice of efficiency rang in her ear. 'Can I help you?'

'Claudia, I've just come from seeing him.'

'Tell me.'

'It's what I dreaded…' And so she told the story, missing out nothing. 'He's very down in the dumps.'

'Frightened his socks off, I should think. And yours too. What will you do? No, that's a daft question. As if you can start to look to the future at this stage. Look, Kathie, if you want to stay on there for a bit, I can easily move in here. Beth will be better at home, I expect, and those two girls seem to know what's what. If Bruce offers I'll let him do the delivering, but otherwise I can drive the van. I took the morning order up to the hall. Really, we're coping.'

'You don't know how grateful I am. If I had to I'd come home tonight, but another day or two and perhaps the worst of the shock will have given way to… to acceptance. He's always been so fit, so strong. If he were some paleface sitting at a desk all day it wouldn't hit him like this.'

'It's a real bugger.' The gorgeous Claudia spoke from her heart. 'But I bet any paleface with a job at a desk waiting for him would feel just as knocked off his perch. You can't imagine, can you? We all want to help – and seeing us milling around him will make him feel even worse. Bert came in after you'd gone and he's coming again this afternoon. He'll know what we ought to be doing out there, won't he?'

Kathie felt a weight had been lifted. Bert knew the garden as well as she did herself. But this was his leave; she couldn't expect him to give up his time to working at Westways. That's what she told herself; but she knew that that was exactly what he would want to be doing.

'Poor Bert,' she said, more to herself that to Claudia. 'He and Stan were always together.'

'I know. But being useful might help him over the initial stage. I don't think he wants to kick about locally – not without Stan.'

'I'll ring again tomorrow. And thank you, Claudia, you're a brick.' Hardly the description the folk in the village would have given the young madam with her airs and graces.

–

Two days later Kathie got off the bus outside the fish and chip shop in the village and walked to the turning to the common.

Out of the tragedy some sort of order had to be found and it had to be up to her to organize it. But hadn't she been doing just that ever since the previous September? Yet somewhere there was a difference in the way she approached her work on the land. No longer was she 'holding the fort'.

On that first evening home Kathie couldn't settle in the house. Leaving Beth to do her homework she came outside knowing she could find plenty to do. Later Beth would join her, but she never gave homework short measure; she enjoyed doing it. Something that even to Kathie seemed unchildlike. Until that time, Bruce had frequently come to Westways if he could spare the time during the morning, but that was the Bruce they were used to seeing: charcoal grey suit, white shirt, silk tie (never a loud tie, always something in keeping with his sober attire) with a matching handkerchief in his breast pocket, well polished black shoes. Claudia had said that he seemed to enjoy being part of the team during the few days she'd been away. On that first evening back after her visit to the hospital he arrived unexpectedly at about seven o'clock, this time wearing workman's overall, short-sleeved shirt and Wellington boots. Hearing foot-steps Kathie turned, her greeting dying on her bps.

'Gosh,' she said as she collected her scattered wits, 'you look ready for anything. Claudia isn't here this evening.'

'I didn't come to see Claudia, I came to offer my inexperience to you. Can you use me? But first, tell me how he was when you left. Is he making progress?'

Rather like 'I'm very well, thank you' being the universal answer to 'How are you?' Kathie was about to say that Dennis was making good progress, he had all the courage he would inevitably need. But something in Bruce's expression stopped her. She shook her head helplessly.

'Can you imagine how he must feel. He is a… is a physical sort of person. That's why he took this place. It was his life – his and mine too. Shall we have to let it go to someone fit and strong, like he used to be?' It wasn't so much what she said as the frightened look in her eyes that drew him to her. Before he reached a hand to her, common sense took hold. She had troubles enough without him confusing her any further.

–

Weeks went by, the school broke up for the long summer holidays. It fell quite naturally into place that Claudia and Oliver came each day to Westways. The village school wouldn't start holidays for another fortnight so with no Beth for company Kathie made sure he was kept busy. Rationing certainly did make it more complicated but lunchtime became a sort of party hour. Early each morning Kathie prepared her cauldron of vegetable soup. No one enjoyed those lunchtimes more than Oliver. Never in his life had he seen his mother as she was here. Always she was pretty, always she loved people and parties, but this wasn't like the parties she used to have in the apartment in London where everyone kept refilling their glasses and the laughter grew louder and yet to Oliver's sensitive ears not a happy sound. But Westways was like another world; the only thing that remained the same was that Claudia took no particular notice of him, but even that didn't hurt like it had before.

Once Beth was on holiday too and the children were free, as he spooned up his daily bowl of soup, he would look ahead to the afternoon, planning what he and Beth would play when they got to the common. That's when the cloud would descend on him: nothing was the same without Jess. He and Beth always had fun, but although they never talked openly about it, they both knew it was because of Jess the bond held them.

There was a quality of unreality in those summer weeks as June gave way to July and July to August. How could Kathie have imagined even six months ago that Bruce would have relaxed into being a member of their working party during the busy period of the school vacation? But then, what man given the chance wouldn't have been drawn there to spend summer hours with Claudia? That's what she reminded herself each time her thoughts strayed out of line. So why did she listen for the click of the gate when he arrived, why couldn't she be casually friendly as she was with any other man? And when she kept her thoughts in control during the day, why was it that dreams of him disturbed her sleep? Did she imagine that his gaze followed her and when their eyes met there was something in his expression that she was frightened to analyse?

Each night before she went to bed she wrote a brief note to Dennis, making sure that he knew exactly what had been done that day in the garden and making sure that when he came home he would be able take up the managerial reins. She was determined that he must feel himself to be part of everything at home.

–

On an evening in late August Kathie was at the far end of their land, near the ditch where, in the days of keeping a pig, she had always emptied her bucket. The light was fading on what had been a beautiful day and she perched on the step of an old stile between Westways and Merry-down Farm. Many years ago the land of the market garden had been no more than a small field and labourers cottage on the western edge of the farm until the farmer had been persuaded to sell it. Nowadays it was leased to Dennis.

'Am I disturbing your daydreams?' She turned as she recognized Bruce's voice. 'I looked in to see how things are going.'

'With Den or with me?'

'I imagine the general answer would encompass both. Now that he's taken the first step' (perhaps unfortunate phrasing but they both let it pass) 'and settled into the rehabilitation unit, the next thing will be he'll be home. No sign of a date yet?'

She shook her head.

'Not yet.' She made sure her voice sounded bright, but he wasn't blind to the fear he read in her eyes.

'I hope it won't be too long,' he said. 'It won't be easy – not for either of you – but better if he can get home before the autumn sets in. Hours in the house on his own while you work outside would be very hard on him.'

He was the first one not to be frightened to acknow-ledge the difficulties that lay ahead.

'I'm such a coward. I'm frightened to imagine what it will be like, even if the days are still warm enough for him to sit outside. Can you imagine, Bruce, just sitting there, watching other people do the work that was always your own? Why, why, why wasn't he an artist or writer, an accountant, anything where he could at least pick up some of the pieces of his life? Supposing he resents seeing me doing the job that should be his?'

'He wouldn't be human if he didn't feel resentment for what has happened to him; but he won't feel it for *you*.'

'Truly I want to be what he expects, not to seem changed. He has so much to bear.'

Her words hung between them. For a few seconds neither he nor Kathie spoke, yet they seemed unable to look away from each other.

'Take it a day at a time, my dear,' he said at last, his voice firm and forceful and not a bit like himself.

She nodded. 'Perhaps I'm worrying for nothing. Just forget what I said.'

He nodded. 'Yes, said and unsaid, Kathie, we must both forget.'

It might have seemed an odd choice of words, but they both understood the full implication behind them.

'Did you see Beth when you came in?' she asked, her tone telling him that their unguarded moment was already forgotten.

'Yes. She's just finishing her book. You know, Kathie, she is a remarkably bright child. I hate the thought of her having to go back to the life she had before she came here.'

'For nearly a year she's been with me, and never once has her mother enquired. Beth says she can't read or write, but she has a neighbour who can. Not a birthday card, not a Christmas card. I sent her our telephone number; surely she could have phoned. But nothing. Once Den is settled, I want to talk to him about adopting her. I'm certain her mother would be more than happy to let her go.' And when he didn't comment immediately, she prompted, 'Bruce? You don't answer. What do you think? Am I being selfish; do you believe blood is always thicker than water?'

He shook his head. 'I didn't answer because I was indulging in pictures in my mind. I don't know your husband so I can't guess how he'll feel. But "tell you one thing"—' and just as she had to Dennis that day in the hospital, so Bruce used Jess's excited tone of voice—'Jess would be delighted.'

His way of answering took her by surprise and before she could hold them back, hot tears sprang into her eyes, overspilling to run down her tanned cheek. Whether he pulled her into his arms or whether she moved instinctively into their shelter neither would ever know.

'Such a mess, all of it,' she croaked, moving her wet face against his neck. 'If only we still had Jess none of this would have happened, I'm sure it wouldn't.' She didn't explain what she meant by that; he didn't need her to. 'I love Den, of course I do. We've been together so long that we've become like two sides of the same coin. So why do I feel like this?'

'Like this?' He tipped her tear-stained face up to his. 'Like I do? As if I'm on some sort of helter-skelter, up, down, no power to stop myself.'

Kathie nodded. 'I mustn't Bruce, and neither must you. You may think Elspeth doesn't remember you but, if you weren't there for her, her life would be changed, she would be lost.'

'I have a friend, a psychiatrist, who told me a few years ago that I have grounds for divorce because of her mental state. The idea horrified me then and so it still does. Marriage isn't just for sunny weather, not yours and not mine either.'

'I *do* love Den, honestly I do. If I could change places with him and be the one never to walk, then I'd do it. But – I shouldn't be saying any of this, I shouldn't and neither should you. That's the God's honest truth. But, before we forget any of this has happened – and we *must* forget – say it to me once, tell me—'

'Tell you I love you? Oh yes, I love you, Kathie. I dread to think of my future without you in it. I think you changed my life the day you strode into my study dressed in your best and ready to put me in my place. Or was it the next day when you looked more like a scarecrow in the field of Merrydown Farm?'

'If you'd only known how angry I was to think you'd caught me looking like that when I'd been to such lengths the day before. You carried the heavy bucket from the sty, remember?' She spoke softly, wanting to hold on to these precious moments and yet ashamed of her own feelings. This was *wrong;* for both of them it was wrong. She pulled back from him. 'We can't let this happen, Bruce.'

'It's too late to stop it.'

'It must be a sort of midsummer madness. Wartime everyone's emotions are upside down, husbands and wives separated, meeting people outside their marriages.' She was clutching at straws, any excuse to make herself believe that once Den was home they would slip back into the way things used to be, their relationship easy and satisfying. But then there had been three of them; now there were two. Den, you've got to help me, she pleaded silently trying to reach out to him. What a moment for the clock at the Hall to chime three quarters: a quarter to eight.

Wherever they were they would all be together in their thoughts. Was he thinking of her now? Was he resenting how dependent he would be on her? Was he longing to get home, certain that her love for him was as solid as the ground under their feet? Help me, help me to love only Den. This is madness; it must be madness. But still she didn't move away from Bruce.

'When I fell in love with Elspeth we were both young,' he was saying, speaking softly, 'she was little more than a child.' She knew he was making an effort to be practical, to help them overcome the sudden emotion that had rocked their world. 'The future was bright; there were no clouds. Under a cloudy sky perhaps we wouldn't have noticed each other. I love her still, for the rest of my life, come what may, I will always love her. But the love I have for you isn't that of the inexperience of youth, it's forged into my soul and spirit. I believe that sometimes, perhaps not often, but sometimes two people are moulded of the same clay. Even if we can never fulfil that love in the way nature craves, nothing can take from us what we have.'

She was no longer crying, but she knew as she looked at him squarely that her face was a mess, her eyelids pink and probably her nose too. Helplessly she shook her head. 'I'm glad about this evening. Is that wicked? No. No, Bruce it can't be. But it mustn't happen again, not even if Den doesn't come home for ages. It must never become furtive and sordid.'

'Darling Kathie.'

'No. No more, Bruce. Listen, Beth's calling.'

–

'Auntie Kathie! Telephone! Quick. Didn't you hear the bell?'

'Run and answer it, Beth. Say I'm just coming.'

Bruce watched her running back towards the house. At this hour of the evening it would be Dennis on the telephone. Already their moment was over and they were getting pulled back onto their own familiar paths. Slowly he walked back towards the cottage and the gate to the lane knowing that on the way back to the Hall he would stop at the lodge. Beth ran to meet him, giving him a full account of the homework she had just done. His life and Kathie's were moving on, those few short moments when the world had been their own were already no more than a memory to be relived in the still of the lonely nights.

'It was just a quick call,' Kathie said as the two came near the cottage. 'It was just to tell me that Den is being brought home tomorrow.'

Eight

In the first moments, as the ambulance reversed back down the lane to the road, Dennis was grateful to be alone. It was nearly six o'clock so the girls must have gone home. Not like it used to be, he thought as, before he could turn his thoughts in another direction, a wave of misery washed over him. Then on a summer evening the lads had liked nothing better than to stay on. And Kathie? Where was Kathie?

Closing his eyes he breathed deeply of the familiar smell of turned earth, and newly cut grass too. Ah, he heard voices. And seconds later Beth and Claudia came into view. That Kathie's waif should be coming back from the bottom end of the field as if she belonged at Westways did nothing to lift his spirits. Trying to cut her out of his vision and out of his mind he concentrated on Claudia. It was apparent she'd been working, evidence of it was in the scarlet gloves and wellingtons, yet she might have stepped straight off the fashion page of some women's magazine under the heading: 'Rural Elegance and Sophistication'.

At that moment Claudia chanced to look in his direction and saw his chair on the grassy patch Bruce had mown that morning.

'Dennis!' she shouted in delight as, leaving Beth, she ran towards him. 'Kathie'll be furious that the reception committee has to be *me*, not her. She put off taking the order to Hopkins for as long as she could, hoping you'd get here. But she'll be back in a minute.' Her pleasure was apparent; her lovely face couldn't stop smiling and the dimples dug deeper.

'You're doing a great job of welcoming me. Kathie has told me what a help you are to her. Just two girls hardly out of the schoolroom… Oh well, nothing I can do, decisions have to be hers in future.' He raised his hands helplessly as he shrugged his shoulders.

'Daa–daa–daa, de–daa–daa–daa,' she sang solefully as she mimed the playing of a violin. Then, her eyes seeming to twinkle with suppressed laughter, she continued, 'Wait while I fetch my fiddle.'

Dennis heard the self-pity in the echo of his words. 'Sorry, Claudia. You make me ashamed.'

Squatting by the side of his chair with the ease and grace of a child, she took his hand in hers. 'I wasn't meaning to do that. Dennis, we are all sorry, *desperately* sorry. But there'll be masses you can do.' Although at that precise moment they didn't spring to mind.

'Never mind Westways; tell me about you. How's the house? I've often thought about it, imagined how it would be looking. All the work must be finished by now. And the garden?'

'The house looks nice but the garden is as you saw it except worse. I've never had one before. From the orphanage to a bedsit, from there to a small flat, then a posh flat, but never a garden. I'd like you to see the things I've had done. Would you let me push you round?'

She was offering to *push* him, a helpless hulk in a wheelchair. He clenched his hands. She sensed his change of mood. That's when she had a sudden idea.

'And anyway, Dennis, it's not just the house I want you to see. I want your advice about the garden. Think of the fun we could have designing what should be done with it. I just don't know where to start. But if you could tell me what to do, honestly I'm not frightened of work.'

He looked at her more closely. She had been a mystery to him on the day he'd gone to the house with her. Something she'd said a few moments ago had given him a clue: 'from the orphanage'. Yet, her speaking voice was a joy to listen to. Children in orphanages surely didn't have elocution lessons? Her voice must be a hangover from her time on the stage. He found himself smiling at her, feeling more relaxed and less in awe now that he knew that under the exotic front lurked a woman as ordinary as any of them. Following that train of thought he opened his mouth to ask her what she'd meant by 'from the orphanage' but that's when he became conscious of Beth standing close by seeming hesitant to say hello and yet not liking to move away.

'Hello Beth,' he forced a note of joviality into his greeting.

'Hello, Mr Hawthorne. I'd better go and lay the table. We all have jobs. That's one of mine.'

'Did you do the chickens?' Claudia asked her.

'Yes. Just four eggs was all I could find. I put them in the kitchen.'

Beth imagined supper with just three of them at the table. She felt uncomfortable.

'Hark! Kathie's back. I'll get my bike and clear off. Oliver will be waiting to get in.' She had sent him on his way walking when he and Beth had got back from an afternoon on the common. 'See you both tomorrow.'

'Go and see to the table,' Dennis told Beth as he heard the slam of the van door. This was the beginning of the rest of their lives. It had to be good, please God help me to find the courage I need.

Seeing him, Kathie ran towards him dropping to her knees in front of his chair. A mistake. He leant forward to kiss her, she raised her face towards his, but for both of them it was an unnatural position, as unnatural as everything else about his homecoming. She got to her feet and moved behind the chair, leaning forward and rubbing her face against his.

'Don't hide behind me, let me have a look at you. Aren't those my old trousers?'

'Indeed they are. You know, Den, wearing them gave me confidence. And this shirt, this is yours too. Where's Beth? Have you seen each other?'

'Yes.' His expression told her nothing. 'She's laying the table.' Then, unable to stop himself, he added, 'Have all the evacuees taken over so thoroughly?'

'She only has us.'

'The way this blasted war is going, we're lumbered with her for a long time yet. How can our young flyers hope to win in the air when day after day droves of bombers make for London? And how long can London hold out? God, Kathie, it made my blood run cold to watch the dogfights. Here in the south west you've no idea what war is like.'

'North, south, east or west we're all one people. Remember Mr Churchill's broadcast? You must have heard it in hospital. You could almost feel the nation pulling itself up tall. What was it he said? The road may be long and hard but we'll *never* be beaten.'

'No use looking to me for help. Bloody useless. About as much good as that van you drive would be without a motor.'

Again she bent over him moving her lips on his cheek. 'That my darling Den is the biggest nonsense I've ever heard. There's nothing wrong with *your* motor.'

'And don't be too sure about that either. Oh hell, Kathie, what sort of a husband can I be to you? I daren't try and look into the future.'

It was a good thing he couldn't see the pity in Kathie's eyes as she rubbed her chin against his head.

'The future is something we have to work at, and we will, Den. Each day you'll find there is something new you can do. I might find myself out of a job.'

'Don't be ridiculous. It's better to look the facts in the face. I don't even think I'm very interested in what's ahead. Yet it's even more painful to look back than forward.'

'Den, we have to look back; we have to remember. Never, never, never forget any of it – of her.'

Den put his arm around her and pulled her towards him.

'The table's all ready, Aunt Kathie,' Beth called. This was usually her favourite time of day, when she sat at the table with Kathie and very often Claudia and, holiday time, Oliver too. She liked Claudia being there, even though the two grown-ups often talked about things she didn't understand enough to join in, but she never felt left out. This evening might be different though. She was sure Mr Hawthorne didn't like her even though he had never smacked her or shouted at her, but his eyes never smiled when he looked at her. If Jess were here it would be different; even not being able to walk wouldn't make him so miserable. Beth opened her satchel and took out a notebook, finding comfort in the feel of it in her hands. Then she opened it and looked with pride at last night's homework. Ten out of ten for her sums and the teacher had written, 'Excellent work. Well done.'

–

Helping Dennis to bed proved to be an awkward job. He had insisted she shouldn't have their things moved downstairs, turning the seldom used drawing room into a bedroom. Instead he reached the stairs using his crutches and swinging his body so that he moved both legs at the same time. Then, gripping the newel post he seemed to throw himself so that he could sit on a stair. From there, painfully slowly, he moved upward, easing himself from stair to stair by taking his full weight on his arms. Kathie stepped forward.

'Let me get round you. From behind you I can help take your weight,' she said, her foot already on the bottom tread of the steep straight flight.

'Stay out of the way,' he told her with a glare. 'I'll soon get the hang of it. In that rehabilitation dump there were lifts.' She knew this was all part of his battle for independence so, even though she longed to be part of his battle, she stood at the bottom of the stairs, her hands gripped into two fists as slowly he advanced to the upstairs landing. 'OK,' he said, a hint of triumph in his voice even though he was out of breath, 'now you can come up with my crutches.'

So he progressed until finally they were in the bedroom with the door closed.

'Remember how we always used to leave it open in case Jess wanted us in the night?' For Kathie there was comfort in talking about the child who had been the centre of their universe.

'Don't! Jess has gone, *gone*, you hear me, like everything else.' He started to undress and she couldn't fail to see how his hands trembled. 'Thank God to be rid of this damned uniform.'

'Amen to that,' she said softly. 'Den, the two of us, we can fight anything. We'll make a go of it however hard the challenge.'

'You can't know, Kathie. Don't help me, but just imagine what it's like: I want to put my watch on the table by the bed but you've leant my crutches against the wall by the door where I can't reach them. I can't bloody move without them.'

She took a step towards the crutches, then stopped.

'What's the saying about necessity being the father of invention? Den, you came all the way up the stairs without crutches so work yourself along the bed using your arms and…' She watched while he did as she said and put his watch on the bedside table just as he had every night they had been together. 'Well done! Another hurdle crossed.'

But the fight had gone out of him. Sitting on the side of the bed he let her undress him.

'Now I need a pee,' he whined.

'Then my darling you shall have one. Slip your arms into your dressing gown. That's it. Now here are your crutches. Off you go. You only need one hand to steer your dinkle, and one crutch to prop you up. You'll be fine.' She knew how near he was to breaking point as she passed first one crutch and then the second to him.

'Kathie,' and at the sound of his laugh she looked at him, her eyes bright with hope. 'Oh Kathie, what would I do without you? Is the kid asleep? Is her door shut?' For his dressing gown was hanging open leaving him to the world displayed.

'Sound asleep. Den – you *won't* – but *if* you want me, just shout.'

'I'll be OK.'

That was another hurdle crossed. He was quite a long time and when he got back she was almost ready for bed. The night was warm and she had pulled back the covers. As he sat on the edge, with one swift movement she lifted both his legs onto the bed.

'You don't want pyjamas any more than I want a nightie. We want just *us*.' She laid down next to him, her body against his. Soon she would have to get out of bed to turn off the light and open the heavy curtains, soon but not yet. It was important they could see each other. There was nothing of the seductress in Kathie, but that they should make love had never mattered more than on that night. She must think just of Den, Den who had been the centre of her world for more than half her life. In that instant she was carried back to those moments by the stile. She mustn't think of Bruce. Den was her past and Den was her future.

'Kathie, I tell you, I can't.'

'Yes you can and you want to. Just look at you.' She spoke softly, her voice affectionate and teasing.

'Yes, look at me.' Hardly moving his mouth, he seemed to be speaking through clenched teeth. 'I want to sink deep, deep into you. But I know when I try to it'll be gone, shrivelled to nothing. I know, Kathie. I've tried often enough but one touch and it's useless. Doesn't work any better than my damned legs.'

She moved to lie half on him.

'If that's the way it has to be, then we can live without that sort of loving. Den we have so much, your life and mine are entwined into one. We'll be fine, you and me.' We can live without that sort of loving… but was that true? Uninvited the thought leapt into her head of the times he had mounted her as if he were serving her like an animal in the field, racing to his goal and leaving her with her body aching with longing for something so often just out of reach. Again she was in Bruce's arms, that same longing thrusting everything from her but her yearning for his love. Tonight was the first night of the rest of their lives; she loved Den, dear Den who had shared her years, Den who had fathered Jess. Moving closer, she raised herself so that she was lying on top of him, his arms around her as he held her close. Above all else she was aware that his desire hadn't retreated with her touch. She drew up her knees and moved to sit taller. His eyes were closed, his breathing quickened by fear. Please let it work for us – for both of us – but especially for Den. She guided him into her and started to move gently on him. With clenched fists he was beating a tattoo on the bed; St George couldn't have fought the dragon with more force than Den did as he battled to hang on to the libido that he knew could vanish with no warning.

She watched him, all thought of her own needs faded. Tonight belonged just to him. If he failed, then the failure would go with them into the future; if he succeeded that would be another hurdle overcome, a high and important hurdle.

And finally it was a battle won.

'You see?' She laughed softly, moving her fingers tenderly through his tousled hair, 'Your legs might not be in working order, but the rest of you is just the man you always were. Right?'

'Seems so,' he answered, still gasping for breath. 'Kathie, I was so frightened. God, but it's good to be home.'

–

In most homes the wives of wounded or disabled warriors would give their time to them. At Westways that wasn't possible. Sarah and Sally had learnt a lot in the year they'd been there, but Kathie contributed a full day's labour as well as organizing the work. For years she had helped; at Den's bidding she had planted seeds, thinned out the seedlings so that when the strong young plants were ready she could plant them out. Doing the work under someone else's watchful eye was a very different thing from thinking ahead, making sure nothing fell behind schedule. In the last year she'd had to learn as she went along, and she had every right to be proud of what she had achieved. On her one and only trip to see Dennis in hospital, Claudia – who in truth knew far less than either of the girls – had taken control and Bruce had been a willing delivery boy plus any other role that came his way Now that Dennis was home, would he still wander down from the Hall in his workmen's overalls and Wellington boots? Kathie knew the answer even before she asked herself the question.

'It's a glorious morning,' she said as, after a slow and difficult descent, Den swung himself into the warm room. Normally she would have been outside an hour or more ago, but having set the girls to work she waited until she heard he was on his way down before she started to cook his breakfast.

'I don't need breakfast. You've got work to do. If you can just put the wheelchair outside the door, I can get myself out there when I'm ready. You can't leave those girls on their own. God knows what'll happen to the place.'

'The arrogance of the man,' she teased, trying not to let him guess the effort it took, 'they may be the fairer sex but they aren't children. They're seventeen years old and they've worked here for a year. When Stan and Bert were that age the extension was being built and I seem to remember you made yourself labourer's assistant.'

'Has the paper come?' he changed the subject.

'I expect it's in the letterbox. It's always late during the school holidays,' Kathie answered at just the same moment as Beth ran in from the garden.

'I'll get it, Aunt Kathie,' she said not slowing her pace as she ran through the room, 'I did the chickens' water.'

'Thanks, love.'

Dennis frowned. The easy and affectionate relationship between Kathie and her waif seemed to make a stranger of him – of him and of Jess too, as if life had gone on without either of them. Slumped at the table he wished it could do just that. What was there to live for? Day after day, year after year, and what was he? Just an encumbrance on Kathie's life.

Running back into the room Beth put the paper on the table in front of him.

'Here it is,' she forced herself to speak and to smile, too, without him being able to guess what an effort it was. When he'd been here before, everything had been so dreadful. Often she had dreams about the accident, the scream of the brakes and then a sort of thud (which in her dreams was louder than it had been in reality) as Jess had been hit, Jess and Fudge. She would wake up in the night and find she was crying; sometimes Kathie heard her and came in, sometimes she just lay there on her own reaching to Jess's side of the bed and trying to imagine she was there. Perhaps he thought about it and was sad too; that's what she told herself as she put the paper on the table in front of him.

Without looking at it, he pushed it away. Watching the scene, Kathie felt her anger rise.

'Beth and I have had our breakfast. I must go and see how the girls are getting on; you can help me, Beth. OK? Just leave your dirty things on the table, Den, I'll come back later and see to them.'

'Or I can,' Beth suggested, feeling that if he saw her as part of the team he might not mind about her so much.

'One of us will. You're sure you're all right to get outside? I've left the chair just near the door.'

'Fine, thanks.' He managed to keep his voice steady, in fact he sounded sufficiently bright that Kathie felt no guilt in leaving him. Already he had found there were things he could manage for himself; each day would get better. Her optimism would have taken a plunge if she could have looked back at the scene in the warm room where he sat with his head in his hands, his untouched breakfast before him.

'The weeds are getting bad at the far end, we'll have a go at them shall we?' Kathie said as she and Beth reached the tool shed where she took a hoe for herself and passed to Beth one which, while she'd been visiting Den in hospital, Bruce had fitted with a handle just the right length for her. Soon they were working together, the little girl concentrating on cutting through the new growth of weeds, then turning the hoe just as Kathie did to smooth the freshly turned soil. Before long Oliver would be here and they would go to their den on the common. What a sad and cross man Mr Hawthorne was. Of course it must be dreadful not to be able to work with the others, but it wasn't Aunt Kathie's fault; he might feel better if he made himself smile at her more.

'Beth, we're here.' As if by magic Oliver came running towards them between the rows of vegetables. 'This morning Mum didn't send me on and then come on her bike. No, we walked together. Good morning Mrs H. Is it all right for Beth to come to the common, or has she got to work? I'll do jobs if you like. Mum's saying hello to Mr H. She said I had to tell you she'll come and see you in a minute.'

'My word, Ollie, I'm spoilt for choice with so many workers. Thanks for offering, love. By this afternoon when were getting the order together for the shop I may be glad of a hand, but you two run off and enjoy yourselves.'

They didn't need twice telling. Like cage birds finding the door left open, they were off. Kathie laid down her hoe and went to change the position of the sprinkler. There had been no rain and she had to make sure not a square foot of the field missed out. This was a job she found more difficult than most. The water hydrant was deep in the ground about halfway down the field and the water had to be turned on and off with a long metal pole. First she turned it off, then she moved the heavy four inch diameter hose further towards the end of Westways' land, then back to the hydrant to turn the water on again. It was as she started back to where she'd been hoeing that she heard the sound of Claudia's laugh. Tempted by the sound she walked to where she had a glimpse of the patch of grass. What a dear Claudia was! There she sat crossed legged on the ground in front of Den's chair, clearly telling him some story that was lifting his spirits.

It was Den who noticed her and called, 'Here a minute, Kathie.' It looked such a happy scene, she was glad to join them.

'I've been telling Dennis about my weedy patch and trying to persuade him to use his brainbox to advise me what I ought to do with it,' Claudia said as Kathie got within earshot.

'And what have you come up with, Den?'

'Nothing. How could I without even seeing the plot and knowing.'

Looking as excited as a child promised a treat, Claudia took up the tale.

'That's easily remedied. I can take him and, once we're there, the brick paths are wide and very wheelchair friendly, he can potter around by himself. You haven't got a spare hoe we can take along have you, Kathie? I tell him I'm open for all the help I can get and if he can loosen the roots, I can grapple with removing the weeds.'

'Do you want anything other than a hoe, Den?' Kathie asked, purposely letting him see that he was in charge of the expedition.

'Maybe a rake might be useful. There are no tools there. What about that length of tarpaulin we've had for years and never use. With no wheelbarrow, Claudia can rake the weeds and dead growth into a pile on the canvas, then she can haul it to wherever looks the best spot for a bonfire.'

'There, you see!' Claudia proclaimed triumphantly. 'Didn't I tell you it makes no difference whether it's peas or petunias, gardening is gardening.'

Dennis's laugh was spontaneous and, hearing him, Kathie realized it was the first time she'd heard that sound since they'd lost Jess.

'I'll get the things you'll need,' she told them, as excited at the thought of the project as they were themselves. 'Can you manage them on your knee, Den? They're awkward and the tarpaulin is heavy.'

'Rubbish. If you'll get them from the shed, I'm sure I can nurse them on my lap.'

With hope in her heart she held the garden gate open for Claudia to push the chair into the lane. This was only day one and already he was starting to get into his stride. Still watching them as Claudia negotiated most of the rock-hard ruts in the unmade track, did she imagine it or did she actually hear Den laugh? What she certainly didn't imagine was just as they were about to be lost to view around a curve in the lane they met Bruce. Briefly they stopped to speak. The previous day, knowing Den was expected to arrive, Bruce hadn't been to Westways, so this was the first time she'd seen him since those stolen moments the evening before last. She had said they must forget, but how could she? If she lived to be a hundred, she wanted the memory never to fade.

'You must feel very proud, Kathie,' he greeted her as she held the gate open for him, his tone telling her that he meant to keep his word and 'forget' their brief moment of forbidden truth. 'I don't think I could accept with his sort of courage.'

'I think you could if you had Claudia to take you out to play,' Kathie laughed, acting her role. Neither of them were prepared to admit to hearing unnatural brightness in their voices.

'As you see, I'm not dressed for labouring. I just called in to tell you that I'm going away for a few days. I have an elderly uncle in Bath. Poor old boy, he lives alone with just a daily. Ethel is almost as old as he is himself and has looked after him for as long as I can remember. I usually have a few days with him during the holidays. He telephoned me yesterday and I could tell from his manner that he could do with company. You'd get on well with him, Kathie. He's over ninety but his mind is rapier sharp.'

'You'll do him a power of good, and I expect enjoy your stay every bit as much as he will.' What a game of lies this was.

'Indeed, yes. As I say, he is remarkably good company. So Dennis is going to give Claudia guidance with that overgrown patch she calls garden.'

Like an amateurishly dull game of tennis with the ball being lightly sent backwards and forwards over the net, no hard hitting, no clever shots, so the conversation continued. Only when he turned towards the gate to leave her did her control snap.

'Bruce!'

Immediately, he turned towards her. Retracing his steps, knowing they were being wrong and foolish, yet neither with willpower enough to put a brake on where they were heading. The small, enclosed porch by the front door was only feet away and instinct turned them into it. Cut off from the world, even though there were no prying eyes to see them, for one brief moment they clung to each other.

'No!' She was the first to draw away. 'We promised.'

He took her hand, a hand hardened by work on the land, and carried it to his face.

'Careful, it's as rough as sandpaper.' She tried to bring a lighter note. Her heart was thumping; she had a million butterflies in her stomach. 'Bruce… we promised, but how can we pretend? What can we do?' She wasn't crying, how could she be when there were no tears? Yet her whole body was shaking as dry, rasping sobs shook her. Tenderly he drew her into his arms.

'I know, my darling Kathie, inside I feel half dead with misery. Years and years ahead of us, making a charade of our lives. Could you play it differently? Could I?' He felt the movement against his cheek as she shook her head. 'Lying awake last night I thought of you with him, of how he must have longed to be as he used to be. I saw you lying in his arms. I even forgot his injuries as I pictured him making love to you. I'd never realized that jealousy could fill me with such hatred. Then, I felt sick with shame that I could resent a man who had lost his future – and, with Jess, so much of his past too. You are all he has.'

This time he knew she nodded.

'And I *do* love him, of course I do. Are we kicking against losing our youth? Are we pining for romance to fill our lives?'

This time his laugh was natural. 'I'm not pining for it; it seems to have taken possession of me. And as for *you*, you have a spark of eternal youth. Never let it die, Kathie.' Then holding her away from him and speaking in a matter-of-fact voice, he continued, 'I had a second reason for coming this morning. There are still three weeks before the Brockleigh term starts. I can't kick my heels at the Hall, keeping away from here as I must. So when I leave Bath I shall take a train to… to… I'm not sure, but somewhere where I can be alone and walk. I have to be back a week or so before the start of term but we *must* have some time apart, where we can't be tempted to see each other.'

She nodded. He had talked of the hopelessness of Dennis's future, but at that moment if she tried to look ahead she seemed to see nothing but years of joyless monotony.

'May Nanny continue to bring Elspeth here? You won't hold it against her that this has happened to us?' His question surprised her. In her mind there was no connection between poor childlike Elspeth and the torment of her own feelings for Bruce.

'Silly question! Of course they're welcome to come as often as they like. Beth looks on walking with Elspeth as her special prerogative.'

'Beth is an unusual child. I have watched them together, and I don't think there is anyone – anyone at all other than Beth – who can bring that look to Elspeth's face. She comes to life. Not as a woman, but with all the innocent joy of a child. Beth was lucky when she was sent into your care; but you are privileged to be her mentor.'

They faced each other as they talked, but they didn't quite let their eyes meet.

'I must get on,' she said with a too-bright smile. 'I have a market garden to run.'

'Yes.' He moved towards the entrance of the porch but stopped before he stepped out onto the front path. 'Kathie,' he said and there was no way he could keep the emotion from his voice, 'don't let us – all this – don't let it get in the way of finding the happiness you and Dennis used to know. He needs all the love you can give. What was it you said the other evening, that this is just midsummer madness.'

243

'Yes,' she said tonelessly, like an obedient child. Then, the words coming in a rush, she added, 'Bruce, don't stay away from us. Even neighbours can be friends. Den hasn't a jealous streak in him and he'd never consider even midsummer madness possible for me. Promise when you come back you'll come – I don't mean to work, you'll be busy at school – but just as a friendly neighbour.'

'He might like some male company.'

She too had moved towards the front garden and for a moment their hands met and gripped before he walked down the short path and into the lane.

–

Although Sedgewood was miles away from the dogfights which were taking place in the skies over the south east of the country, people everywhere listened to each news bulletin and despite an underlying fear for what might lie ahead, a new pride was being born. And when late in September Winston Churchill's voice was carried to every corner of the land proclaiming that 'never had so much been owed by so many to so few' there was a surge of hope. The end may be a long way off, but this was the end of the beginning. The threat of invasion had been lifted by the courage of young fighter pilots. The newspapers referred to the Battle of Britain, a battle fought and won in the skies and, coming so soon after the retreat from Dunkirk, it added steel to the people's determination.

At the start of a fresh school year in the third week of September a new working party took up the cudgels in the market garden. On the first Saturday morning of term Bruce came to introduce them to their first insight into the working world. Sally and Sarah looked on from behind the shield of runner beans; they were seventeen and considered themselves too adult to be attracted to mere schoolboys. In fact, back in June when Bert had spent much of his leave working at Westways, Sarah had brought her Brownie box camera to work with her. He had given her no encouragement, neither had she needed any. Ten years older than her, perhaps he had a girl-friend in the village. Sarah knew nothing about his life and she was young enough to find all the excitement she craved in keeping his pictures, listening to his name being mentioned and weaving her dreams around the time when another leave would bring him back to Sedgewood.

'Here, Sal,' she hissed to her friend further along the row of beans, 'look at the one talking to Mr Meredith. Bet he's outgrown his school cap! Gorgeous, isn't he.'

Sally had already noticed the good-looking dark-haired lad with the headmaster, but she wasn't going to admit to her interest, not even to Sarah.

'Hope he's as strong as he looks. That's what we need here, Sarah, someone with brawn to help with the winter digging. Mrs H'll have to use the digger like she did last year but think how rotten it'll be for him to have to sit doing nothing while she struggles with it.'

'Maybe that's what she'll set the boys to do. She won't have that much time herself, not with him to look after. She must have to do everything for him – however could she get him in a bath? If he were mine he'd have to stay dirty.'

They laughed good-naturedly, enjoying the images that sprang to mind, but not without sympathy. Then, sizing up the spoils of their labours, they decided that they had plenty to box up for the school delivery.

'Claudia's come,' Sally observed, 'but she seems to have given up helping in the garden.'

'Got a garden of her own these days. She looks so sort of posh and better than everyone else, but when you get to know her I reckon she's great. I miss having her working here, don't you?'

'Yes, she – what was it my old gran used to say about anyone who made everything seem like fun? It was something like being "a bit of God-given sunshine that warms the soul".'

'A bit mushy, but it's sort of right. See how Mr H perks up when she comes for him,' Sarah said, having a good view of the patch of grass from behind her shield of runner bean leaves. 'I wonder Mrs H doesn't feel her nose is being put out of joint.'

'Don't be a nit,' Sally laughed. 'Claudia may be a bit of God-given sunshine, but she's not likely to fall for poor Mr H. And I expect it's a relief to have him occupied for the day; it must be an awful strain on Mrs H to watch after him and work in the field too. Let's go and weigh up what we've picked and put them with the other things for the school.'

The handsome young lad with Bruce was forgotten as Kathie bore him away to initiate him and the other two who had come for the first shift into the tasks she had lined up. Claudia wandered over to say hello; Bruce went to talk to Dennis before returning to the school, then while Kathie and her team of three boys and two girls set to work, Claudia went back to Dennis.

What a relief it was to Kathie to hear them talking, even laughing. Claudia had always been a welcome visitor, but never more than now.

With autumn the weather broke, something that Kathie had been dreading. To sit outside was a thing of the past, but there were plenty of gloriously bright days. What was the magic in Claudia that made Dennis fall in with her plan that they should walk – or in his case sit – to the Boatman's Arms, an ancient inn by the River Dere. It was quite two miles away, and once out of the village there were no footpaths, but the road was smooth.

'We might get there and find it closed with a sign on the door telling us there is no beer,' Dennis warned her.

'Then we'll have enjoyed the walk anyway,' she answered cheerfully, forgetting that 'walk' was hardly an accurate description.

'Claudia, you have much better things to do with your days than push a useless hulk like me around. I feel—'

'I'm not pushing this chair just out of kindness, Den. I thought we had fun together. Stop grizzling and keep your fingers crossed that the pub's open. Which way do we go at this T-junction?'

Occasionally there would be a day when Claudia didn't come to Westways. She had other things to do – a trip to Exeter, a hairdresser appointment, a visit to the manicurist to have her nails painted, fingers and toes too. Like a lost soul Dennis would stare into space, his mouth turning down at the corners, his eyes seeing nothing. Kathie tried to arouse his interest in the work she was doing in the field, ask his opinion even though she had been managing very well without it while he was away. With a bored shrug of his shoulders he would answer her questions then pick up the newspaper and make a pretence of reading. On the days he had Claudia for company, whether in her garden, being pushed for a walk to the Boatman's Arms or playing Monopoly in the warm room his spirits were lifted and he forgot his frustrations.

That was part of the reason for Kathie's troubled conscience. The other part was less complicated but just as hard to bear. Bruce's visits were rare; sometimes he would look in on Saturdays on the pretence of seeing that the boys were helping; sometimes he would just 'happen to pass' the gate and drop in to have a few words with Den as he did around teatime on a Saturday in early December. Like Kathie, he too was troubled by conscience even though for weeks they had had no time alone. He had enormous sympathy for Den, a man who had gone to war leaving a wife and daughter and the happiness that had been so apparent at Westways, only to return crippled, with no daughter and a wife who had moved on from their old life just as surely as he had himself. How was it that Bruce was so certain Kathie and Den hadn't slotted back to the way things used to be, 'two sides of the same coin'? It was a question he didn't ask himself, for he only had to be in the same room with her to be aware that for her, as for him, what they felt had been no midsummer madness.

'How are you getting on with this year's party from the school, Kathie?' he asked her on that December Saturday.

'They're great. Clive got the mechanical digger out this morning and worked with it. It's heavy work, but he's as strong as an adult.'

Bruce nodded. 'Clive Dunster. He's head boy, you know. I have great hopes for Clive, he's a bright lad. He came to me when he was six, the youngest boarder I'd had. Now he's just eighteen. I trust by the time he comes out of university this wretched war will be over.'

His eyes met Kathie's, both of them thinking along the same lines: the war over, evacuees sent home, Brockleigh gone from the Hall.

Dennis shrugged his shoulders. 'Bloody war!'

'I must go. Young Marley was in the garden with Beth, I believe. I'll take him back with me, it'll be getting dark soon. Don't bother to see me out, Kathie, I'll use the back door and collect Marley.'

'I expect he's helping her with the chickens.'

—

They dreaded Christmas, always a time for heightened emotions. No Jess, Den so changed and with his resenting Beth's presence even more than for the rest of the year. Under Claudia's casually cheerful manner lurked a spirit more sensitive than she was prepared to show, and it was she who suggested they should spend the day with her.

'I expect I'm being selfish,' she chuckled, 'but I've ordered a turkey and I haven't a clue what I have to do with it. Will it come with its clothes on? It won't, will it? If you're there you can tell me what to do, Kathie. Please come. Bruce has promised to help me pretty the place up, I bought lots of sparkly bits when I was in Exeter.'

They agreed with no hesitation. Like Kathie and Dennis, Beth had been dreading the festival. Mr H could make everyone feel miserable without even saying a word. But if they all went to Ollie's house, and nice Mr Meredith too, it would be new and different, not like last year when they'd gone to the common to cut the holly and she had learnt about the spirit of Christmas.

Good times and bad, they all pass. Somehow they lived through that first year without Jess. Claudia had a piano but no great expertise as a pianist, so she persuaded Bruce to accompany their sing-song. Surprisingly she had quite a lot of sheet music, well known songs, some old and some new. She led the singing, performing with no more skill than she had in the repertory company but looking even lovelier than she had in those days ten years earlier. They played games, charades being the children's favourite, and somehow the day melted into history. At Claudia's suggestion, Beth stayed the night so that the others didn't have anything to hurry home for and when at last they left it was already Boxing Day. Bruce pushed the wheelchair and insisted on coming right along the lane to Westways before, by the light of the moon, he managed to see to undo the padlock, then with his pocket torch aimed at the ground, make his way through the wood and back to school.

After four months at home Den had become more independent and managed the stairs in half the time he had originally. Once he was in bed, Kathie pulled back the curtains and opened the window, then climbed in by his side.

'Didn't she do well?' she said in little more than a whisper, the effect of the silence of night. Her words carried an unspoken message. Somehow they had got through the day without Jess. The pain never got any less, and neither could they talk to each other about her.

Lying on his back Den put his arm around her, easing her towards him. She recognized that he was unsettled and read the message in his action. Tonight she had wanted to lie awake in the isolation of the dark bedroom. She wanted to remember every moment of the hours that had gone, the brief exchanged glances, the surprise of Bruce's ability on the piano. She wanted her mind to reach out to his, for he would be thinking of her just as she was of him, of that she was sure. Instead she raised herself to lie on Den, answering his need of her. Then, just as he wanted, she drew her knees up and sat straighter, so that she could guide him. Bruce, Bruce, she cried silently as she moved slowly and firmly, forcing Den deeper into her, I want this to be *you*, nearer, deeper, you, you. She kept her eyes closed cutting her off from everything but her dream of being one with Bruce.

'Quicker, Kathie, quicker, yes, yes, aahhh…' It was over, her illusion gone. Duty done, she climbed off him and lay down by his side. Dear Dennis, consciously she brought the thought to the top of her mind. She had never felt so full of self-contempt, nor yet so frightened of the future.

So the days went on. Kathie told herself she was a realist, and if when she looked into the future she could see no shape, no hope, then it had to be up to *her* to set the scene. Work was her salvation and in the early weeks of the year she threw herself into it wholeheartedly. Perhaps that was what made her so blind.

It was a day during the Easter school holiday when, working with her seedlings in the greenhouse (surely Den could have done this, some evil spirit whispered to her) she heard an unfamiliar sound. Raising her head she listened again. Beth and Ollie were at the Hall where Bruce had given them permission to play during the school break. Anyway, this wasn't a child's cry, it was a woman, a woman who was being swept along on a tide of despair.

Following the sound, Kathie found the girls at the far end of the field. Sally was sitting on the stile, bent forward so that her head was almost on her knees, her whole body twitching and shaking as she pressed her clenched fists against her face as if that way she could force her out-of-control outburst into silence. In front of her knelt Sarah, and whatever it was she was saying was lost to Kathie who could hear nothing above the wild hysteria. Glancing helplessly at Sarah, she too dropped to her knees pulling the shaking body into her arms.

'Whatever is it, Sally? Nothing can be *that* bad. Come on, love, tell me. Whatever it is, we'll sort it out.'

'Can't sort it out. Oh Mrs H, I don't knows what to do. Mum's found out. And I can't do what they say. I won't!'

To Kathie it made no sense. 'Start from the beginning, Sally.'

Making a huge effort and accompanied by spasmodic snorts and gulps, and a quick glance at Sarah who nodded her silent reply, Sally began at the beginning.

'Right from the first Saturday he worked here, Clive and I have been going out when he's free. Lately it's been more that just "going out". It just seemed to happen, Mrs H. When we were walking ages ago, back in the autumn it was, we found an old barn on the lane going down to the river. There was never anyone there, no tools in it or animals or anything, just a pile of old straw. We went in to shelter when it suddenly rained. Then when the days got colder that's where we went. It was sort of *our* place. We just talked most of the time. You don't really know him, Mrs H, but if you could hear him, the things he believes, the things he means to do with his life, then you'd understand. I'd never talked to anyone like him. I hated the Christmas holidays when he wasn't at the Hall and he said he felt just the same.'

'You fell in love with him. And does he feel the same about you?' But they were hardly more than children. And what would this sort of trouble do to his school leaving exams?

'Yes, yes of course he does. That's how it all happened. Mum's been watching me, then yesterday she asked me straight out why I was late, if I'd been doing anything I shouldn't.' It was hard to understand her words as her crying took control again. 'What we did was right, it wasn't dirty and beastly like they said. Called me a whore, a child of Satan, and Clive too. Said I had to go away till my baby gets born – they'll tell lies that I've got a job somewhere – then I have to have it adopted. I won't! It's mine and Clive's.'

'They've told her that unless she does as they say they will finish with her,' Sarah took up the tale. 'They say they can't stay in Sedgewood become of the shame.'

'They're going to stay with Uncle Matt and Aunt Ivy. They lost Gerry, their son, trying to get home from France. They want Dad and Mum there. Would have gone before except for the chapel and all Dad does there. Now I've spoilt all that for them. But I won't do what they say. They can't make me. I want our baby.'

'And Clive wants it too?'

'Of course he does. He's asking his people to write permission for him to get married – when the exams are over. I asked Dad and he nearly went mad.'

'There's no one indoors, love. Claudia's taken Den to help her with her garden. Go and wash your face and leave me to go and talk to them.'

'They won't listen, Mrs H. And I don't care. I couldn't get big and fat with them looking at me as if I'd done something dirty. Don't know what to do.'

Taking herself by surprise Kathie kissed the girl's wet cheek.

'You're Mrs Hawthorne, aren't you,' Ewart Brent greeted Kathie when he opened the door to her knock. 'I suppose you've heard the disgusting way they've behaved. It's no use your looking to us to sort her out.' Not an auspicious opening to the interview.

'It must have been a shock for you, but if we all help them it needn't be a calamity. And honestly have they done anything that we wouldn't have when we were between the innocence of childhood and being in love for the first time?' Kathie was rather pleased with her reply, it told them that she knew the situation and at the same time showed that she understood.

'How dare you insinuate such things!'

'I dare because you're her parents and you love her. Surely love overrides convention – it does in my book anyway.'

'Then, madam, I suggest you change your reading. The good book lays down strict rules and if the world obeyed them it would be a better place.'

'Yes,' she agreed, 'of course it would. But I thought ours was a god of love – love between parents and children which lasts a lifetime, love between a man and woman which, when you first experience it is a… is a… soul-consuming emotion.'

'Madam, you forget yourself. I will not be preached at by a woman who condones their shameful behaviour.'

'They are children,' Mrs Brent interjected, 'a nasty, smutty boy fumbling, exploring…'

'He is a fine young man. Mr Meredith, the headmaster of Brockleigh School, is a friend of ours and he has talked of Clive, the head boy, with enormous admiration. Home for his school holiday he is getting his parents' consent to his marrying at the end of next term.' She momentarily crossed her fingers for luck as she said it. 'Can't you give the same consent to Sally? Think of the joy of having a grandchild to love.'

'We're not interested.' Ewart Brent didn't mean to be preached at by this gypsy-looking woman in her workman's overalls (for Dennis's old trousers had at last given up the ghost). 'The girl seems to have no conception what her condition would do to us if she were to stay in Sedgewood. If you want to do something to ease the situation, then I suggest you use your influence to persuade her to do as we say.'

'I can't do that. Imagine, Mrs Brent, if you were carrying a child, even if you'd conceived before you were married, that child is part of you, part of you and part of the man you love. Could you go through all those months, feel its first movements in your womb—'

'Enough!' Ewart Bert blustered. 'Where's your sense of decorum, madam? There are some things one doesn't discuss. Perhaps it's *your* influence that has done this to the girl. Love, you say! As if love has to be expressed by… by… by…' He found it difficult even to say the words 'sexual gratification'. 'Just to say the words fills me with shame. We've given her every chance. If she does as we say and has a few months away, hands the child over for adoption, and humbly prays for forgiveness, then we are prepared for her to come home.'

'That's your final word? And you, Mrs Brent?'

'Of course that's the wise thing to do and we'd look to you not to spread the word in the village. But Ewart and I have talked for most of the night and we have made our minds up. If she refuses to do as we say, we shall have to move right away. I won't, no, I will *not* have Ewart's position jeopardized in the village. He is thought very highly of, and so he should be. To leave Sedgewood is a sacrifice for both of us, but it's what she has done to us with her dirty, immoral ways. No schoolboy is going to let a romp on the hay cast a long shadow over his life, especially a boy with good prospects. We've told her just what she is letting herself in for, but she is stubborn as a mule – and has no thought for her parents or what this will do to them.'

It seemed hopeless. Anger, disappointment, hurt, these things Kathie could understand, but this cold laying down of rules – rules that didn't consider Sally's feelings – put an unbridgeable distance between them.

'We're going round in circles,' she said. 'I'm sorry you take the unsympathetic attitude you do. But just in case once you settle in your new surroundings you have a change of heart—'

'Never!' Ewart thumped his fist on the table. 'It's not easy to live by the commandments from on high, but ours is not supposed to be an easy path. Never, never will we condone her sin. That you even suggest it tells me the sort of woman you are.'

'If you want to drive her away, at least write a letter of consent to her marriage.'

'Woman, are you deaf or stupid? To do that is tantamount to forgiving the sin.'

Kathie turned and left them, slamming the front door behind her. She found herself shaking with anger and frustration.

Instead of going straight home she went to the Hall where she was told that Bruce was in Exeter and wouldn't be back until after lunch.

That evening just as she was clearing away their meal, there came a loud knocking at the door that pushed everything else from her mind. It must be Bruce; occasionally he came in to sit with Dennis who was so deprived of male company.

'I'll get it, Auntie Kathie,' and Beth was already halfway across the passage. Kathie listened for the voice she wanted to hear.

'Beth, can you get Mrs H. I've got to speak to her.' Hearing Sally's words Kathie knew what the next step must be.

'Den,' she whispered urgently, 'I'll explain everything later. But please, *please* trust me and be kind to Sally.'

'I've no idea what you're talking about, but whatever it is you'll have your own way.' Today had not been good. Claudia had spent it in Exeter having her hair done, her hands and feet manicured, her perfect teeth checked and trying on numerous skirts before finally deciding that none were worth using precious clothing coupons for.

Although Dennis's reply irritated Kathie, she was touched by his expression of forlorn hopelessness. Leaning over the back of his chair as she passed him on her way to the passage, she rubbed her cheek against his. 'Good chap. I can't explain till we're on our own, but you'd do just the same as I would.'

'Makes no difference whether I would or I wouldn't. Go and see what that girl of yours wants.'

'You old grouch!' She forced a light note into her voice as she ruffled his hair. Then her mask of light-heartedness dropped.

Nine

'Sally, come inside. Yes, bring your case. Beth, love, can you finish drying the dishes for me and put them away.'

Something was afoot and Beth would much rather have stayed to hear why Sally had a big case with her. Was she going away?

'Is that girl still here?' Dennis asked her as she hurried through the warm room to the kitchen. 'Did she say what she wanted at this time of the evening?'

'No. But she has a huge case with her. They've gone into the sitting room.'

The minutes ticked by. Beth dried the dishes then put everything away. Wanting to give Kathie a pleasant surprise she even made a valiant effort at cleaning the sink; or was she just killing time rather than go back and wait with Mr H who, even after all these months, made her feel uncomfortable? If only he wasn't sitting and staring at nothing in the warm room she would creep through and listen in the passage outside the sitting room.

She was rescued by Kathie's voice calling, 'Beth, can you come here a second.' She hurried past Dennis, but he seemed not to notice. 'Beth, shut the door love. Now listen...'

A minute or two later, as the girls bumped their way up the narrow stairs with the suitcase Kathie went back to Den. 'Now I can tell you. Don't say a word, Den, just listen and you'll feel the same as I do, I *know* you will.'

So she told him the story.

'We have to help her. She can't get married, her parents are adamant they won't give their consent, even if Clive's approve. And that dreadful father of hers sees himself as a Christian!'

'This is fast becoming a home for waifs and strays. There's no alternative; I can see that. You have a responsibility; they both worked for you and you were too wrapped up in your own affairs to see what was happening.'

She couldn't have been more surprised if he'd struck her, but at least he was in agreement that they must take Sally in.

'Once we've got a second-hand bed she can use the sitting room,' Kathie planned.

Clearly that was a step too far. 'Let her stay with Beth, keep all your do-gooding in one room.'

She pretended he had made a joke and managed to laugh.

'Imagine what I was like when I was expecting Jess,' she reminded him. 'The pennies I had to spend in the night.'

'Don't!' He pulled back from her. 'Don't bring Jess into this. I still say, pregnant or otherwise, if we have a responsibility to house her it shouldn't mean we have to ruin our home.' Fortunately at that second there was another knock at the front door.

'I'll go,' she said, getting up from her knees, 'Sally and Beth are upstairs.'

With her head held high and her shoulders squared ready to do battle she opened the door expecting the caller to be either one or both of Sally's parents. Relief and joy swept through her as she faced Bruce.

'I've only just been told that you called while I was in Exeter.'

'I have to talk to you. Thank goodness you've come; you'll know what to do.'

'Kathie.' He gripped both her hands in his, speaking so softly she could scarcely hear him. 'Is something wrong?'

'Not with us. But you're as involved as we are. Come inside and I'll tell you the whole story.'

In the warm room Dennis greeted him with something akin to pleasure, smiling for what Kathie was sure was the first time that day.

So Kathie told Bruce all she knew, while he listened with no more than the occasional nod. 'Her parents are the most bigoted and sanctimonious couple I've ever had the misfortune to meet.'

'They are her parents and they must be very hurt by what has happened.'

'It hurts a lot of people,' was Dennis's opinion, 'her parents, his parents, the boy's future, to say nothing of the unborn child.'

'To my mind,' Kathie said, 'it isn't for any of us to condemn. Whatever happened it came from a natural and innocent first love. We *have* to give them both all the support they're going to need.'

She was conscious of Bruce watching her.

'Amen to that,' he said. 'You realize I can't have Dunster back as head boy of Brockleigh next term? I shall phone his home this evening and hope to visit them tomorrow.' Kathie gripped her hands behind her back while every instinct was to reach out to him. She knew just how much he cared for Clive Dunster, a boy he'd guided with pride for a decade.

The odd-job man employed at the hall by Brockleigh School arrived pushing a cart on which was a single bed, a small wardrobe and a bedside table. He'd been instructed by the headmaster to help Mrs Hawthorne get the room ready for a visitor.

On the first day of term Bruce announced at assembly that for family reasons Clive Dunster would not be returning to school and the head boy's responsibilities would therefore be taken by the deputy. So after a successful twelve years at Brockleigh, Clive's name was painted out of the head boy's panel in the assembly hall and life went on as if he had played no part in it. But not for Bruce. Twice a week he posted a large envelope to the pupil for whom he had had such high hopes – and genuine affection too – keeping him abreast with his work, helping him with revision and finally with arrangements where he should sit his examination. Clive's work was returned promptly – and always at the same time he posted a second envelope addressed to Miss S. Brent, Westways. Not even to Sarah did Sally divulge what he wrote or what his true feelings were about his changed life.

Dennis had been back at Westways for almost a year on the day that Bruce brought news that Clive Dunster had gained his Higher School Certificate with a credit.

'I spoke to him on the telephone – to him and to his father. Cambridge was always his ambition but it seems he has already volunteered for the army. He's had his medical and expects his papers any day.'

To know he was at home studying for his exams was one thing; for him to be in the army quite another. To Kathie, it seemed a far cry from the boy who'd worked so hard in the garden on Saturday mornings. Was that how Sally felt too? Her expression gave nothing away as she left the others gathered on the small grassy patch in the evening sunlight.

'I must write and congratulate him,' she told them as she left them. There was a new reserve about her.

As Clive went through his initial training his letters still came, but less regularly.

–

'What's going to happen to them, Den?' Kathie said one evening in September. 'Another few weeks and the baby will be here. Suppose he lets her down.'

'Well, baby or no baby they can't marry. And God knows what his future will be – if the poor devil even has a future.' Then, folding his unread newspaper, he added, 'Kathie, I have to talk to you.'

Lately he'd seemed to have retreated even further into himself. Now his 'I have to talk to you' gave her a great surge of hope. Was he at last going to break down the wall of misery that seemed to cut him off from her and from everything that went on at Westways? More and more she was thankful when Claudia arrived to take him to 'help' her in her garden; only then did she see any sign of the pre-war Den. It was because there, with long-handled tools and the wide smooth paths for his chair he felt he played a useful role. Eager to hear what he had to say, Kathie stopped chopping the vegetables for tomorrow's lunchtime soup, washed her hands and pulled a chair nearer to his. Looking at him she expected something in his expression to tell her what was on his mind, but he seemed distant, almost frightened.

'We can't live like this. Perhaps you can, you have a full life, people depending on you. I have nothing. As long as we stay in this place I have nothing but reminders of what I've lost. I'm giving notice; we'll leave Westways. After the value we've added by the work we've had done, they ought not to hold us to three months' notice.'

'Leave Westways! And where do you think you'll suddenly find everything changed and easy? I know that sounds hard, but the grass isn't going to be greener somewhere else. We all work together—'

'*You* do. I don't. I want to get away, away from Sedgewood.'

'No!' Something in her snapped. Away from Sedgewood… away from Bruce.

Fear fuelled her pent up anger. 'You could do lots of things if you wanted to.' At her change of tone he looked at her in amazement. 'What do you do when you go to Claudia's? Do you sit all day feeling sorry for yourself? Of course you don't. You could look after the greenhouse; you could have mended the latch on the garden gate last week. But did you? No, you left it to me.' She felt tears welling up. She mustn't cry; she *wouldn't* cry. She'd tried so hard to give his life a purpose, but it was as if he was frightened to have anything to do with the old life.

'Kathie, I can't live as we are. Here, I am nothing.' He started to bluster. 'A few more weeks and that girl will be draping her illegitimate brat's nappies and God knows what to air on the fireguard. Whose home is it? Ours or hers? She must find somewhere else. And Beth must be given another billet. We shall leave here, get right away, somewhere new.'

'If *I* can't make you think differently, what about Claudia? It's been good for you to spend so much time helping her, but what about her? She needs to feel wanted; you have been as good for her as she has for you. She'd be lost if we went. You can't expect us to drop her as if friends don't count.'

'For Christ's sake, Kathie, how blind can you get? Don't you ever see what's going on before you? If we have any chance, we have to move right away.'

'I don't understand.' She saw how his hand was shaking as he lit a cigarette. 'You might offer me one of those.'

He passed her the packet and the matches, leaving her to take one and light it herself.

'Kathie, oh hell, Kathie I'm sorry. It just happened, I don't know when or how. Just when I thought I'd never know what it was like to enjoy being alive, I found myself looking forward to her arriving to take me to her garden, or sometimes just to play silly childish games here while you were running the show out there. But Kathie, marriage is important; we can't throw it away like changing a job. So that's why I want us to get away, somewhere new, away from your lame ducks, away from Sedgewood – and away from Claudia. If you agree, that will give me the… the *guts* to do what I know is the right thing.'

For a long moment Kathie said nothing while he watched her and waited, unable to guess where her thoughts were carrying her.

'How does she feel? She and I have been good friends. Yet I had no idea.'

'You sound very calm.'

'Answer my question, Den. Does Claudia feel the same as you do or are you just dreaming dreams?'

'What's the point of answering your question? I can't walk away from our marriage. But yes, Claudia feels just as I do. Here I am, lamer than any of your ducks, yet she wants to spend the rest of her life with me. In marrying again she'd lose her alimony, but it seems she sees me as worth that.'

'And Ollie?'

'The kid? Oh, kids get used to things.'

Kathie seemed to stand outside herself as plans started to take shape in her mind. He watched her, knowing her so well he recognized she was working something out.

'I shall stay at Westways,' she said, speaking with no emotion and leaving him in no doubt. 'You say I'm blind, but I'm not so blind that I don't realize you won't try to do things here because deep down you are unhappy; you're frightened to hold on to the past. Our marriage is over. It has to be. Even if I agreed and we went somewhere else, what we had is gone. I want you to arrange for the lease to be transferred to my name. I shall carry on here.'

'I can't believe it, Kathie. I've been putting off talking to you for weeks – months. You seem so calm.'

'I may be calm, but I'm not soft. We used to be so happy here – but nothing is the same, nothing can ever be the same. It's as if we're different people…'

'We've got to look to the future,' he cut in.

'The past is precious too; it's the one thing no one can ever take from us. If you can't hold on to memories, then you get frightened and bitter. Don't let that happen, Den. We're not the same people we used to be when we were young, full of hope. And then the joy of our darling Jess—'

'Don't, Kathie!'

'Take her with you into your second chance; take memories of our good years. If you don't – I wish I could think of the right words – if you shut part of your life away and are frightened to remember the good things, then you won't be *whole*. Claudia has a past too, we all

have. We are what we are today because of our yesterdays.'
She stood up, seeming to put an end to the conversation.
'I must finish getting the soup ready. I'll move in with
Beth tonight.'

'You don't have to do that. I won't—'

'Oh for Gods sake, Den!'

From the kitchen she heard him making his slow
progress upstairs. She knew just what she meant to do
– what she *had* to do. So from the open door of the
warm room she listened for the clump of his crutches
on the landing and finally the closing of the bedroom
door. There was finality in the sound. Could this really
be happening to them? 'I love Den, I'll always love Den'
came the echo of her words. Were they true? Yes, even
now – and always – she knew she would love him. He
was part of every haunting memory. It seemed a lifetime
ago when she'd found Jess crying on the night he went
away. 'I want to say goodnight to Dad.' She must never
let those memories of Jess fade, and Den was part of every
one of them. But it was all past, gone as surely as snow in
sunshine.

Picking up the telephone receiver she waited for the
operator then asked for Sedgewood 172.

'Bruce?'

'Kathie, something's wrong! Kathie, what is it?'

'Not wrong, Bruce. I think it had to happen. I can't
tell you on the phone. Can you come through the woods
and I'll meet you by the gate.'

He was there ahead of her, waiting outside the gate in
the lane. It was a moonless night but after two years of
blackout their eyes had become used to adjusting. When
she saw the outline of his body she ran towards him and
found herself held in a close embrace.

'Tell me, darling.'

'Den is leaving me.'

'Claudia? Yes, of course, Claudia.' He couldn't have said anything that surprised her more.

'Has she talked to you? How did you find out?'

'No one has talked to me. I've seen the change in Claudia. To begin with it was because she fell under the spell of Westways, but latterly it has been more than that. I believe she truly loves him. But it's not them I care about; it's you.'

'He wants to be free to marry her. Bruce, I'm ashamed. All the years – such *good* years before the war – and all I can think of is that I've been given my life back. He says we must look to the future.'

'Years ago, I was told that because of Elspeth's irreversible mental state I could get my freedom. I couldn't do it then – I had no reason to want to – and Kathie, my darling precious Kathie, I can't do it now.'

'And if you could, you wouldn't be the man I love. Elspeth needs you even if she doesn't realize it.'

'And you?' he asked softly, knowing the answer.

'Oh yes, I need you. I know we can't marry, but Bruce love isn't confined to those who have a certificate to make their union legal. You once told me that when you fell in love with Elspeth you were young and inexperienced, but you and I are—'

'Moulded of the same clay,' he finished the sentence. 'Perhaps I could better liken us to tempered steel. We know about sadness, pain, loss, they are woven into what we feel for each other. Darling,' he whispered, and she knew the moment was something that would stay with her always, 'I can't offer you marriage, but I give you my undying love.'

'I know and you have mine. I love you with my mind and spirit, but Bruce that can't be enough.' In the near darkness he could just see her face was raised to his, her lips parted as his mouth covered hers. Her heart was pounding, every nerve in her body was crying out for his touch. What a moment for her to think of that mountain she had so often strained to climb and so seldom reached the summit. Now, she was almost to the peak as she stood with her body pressed tightly to his. One day she'd tell him about that mountain; somehow, somewhere, they would climb it together.

—

'Kathie, I didn't mean it to happen,' Claudia said as, the next morning, she approached where Kathie was working at the far end of the field. 'You won't want even to look at me after what I've done. It sounds so feeble to say it just happened.'

'If he had to fall for someone, I wish it hadn't been you. It must make things different for you and me, and that's a pity. Already we're different, guarded.'

'I feel such a heel.'

'That'll pass,' Kathie said with a laugh that held no humour. 'I must get on, I'm short of workers. There used to be a lady in red wellies.' Then, stopping work and leaning on her hoe, she added, 'Claudia, are you truly prepared to give up your comfortable lifestyle, your good income?'

Life would be very different for Claudia Marley, the glamorous 'stuck-up bit' as some of the villagers still thought of her. But they didn't know her. Living comfortably on more than enough alimony to finance her lifestyle in London, let alone in Devon, with a house bought for her by her ex-husband so that she would be near Oliver's school, the changes made the future look bleak. But bleak wasn't a word in Claudia's dictionary.

'I've never been so sure of anything, Kathie,' she answered. 'You know what I've learnt these last months? The most important thing isn't to be comfortable and worry-free. It's to matter, really *matter* to someone – and to care about that person more than you do about yourself. Doesn't that sound mushy,' she said with a laugh, suddenly embarrassed, 'and fancy having the cheek to say it to you of all people.'

Kathie shook her head. 'You've taught him to laugh again. Only when he's with you, I admit, but it's more than I could do. But Claudia, what you and Den are doing is right, right for Den and right for me. We couldn't have gone on as we were, we're different people. None of it would have happened if Jess were still here.'

'Well, Oliver's a good enough kid, but I'm damned if I'm going to run my life to please him. He's a funny lad; I've never told him about Den and me – well of course I haven't; until today there has been nothing to tell – but he knows jolly well what's going on. And he's really got the hump. Well, he'll just have to put up with it. I say, Kathie, you won't mind me poking around in your bedroom, will you? I've promised Den I'll help him shift his stuff.' Then with a mischievous twinkle, she continued, 'And please ma'am, may I borrow the delivery van? We can't walk down the High Street with his luggage on his lap. All his worldly goods.'

How it brought back memories: Kathie seeing him off at the end of his disastrous embarkation leave, all his worldly goods in that kitbag bearing his name and number. For them, the change had started even then.

'Of course you can. Bring it back in time for Hopkins' run though, won't you.'

She was glad when Claudia left her. She ought to be distraught, her husband of nearly twenty years, dear Den who had been her life, was leaving her for another woman. The thought suddenly came to her: was he perhaps not as blind as she had been? Had he seen what was happening to Bruce and her? Then her mind was cleared of all thoughts of Den and Claudia too; her imagination leapt ahead to the evening to come. She was leaving Sally and Beth and going out to dinner with Bruce. And after that?

–

She had nothing suitable to wear. The dress she looked on as best and had worn last Christmas at Claudia's would have to do. But she took extra care getting ready, bathing, washing her hair, putting on her best underwear and finally the cherry coloured dress. She looked at her work-worn hands, by contrast imagining Claudia's, and was ashamed.

Bruce collected her in a taxi and they were taken to the Pendragon Hotel on Picton Heath near Deremouth. She realized that never in her thirty-eight years had she dined in a hotel. The evening had all the ingredients of magic. Then, having asked for a taxi to be called, they drove back to Sedgewood Hall and to the wing known as the Headmaster's Lodge. With the door locked and the blackout curtains securely closed, the world was their own. He put records on the radiogram, a modern machine powered by electricity and set so that one record would follow another. The volume was low, no more than a background to what they both knew was ahead.

In the bedroom item by item they undressed, she taking off his clothes, he taking off hers, just as she'd dreamed. There was no wild tearing off of garments; what they did had the quality of a religious ceremony, until finally they stood naked in front of each other. That was when she caught sight of herself in the mirror on his mahogany wardrobe.

Instinctively she folded her arms across her thin and sagging breasts. Gently, he moved them, holding her hands to her side.

'Wish I was different. I wish I was beautiful for you.'

Suddenly his Adam's apple seemed to have doubled in size.

'Kathie, my precious Kathie, you are just as I dreamed you would be, just as I've longed to see, to touch. I can't marry you, but I can't think of my life without you. No church, no one to hear our vows and bind us legally, but I promise with all my heart that I am to love you and be faithful just to you for the rest of my life.'

'I promise too, for the rest of my life and when my body is old and dies, then for all eternity.' She knew about these things. As she was drawn almost reverently into his arms she seemed to hear that piping childish voice, 'Tell you what, Mum – you're going to be ever so happy. He's nice and he knows about things.'

Later, lying in his arms, she thought of those words. At the mountain top she had found joy and fulfilment she had never known possible.

–

'Mother is leaving Sedgewood – Mother and… and him,' Oliver told Kathie a week or two after Den had moved in with Claudia. 'She… they—' the way he said it made Kathie look at him anxiously— 'they are going to live in Hampshire. She says I shall like the house they've found. I won't; I'll *hate* it. We were fine with things like they were, her helping you here, me coming as if – well, as if we were all sort of one family. I don't want to go there, Mrs H. She can't make me, can she?'

'She might be very hurt if she thought you didn't want to.'

'Not likely, she wouldn't,' he said with an unchildlike sneer in his voice. 'I don't care what she does,' he tried to convince himself as well as Kathie, 'except that if she wanted to steal someone else's husband, she ought not to have taken yours.' His view was firm and Kathie was trying to think of something to say that would lessen his hurt, when he went on: 'I told her when she came to school to say goodbye. And I said I wanted to write to Dad but didn't know where he lived. She didn't like it, I could see she was angry. But she wrote down his address. And I wrote to him. So there!'

'Is someone buying her house?' Kathie changed the subject.

'She has people coming to live in it. Pleased as anything she was because it means she will have some money from the rent they pay and the house is still hers.'

It wasn't Kathie's responsibility to worry but how would Claudia cope with having so little money? Den had a pension, she had the rent of the house, but once she and Den were married her alimony would be cut leaving just enough that Oliver wouldn't suffer. But it seemed Oliver wanted nothing to do with them.

'I've finished the chickens,' Beth shouted. 'All right if we go to the common, Aunt Kathie?'

And just as always, Kathie told them, 'Yes of course. Listen for the clock to strike twelve.'

–

'It must be something to do with the work here,' Kathie said laughingly to Sally, 'you look positively blooming.'

'I'm getting as big as a house, but I feel sort of – oh, I don't know Mrs H – bountiful. Is that silly?'

'It's wonderful. But, Sal, it's time you did less. Another six weeks and you'll be a mother. The lad who rides the delivery bike for Jack Hopkins is coming in for a few hours each day and I've had a letter from Bert Delbridge saying he wants to help out when he's on leave in three week's time.'

Sally chuckled. 'Bet Sarah's chuffed. Do you reckon that's why he wants to spend his leave here Mrs H?'

The suggestion came as a surprise to Kathie. But hadn't Den told her she must be blind and never looked beyond her own affairs!

–

On the 1st November Sally had a son. It was Bruce who went to Deremouth to register the birth: Steven Clive Dunster, son of Sally Muriel Brent and Clive Anthony Dunster. He was born at Westways, a home with freedom for anytime visitors; but apart from those who lived in the house there were few to come and admire the new arrival. Sarah came at every available moment, Bruce came, Nanny Giles even brought Elspeth but the baby didn't attract her interest. It was some weeks before Clive knew he had a son, for on the 1st November he was already on the high seas, destination unknown.

History was repeating itself as Steven's pram was put on the grass for him to sleep when he was very tiny; then as he grew strong enough to be propped on his pillows he liked to be wheeled to where the action was taking place; from that stage it seemed no time before he was staggering after the workers with his seaside spade, wanting to help. Sometimes Kathie drew comfort from seeing him following the pattern set by Jess; sometimes it hurt unbearably.

When word first got around that Dennis had walked out on her for 'that Marley woman', the gossips enjoyed the excitement. But soon the waters closed over the incident and Kathie probably gained a little unmerited respect for carrying on with no visible self-pity. Nanny Giles continued to bring Elspeth to Westways; Oliver spent every available hour there and even persuaded Claudia that he could stay at school for part of his holidays and spend each day 'helping' in the market garden. School holiday times were very special; there was plenty of work for everyone, and that included Bruce and Oliver.

'I had a letter from my father this week,' Oliver would sometimes say with pride when he arrived on Saturday morning. Kathie had worried when the child had first written to his matinee idol father, fearful that Richard would be as casual as Claudia always had been. But she was wrong. Letters came regularly and between father and son a bond was developing that was to shape Oliver's life.

Nanny Giles loved Elspeth as if she were her own, but that didn't mean she had no sympathy for Bruce. She was a wise woman and one who missed very little so, whilst in the village Kathie was looked on as a hard-working woman whose husband had left her after she'd given him her best years, Nanny saw deeper. If Bruce and Kathie cared for each other, then it was no more than he deserved and each night when she knelt at her bedside and prayed that her darling Elspeth should always be happy, she added a rider that the love between Bruce and Kathie would find favour.

'Have they suggested at school that Beth tries for a scholarship for Deremouth Grammar?' Bruce asked Kathie as he carried a box of runner beans into the shed for her to weigh. It was early summer of 1943. By the end of the year Beth would be ten.

'Isn't it too soon?'

'Too soon for the exam, but not for her to be primed for it. If she likes to come up to me, say a couple of evenings a week we could work together. I have enormous hopes for her.'

'Bruce, you know we talked once about me persuading Den to see if we could adopt her. It's not Den now; it's you.'

'I don't think the adoption society would see it like that. In their eyes my presence in your life would be decidedly detrimental.'

She frowned, realizing that what he said was true. If hard and fast rules had to be adhered to, then the last months of her marriage to Den would have presented a better chance of adopting Beth than putting her in the care of a divorcee with a lover. Hard and fast rules be damned!

'I shall go to see this Tilly woman and see if I can get her to give her permission.'

'It's half term next weekend. I'll come with you. With Sally here, we could stay in town for the night.'

She nodded, her dark eyes saying more than any words.

That same day, just as she often did, after she'd taken her daily delivery to Jack Hopkins she drove on up the hill to the lodge to spend a few minutes with Nanny Giles.

'I'm going to visit Beth's old home on Saturday.'

'That woman! Not fit to care for a dog, let alone a child. Mr Bruce has talked to me about it. He's really fond of that child – well, how can you help it? Breaks your heart to think when peace comes she'll be sent back. Bad enough for the poor mite when she'd seen no other way of living, but how can she slot back now after all this time in a home with love?'

'That's why I'm going. She belongs here with all of us. Bruce is coming with me. We shall be home on Sunday.' Her words seemed to fill the room and she waited, unsure of what Nanny would read into them.

'Ah. Well, my dear, you won't need a ration book for a night's lodging, but just in case you get asked for your identity card it's best you pop little Elspeth's in your bag. We don't want to throw a spanner in the works just when you hope to be able to take Beth as your own.'

For Kathie it was one of those moments that would stay with her. Her eyes stung with tears, not of sadness but of a nameless emotion that prompted her to take the elderly hand and carry it to her lips.

'Nanny, I truly love him…'

'I know that, my dear, or I'd not give you my little one's card. And he loves you too. I don't need telling. How long are you willing to live as you do now?'

'Divorce, you mean. He will *never* do that. Even if she can't know, he would never do it. And I wouldn't want him to. She's more than a duty to him – but I don't have to tell you that. He once told me that sitting with her, knowing her contentment, he finds peace.'

'Well, if ever a man deserved it, it's him.' Then turning to Elspeth, she said, 'Now then, duckie, I'm going to get you your tea. How about a nice toasted muffin with some honey? She likes that, bless her, she always did even as a child. I'll just run and get that card for you.'

–

To Kathie, London was another world. She hated to feel out of her depth with any challenge, but she admitted to herself that she was glad Bruce was with her and seemed to understand the routes of the tube trains. Just as she was glad he was with her as she confronted Tilly, who wasn't a bit what she had expected. She had imagined a young woman, over made-up, smelling of cheap perfume, dressed in a way that advertised her profession. In fact she was older than Kathie, with teeth stained yellow from cigarettes, with badly kept nails where one coat of varnish had covered the last probably for years. Over-weight, wearing clothes that were too tight and with laddered stockings, it was hard to imagine any man paying for her favours. The only odour that came from her was from her unwashed body.

Please God, don't make Beth have to come home to this! Kathie's glance locked with Bruce's and she knew his thought was the same as hers.

Tilly listened to all they had to say.

'Well,' she observed thoughtfully, 'tell the honest to God truth I'd as good as forgotten the kid. More likely tried not to remember. Funny kid she was too. And you want to hang on to her? Bugger me, that's a turn up for the books. Here, have a fag.' She pushed the half empty packet across the table.

'Kind of you,' Bruce answered, 'but they're hard enough to come by without handing them around. I am not Mrs Hawthorne's husband, I am headmaster of a neighbouring school and have really come to give you reassurance. At Westways, where Beth is living, she is well cared for, loved and extremely happy. When this war ends there will be many children who've been away from home so long that they will find difficulty in adjusting. I foresee a lot of unhappy homes as a consequence. If you are prepared to let Beth stay where she has settled you would be doing her a great kindness. To look back to 1939 is like looking to another world.'

'Ah, buggered if it isn't. And when this lot ends and the blokes go home, what's to become of poor sods like me. Ain't getting any younger. Some of us, the young ones with a bit of the Hollywood look about them, they make a good living. But not everyone can pay their prices. But like I've always said, you don't look at the mantelpiece when you poke the fire.'

'So what do you say about Beth,' Kathie prompted, expecting that Tilly was softening her up for a financial arrangement.

'Never wanted the kid, well of course I didn't. And she was a funny one, like I said before. If you know how to set about getting it all legal, then I say good luck to you. I don't expect she remembers much about me and, like I said, I'd as good as forgotten her. I don't wish the child no harm, but bugger me, the last thing I want is some prissy miss coming back 'ere.'

So with not a penny exchanged, the wheels were set in motion. Of course there were formalities and a visit from a representative from the department responsible, a prim and humourless woman.

278

'You say you are in charge of this market garden?'

'Before the war my husband and I ran it together. But he was in the Territorial Army so, of course, as soon as the war started he had to go. Since then I've coped. It was hard going at first, but I'm lucky and everyone who works here seems part of one team. Right from her first day Beth wanted to help. She and Jess, my daughter, were the same age. They looked after feeding the chickens and collecting the eggs.' Looking back and picturing the scene Kathie had walked straight into the unforeseen trap.

'Were? Were the same age? Where is your daughter now?' Officialdom smelt a rat.

'Jess was killed in a road accident.' Kathie wished she had never mentioned her; she hated discussing her with this unsmiling creature.

'How sad,' and a note was made on her pad. 'Well, I think that will be all, Mrs Hawthorne. I've seen for myself that the child is well cared for here. You will be hearing.'

It was a month before the official papers came with confirmation of the adoption. Brockleigh had already broken up for the long summer vacation but Oliver had been allowed to stay for the holiday.

'After all, he's heir apparent to Sedgewood so he might as well get used to the miserable great morgue of a place when it's not full of noisy boys,' Claudia had said laughingly to Den. The arrangement suited him perfectly. Den sometimes wished that Kathie could see how well he was doing. Their rented bungalow was convenient, he could move about independently. And outside he and Claudia had transformed yet another wilderness.

On the morning the official document arrived the post lady was late and Beth had already gone to school. Bruce and Oliver walked down at about ten o'clock prepared for a day's work and at twelve years old the boy had become an asset to Westways. Bruce would never make a natural gardener, but no job was beneath him. On that day Bert Delbridge was home on seven days' leave and by that time even Kathie – blind to everyone's affairs but her own, as Den would have said – knew who it was attracted him. It was two months since his last forty-eight-hour pass, the weekend when he and Sarah had gone shopping for an engagement ring. Yes, the workers in the field at Westways had much to be grateful for on that July morning, not least for Steven who staggered after his mother waving his seaside spade.

Kathie and Bruce said nothing about the document which had arrived that morning, but he walked to the village to see what it had to offer by way of making a teatime celebration. The best he could find was lemonade, biscuits (for which he passed up his ration book to have the points taken) and one bottle (no more allowed to any one customer) of British Type Port. The trays were prepared in the kitchen and the table put to the middle of the grass in readiness.

'Hello, Aunt Kathie, I'm home,' Beth called as she slammed the garden gate, then not seeing Kathie in the garden she went into the house.

'Gosh, what's all this?' she asked seeing the laid up trays. 'Hello, Uncle Bruce. It looks like party time.'

'You could say that,' he answered. 'Can you go and fetch everyone over to the grass and I'll carry the trays out. Kathie's just finishing cutting some cucumber sandwiches.'

'Is it someone's birthday?'

'Even better. Round them all up – oh and here come Nanny and Elspeth. Bring them too. Don't take Elspeth walking till after party time.'

It was quite a gathering: Kathie, Bruce, Beth, Sally, little Steven, Oliver, Sarah, Bert, Nanny and Elspeth.

'I wish we had champagne, for if ever there was an occasion to merit it, this is it.' Bruce said as he poured a not-quite-as-full-as-they-should-be British Type Port into six glasses for the adults, then three glasses of lemonade for Elspeth and the children. Steven hadn't reached the age for lemonade so he had milk in a feeder cup. 'We want you to drink to Beth and the wonderful news that arrived this morning. She is now officially Kathie's daughter, chosen and adopted. To Beth.'

In the clamour of excitement Beth could do no more than look at Kathie in wonder. Chosen and adopted, never to have to go back to the place she only half remembered.

'Chink!' Oliver tapped her glass with his. They looked at each other, neither knowing quite what to say on such an occasion yet feeling the excitement of the moment. Later she would be alone with Kathie, she might find the words to tell her how much it meant. But when Oliver took both her hands and pulled her away from the group, by one accord they started to do a 'twister'. Round and round they went, faster and faster until at last they fell to the ground in peels of laughter.

'I had a letter this morning too,' he told her when they got their breath back and still lay sprawled on the grass. 'From my father. He said as soon as the war finishes he is coming to see me. We'll have so much to talk about. I'd told him I've decided what I want to do when I leave school. Bother the silly exams; I don't care about those. I'm going to be an actor. I'm going to be just like him

– except I'd rather be on the stage than work in a film studio. But imagine, Beth, taking a part, getting to feel how another person feels, saying their words, *being* that person.'

'I expect you'll be splendid, Ollie. But I wouldn't like that sort of work.'

–

It was towards the end of that year that when Beth collected the morning paper from the letterbox she looked at the front page in horror.

'Aunt Kathie, look what it says.' She passed the paper to Kathie. They had become used to the broadsheets being no more than four pages, but on that morning the top half of the front carried a banner headline: SUDDEN DEATH OF RICHARD MARLEY and below that a picture of him with an account of how he had collapsed and died on the set of his latest film. 'Aunt Kathie, what about poor Ollie? It's not fair. His mum never bothered about him, now he's got no one.'

But of course his life would go on unaltered; he had *them*, he had Bruce and he had most of his father's not insignificant wealth held in trust for when he was twenty-one and would become master of Sedgewood Hall. In the meantime the rent paid by Brockleigh School would add to his fortune. Nothing detracted him from his certain intent; the name Marley was already held in esteem in the acting fraternity and Oliver meant to raise it to further heights.

There had never been any doubt that Beth would win a scholarship to the Grammar School. Sitting with Bruce in Deremouth Town Hall, Kathie wondered what Den would make of her waif if he could see her on her first speech day called to the platform to receive one prize after another. Oliver made no such trips at Brockleigh and was determined to leave as soon as he had taken his School Certificate and attend drama school. He never wavered in the path he meant to follow.

–

Like communities up and down the country in May of 1945 Sedgewood village gave a street party for the local children to celebrate the end of the war. Locals were the only children there by that time, for as the country had become safer the evacuees had gone home. The local policeman closed the road and there were games and races. Beth was too old to join in the fun but she held the rope at the finishing line and took the name of each winner. Then came tea, every household having dug deep to contribute something. The evening was for the adults, dancing in the street to the strains of an amateur band from Deremouth.

'They're growing up, Kathie, our young people,' Bruce said as he led Kathie into a waltz and nodded his head in the direction of where Oliver was dancing with Beth.

Kathie nodded, remembering Den's warning that as the others changed so the spirit of Jess she 'imagined' spoke to her would be left behind, too young to understand an adult world. With her head on Bruce's shoulder she longed to hear that voice, to know that Jess was still with her. She heard nothing, nothing but the clamour of happy people enjoying themselves. Bruce held her closer and whispered, 'She'll always be there for you, Kathie.' But how had he known where her thoughts had taken her? 'When you're old and grey, she will know and understand because she speaks to your heart.'

'How did you guess what I was thinking?'

His serious moment had gone and holding her away he looked at her with a teasing smile, 'Be warned, woman, you can have no secrets from me.'

'So you know what I'm thinking now?'

'The same as I am. Yes, we'll go back to school but not until later, later when the world is asleep.'

-

There was nothing in Sally's countenance to hint that each morning she watched for the post lady, but then over the last years she had learnt not to wear her heart on her sleeve. The fighting in Europe was over, but Clive hadn't been in Europe. 'The atom is split' read the newspaper sellers' placards and, only half understanding, the nation waited in anticipation. Days later on the 16th August the final peace treaty was signed. Even then the full horror of what had happened in the Far East wasn't known. Still no letter came from Clive.

'Sally, quick Sally, there's a phone call for you,' Beth shouted. 'I'll stay with Steve.'

It was a long distance call and it was brief. When Sally came out of the house her vision was blurred by tears she had held back for so long.

'What is it, love? Who was it?' Kathie was waiting, frightened to hear the answer.

'It was *him*, Clive. He's home. He's had malaria, that's why he couldn't write. Came home on a hospital ship. He's home. Soon as he's fit to travel he's coming to get Steve and me.' She had never known such aching joy – yet she couldn't stop crying.

Before that summer was over the day came when removal vans were at Sedgewood Hall and finally the convoy left. Removal lorries, coach loads of boys and staff, then a private saloon with Bruce in front at the wheel and behind him Nanny Giles holding Elspeth's hand. They were going home.

1954

Ten

Replacing the telephone receiver Kathie looked around her at the tidy room. The weekends were precious; she lived through each week waiting for Saturday teatime. Usually Bruce arrived around five o'clock, leaving London-based Brockleigh as soon as Saturday morning classes finished, the day students went home and the boarders filed in for their lunch. He stayed just long enough to say a quick grace and then he headed westward. When she'd paid Bert and his two young helpers and wished them all a good weekend that's exactly what she had anticipated for herself. Each evening Bruce phoned her and she had known that Elspeth had a chesty cold, even that she had trouble breathing, but neither of them had thought it was anything serious.

'Nanny fetched me to her in the night,' he'd just told her. 'I called the doctor out; she could hardly breathe. He's brought in a nurse to stay with her but she's so frightened. Poor Nanny seems to have gone to pieces. She's been up all night of course, poor old dear. Kathie, I can't leave Elspeth, not like this. She always smiles, you know she does. But today she's crying, she sounds like a hurt animal.'

From his voice, Kathie could tell how upset he was. 'Of course you can't.' And she had meant it, for she wouldn't have him any different. 'Is she in pain?'

'How can one tell? The doctor says it's pneumonia and now pleurisy. It must hurt her to try to breathe. I feel utterly helpless. Nanny's holding her hand while I talk to you, then I'll take over. Can't believe it. Never seen her so… so… alone. She's always happy, contented. Now she seems lost. She whimpers, she fights for breath, she looks like a trapped animal. A chesty cold, a nasty cough, that's all it was. She still smiled. Now suddenly… it's like seeing a child suffer. Oh God, if only it could be *me* not her. She doesn't understand.'

'Go back to her, darling. She won't be frightened if you are with her.'

After the call ended she looked around her and shivered not so much with cold as with an uncharacteristic fear of the unknown.

'Pull yourself together,' she chided herself, speaking aloud, the sound of her own voice making her feel even more alone. As she climbed the narrow flight of stairs, without warning the memory of Den pushing himself up one stair at a time came into her mind. According to what Oliver told her fairly recently after making a brief visit to the bungalow in Hampshire, Claudia had brought alive his enthusiasm for living and achieving. Together they ran a small business crafting leather goods, handbags, purses, wallets. Imagining them Kathie smiled with satisfaction. If Den could pick himself up to that extent, then who was she to worry about one disappointing weekend? Like a child, Elspeth wouldn't need time to convalesce; once she felt better her illness would be forgotten.

But Kathie was wrong. Late that same evening Bruce phone again.

'It's all over, Kathie. Her breathing got worse, just an unearthly rattling noise while she stared at nothing. She didn't cry anymore. It was as if she'd already left us. Then her breathing stopped. She'd gone.'

'Bruce…' But what could she say? 'Are you all right?'

'Better than I was when I spoke to you earlier. I worried about Nanny, but she is remarkable. Elspeth was her life. She loved her with a sort of completeness. Now she says she is thankful. What were her words? "My darling child, now she is herself again." I felt humble.'

On the Sunday morning he phoned again, and late that night too. Between those two calls something happened to change the shape of all their futures.

'Morning, Aunt Kathie.' Immediately she recognized Oliver's voice and threw down her hoe. 'Working on a Sunday? All on your own?'

'Bruce couldn't come.' And she told him why.

'That's going to put a different complexion on your carrying on here surely? And just when I have some exciting plans to share with you. Get your bonnet on and I'll take you down to the Boatman's Arms.'

At twenty-three Oliver was as handsome as his father had been and was already making a mark on the West End stage. As he'd always said, it was the stage that drew him, he had no wish to be like Richard and become a movie idol. But the money he had inherited from that movie idol was what made possible what he proposed to do.

'The hall stands empty,' he told her as he put half a pint of local cider in front of her, 'I can't imagine I shall ever make it my home. But it's ideal for a school – and this time it will be a school of stage and drama. The Marley School. It's my father's money that makes it possible. You have to be in films to get to be a household name and that holds no appeal. But what do you think, Aunt Kathie?'

'You want to teach?' She was surprised.

'No,' he laughed, 'can you imagine it? No, but I've put out a few feelers and staffing would be OK. Somehow, when I dreamed it up I always pictured you at Westways working your magic on some of the students like you did on me. Funny how things work out, isn't it? Because of being able to come to Westways I learnt to adjust to school – and to know Bruce Meredith so much better.'

'And it's because of *you* – like an animal in a cage…'

'I remember. Jess took me under her wing.'

'She knew no other way,' Kathie said lovingly. 'And it was because of you and the row when you got back to school that I met Bruce. Do we weave our own pattern, Ollie, or is it ordained and we have no choice?'

'I don't know, Aunt Kathie, but if it is I'm sure we are in good hands. Have you seen Beth lately?'

'She comes over most weeks. She's been busy with her new flat.' Beth had lived up to Bruce's high expectations. After seven highly successful years at the Grammar School she had gone to London to law school, leaving with high commendation. London held no appeal for her. She loved Devon, and perhaps above all she loved Westways. So she accepted a post with an Exeter firm and moved into a flat with views of the river. 'She never tells me when she's coming, but very often it's Sunday evening just in time to see Bruce before he sets off back to London.'

'You and he,' he hesitated, his sensitive nature making it difficult for him to go on, 'I mean now that Mrs Meredith has died…'

'Shall we get married? As far as the two of us are concerned, Ollie, we've been married for years. Whether Elspeth knew he was always there for her we were neither of us sure, but he would never leave her.'

Oliver nodded. 'That's what I thought. He's a great guy. Drink up your cider and we'll go and find somewhere for some lunch.'

It was turning into quite a day. But it hadn't finished with her yet. They were back at Westways when Beth arrived. The skinny waif of yesterday had become an ethereally beautiful young woman. She and Ollie walked together to the hall, they even looked at the weedy mound where Fudge was buried before they went into the great house, going from room to room while Oliver expounded his plans.

'With Mrs Meredith gone, Aunt Kathie is sure to give up Westways. I suppose she'll be the headmaster's wife at Brockleigh. It won't be the same here, Beth. It's been the base we've built our lives on.'

This was on their minds as they walked back through the wood and over the gate to the lane. Even then they didn't come straight indoors. Just as Den and Jack Hopkins had all those years before, they sat on a couple of old oil drums. Through the window of the warm room Kathie watched them. The fading daylight seemed to bring a thousand memories flooding through her mind. Soon all this would be no more than another memory. The Head-master's Lodge, part of the school, would be her home. Remember the past, she had told Dennis, your future is built on it. All this, every clod of earth, every blade of grass. 'I've done the chickens, Mum, and I tell you what! I got six huge eggs today.' Her eyes stung with tears, no longer tears of sadness but of unchanging love.

She wondered what Ollie and Beth were talking about so seriously. Soon they'd come in for an early supper before he started back to London. They were sure to tell her.

But they didn't. That was the last day of September.

–

It wasn't until a date at the end of term had been fixed for the wedding that Kathie found out what Oliver and Beth had been discussing so seriously on that September evening. He was to take over the lease of Westways.

'But your career?' Kathie had looked at him in amazement when he told her.

'I may have been a willing worker when I was a child, but that's about all,' he laughed. 'This is the idea: I've sounded Bert out and he's talked to Sarah about it. You know how it is for them, still living with her people and precious little hope of getting a place of their own.'

'Awful. They say the waiting list for housing in Deremouth is hopeless.'

'There and everywhere else. And there's nothing to rent in Sedgewood. They can't have a family living in one room over the pub. Anyway, I've said I haven't talked to you yet but I was sure you were going to give up the lease. He will be responsible for carrying on here – and supplying stuff to the hall just like you did – and he and Sarah will have the house.' Then with a hopeful but not entirely confident smile that seemed to take her back years, he asked, 'What do you say?'

'You've swept away the only cloud in my sky. What did Beth say?'

'To be truthful Beth put the idea in my head – you know what women are like for suggesting a thing and making a chap believe it was his idea. But we both hated to think of Westways not being there for all of us. I think it's great – here, the Hall, all of it put to good use. And still *ours*, still yours. It sort of brings yesterday along with us to tomorrow.'

She was ashamed at the way her mouth was twitching. He put his arm around her shoulder. 'You know something? When you and Bruce (I should say Uncle but he doesn't mind being just Bruce) were out last Sunday I went to talk to Bert and Sarah. Then Beth came over and we met up outside here and walked to the common talking about all of it. Silly, wasn't it, but we even found our den. What makes people cry when they're happy?'